Persecution

RC Bridgestock is the name that husband and wife co-authors Robert (Bob) and Carol Bridgestock write under. Between them they have nearly 50 years of police experience, offering an authentic edge to their stories. The writing duo created the character DI Jack Dylan, a down-to-earth detective, written with warmth and humour.

Bob was a highly commended career detective of 30 years, retiring at the rank of Detective Superintendent. He was also a trained hostage negotiator dealing with suicide interventions, kidnap, terrorism and extortion. As a police civilian supervisor Carol also received a Chief Constable's commendation for outstanding work.

R.C. BRIDGESTOCK

PERSECUTION

CANELO

First published in the United Kingdom in 2021 by Canelo

This edition published in the United Kingdom in 2022 by

Canelo
Unit 9, 5th Floor
Cargo Works, 1–2 Hatfields
London, SE1 9PG
United Kingdom

A CIP catalogue record for this book is available from the British Library.

Print ISBN 978 1 80032 978 2
Ebook ISBN 978 1 80032 501 2

This book is a work of fiction. Names, characters, businesses, organizations, places and events are either the product of the author's imagination or are used fictitiously. Any resemblance to actual persons, living or dead, events or locales is entirely coincidental.

Look for more great books at www.canelo.co

Printed and bound in Great Britain by Clays Ltd, Elcograf S.p.A.

1

The COVID-19 pandemic continues to savage countries, and whilst battles are won the war against this plague is far from over.

We dedicate this book to the Covid heroes – ordinary people doing extraordinary things and those who support you in these unprecedented times. Your selflessness and courage is truly humbling.

Although there are no words to adequately say thank you, we are indebted to you for protecting us and being brave, and for the daily sacrifices you make.

May you never lose sight of the inspirational work that you do, and the difference you make.

Prologue

The pounding of Dani's head competed with the pumping of her heart, the result of an adrenaline-filled reaction to her sudden wakening that left her feeling hot and shivery all at the same time.

Her body stiffened as she listened, wondering if it was merely a terrible dream that had interrupted her sleep, leaving her feeling vulnerable and worried for her safety. She held her breath.

In the darkness, Dani sensed that she was not alone.

A paralysing fear suddenly grasped her, and she twisted her shaking head towards the door. Had a friend sneaked back to the halls to check on her?

The full moon slid from behind a cloud, and its beams streamed through the curtainless window and settled at the bottom of the bed, where she could see a man, motionless, his hands clasped between his legs. His terrifying stare locked into hers.

She let rip a blood-curdling scream as terror flashed through her. The high-pitched sound seemed to her to kick up a notch as the noise bounced off the walls.

What the fuck! The words echoed soundlessly around her head.

Panic, hot and terrifying, blurred her vision.

Get out! her instincts screamed. *Get away from him.* But how? He blocked her only exit.

Dani's heart and lungs rushed with blood. When her central nervous system kicked in, and the blood supply brought about another injection of adrenaline to her system, she sat bolt upright in bed and whipped her knees to her chest. She could taste the salt of her tears spilling into the cracks of her open mouth.

She could feel the closeness of death in the room, and her body prepared itself.

I'm going to die.

When the intruder didn't move, she screamed again, louder, until she had exhausted all the air in her lungs.

She hoped and prayed that someone would hear her and run to her rescue soon.

No one came.

The moon disappeared again and the room was thrown into darkness.

With all the force she could muster, Dani slammed her trembling hand down on her touch lamp that sat on her bedside table. The light threw long shadows across the room. Shaking, her eyes never left the intruder's face. Every inch of her body pained her, as she dug her heels into the mattress and scrambled towards the headboard until she was backed into a corner like a caged animal.

The man was naked.

Her fear soared but the man's only reaction was to tilt his head, his face expressionless, as if he questioned her reaction to him.

Dani's breathing was quick, and shallow. *If I stay quiet, if I don't move, maybe he will go.* Her rational mind was regaining control.

She sat frozen, watching and listening as the intruder rose from the bed, scooped up his trousers from the floor and calmly stepped into them, tying them at the waistband in a bow. He slipped a sleeveless T-shirt over his head. All the while his eyes remained focused on Dani.

He turned and walked backwards the few steps to the window, hesitating for a moment before putting his foot on the windowsill, and with that he disappeared into the night.

Dani started crying.

'I suggest you take more water with it next time, love,' the campus security guard said, almost laughing down the phone. 'Not even Spiderman could climb up to your room.'

With emotions running rampant, Dani wiped away a tear. 'But, you don't understand, I haven't been drinking.'

'Are you on medication?' The security man's voice deepened. 'Have you been taking drugs? They frown upon drug users here, you know.'

Dani shook her head. 'No,' she whispered. 'I'm not on any medication, and I don't take drugs.'

He scoffed. 'I've heard it all before.'

'But I'm telling you the truth.' Why wouldn't he take her seriously? 'There was a naked man in my room. He was right there! He could have…' She trailed off, unable to finish the sentence.

'Well then, if you're sure. I think you'd better ring the coppers and see what they've got to say.'

And with that he hung up.

As she waited for the police to arrive, she curled up on her bed and looked at the photograph of her parents on the desk. She reached for it.

'I miss you so much,' she whispered. 'I wish I could call you to help me…' Tears welled up in her eyes once more. She held the photo close. Several tears tumbled down onto her cheeks unchecked. It felt as if she had been away from home for such a long time, but family life as she knew it would never be the same again. She hadn't been home since her dad's funeral. She felt tears threatening to fall and she squeezed her eyes shut.

In that moment she heard short, sharp footsteps on the corridor which suddenly stopped at her door, and her heart quickened. As she reached the door a knock came. Still shaking, she put the photograph down and peeped through the spy hole to see two female officers. She fumbled with the lock such was her trembling.

'PC Helen Weir and PC Lisa Bayliss. Can we come in,' Helen said, with a reassuring look on her face, as she took a step forwards.

Dani moved to one side to let the officers pass. It was a tight fit in the small room, but their presence gave her a sense of relief.

She pointed to the bed and her chair, and invited them to sit. A tear broke loose, and fell onto her bare arm when she reached for a chair. She grabbed a tissue to dry her eyes, and when she had done so she clutched it tightly. Her instincts told her there would be more to follow.

'We'll stand, thanks, if it's all the same with you,' said Helen.

'We don't want to disturb the scene, or touch anything which may ruin any chances of recovering evidence,' Lisa said, by way of an explanation.

Pens poised over pocket books Helen asked her, 'In your own time, can you tell us what happened?'

At times Dani's shaking became uncontrollable, and she found it difficult to speak. 'I'm sorry,' she apologised, on several occasions when her spirit broke and her speech faltered.

Helen looked into Dani's eyes with compassion. 'Take your time, it's important to remember as much detail as you can,' she said softly. 'We're here, and you're safe now.'

There was a pause, and Dani's eyes followed PC Lisa Bayliss as she walked across the room to the window. The officer looked this way and that, and down at the street below, which was awakening to the start of a new day.

Dani's eyes focused on the window catch. Helen saw her hand tighten into a fist, and her breathing quicken. 'It was open, I closed it when he'd gone,' said Dani.

Lisa glanced back at Helen. 'I'll go and look around outside,' she said.

Helen nodded. 'Check the possibility of us obtaining CCTV.'

'What woke you, Dani?' Helen asked softly. 'Do you think the man might have touched you?'

Dani dipped her head, and shook it slowly. 'I don't think so.'

'Where did you first notice the intruder?'

'I saw his outline, sitting at the foot of my bed. He was staring at me.'

'What did you do?'

'I tried to get as far away from him as I could. I panicked. I— I think I screamed. I prayed harder than I have ever prayed in my life. I… I… really thought I might… that I might die.'

'You told our control centre that you managed to raise the alarm?'

'When he'd gone, I phoned the office. The number's on the poster behind the door for emergencies,' Dani paused for a moment. She swallowed hard.

Helen nodded.

Dani felt tears threatening again. 'The security guard told me that I must have been dreaming, drinking, or taking drugs, because even Spiderman couldn't climb up here to the fifth floor.' Dani eyed Helen beseechingly. 'I know it sounds unbelievable. You must think I'm mad, but it's true.'

'Did the intruder say anything?' asked Helen.

'No, not a word. He wasn't fazed by my screams. It was like he wasn't human.' Dani ran a hand through her tangled hair, and again swallowed hard. 'I didn't know what to do.'

Helen breathed in deeply. 'You did the only thing you could do.' The police officer bent down and caught Dani's trembling hand in hers. 'It's over now, Dani, you're safe.'

Dani looked up at her, dabbing the tears that fell from her eyes with the soggy tissue. 'He was weirdly calm. I mean, his face didn't change at all, not even when I screamed. When I realised he was… he was naked, I panicked. I— I tried to get away from him, you know? I thought, I thought he might…' She paused for a moment and wiped at her eyes. 'But, he just casually put his clothes back on, and walked to the window, like he had all the time in the world. He looked at me and then he climbed out…'

Helen continued to write in her notebook. 'Can you describe him for me?'

Dani nodded. 'Early twenties, white, short light-coloured hair. Physically fit.' Dani shuddered. 'I've never seen him before, and I never want to see him again.'

'Was his penis erect?'

Dani gasped. 'Oh my god, I have no idea. I was too frightened of doing something, anything, that might upset him, and thinking if I did, what his next move might be...'

'I think we ought to get you checked for sexual assault, for your peace of mind.'

Dani stared at her, feeling sick. Helen nodded towards the window. 'We'll get Crime Scene Investigators to look for prints.' She cast her eye towards the bed. 'We'll need to take your bed sheets so that they can be examined. CSI will also examine outside at ground level.'

When PC Lisa Bayliss let herself back into the flat she was smiling. 'Good news,' she said to Dani. 'There are fresh partial footmarks in the flowerbed directly below your bedroom, and we've found scuff marks on the wall both sides of the drainpipe which runs parallel to it.' Involuntarily she shuddered. 'It looks like someone shimmied up it to enable them to climb to the window.'

Dani went cold at the thought – someone had gone to extreme lengths to get into her room.

'And, the bad news?' Helen knew her partner well.

'The gubbins of the CCTV cameras are present...'

Helen signed. 'But, some think it's not acceptable for big brother to be watching, so take it upon themselves to disable them by throwing stones.'

Lisa nodded. 'Let's just say they won't be any use to us.'

Helen was determined to focus on the positive and hopefully on a clue to the intruder's lifestyle. 'The mode of ascent suggests that we are looking for an experienced climber.'

'Definitely a confident one, who has no fear of heights. CSI are downstairs now, taking photographs.' Lisa turned to

Dani. 'They'll be up here soon to dust the windows, and the room...'

-

When they had gone, and she was alone, Dani caught her reflection in the mirror. She looked surprisingly normal, even though she felt completely changed.

With the tips of her fingers, Dani wiped the moist fog from the bathroom mirror. Then she adjusted the shower. For several moments she stood motionless under the pelting spray of warm water. That's when the realisation of what had happened finally set in and her pent-up feelings rushed forth. A heart-wrenching cry shook her body. She turned her face directly into the spray, as she desperately fought to rein in her emotions. Her tears mingled with the warm water, her crying turned to choking sobs, and when her knees sagged she gave way to the feeling of helplessness and slid down the wall onto the shower stall floor. For a while, laid in the foetal position, the cascading droplets pulsed against her skin from a great height, like relentless needles. Until she found the presence of mind to turn the water off, and drag a towel from the rail to wrap around her shivering body, and pat her body dry.

Standing with the help of her hand on the sink, she ran a brush through her hair. 'Pull yourself together,' she muttered, leaning into the mirror for a closer look at her face. 'Nothing actually happened for God's sake.'

-

With the flat window secured, and it unlikely that anyone would try and scale the drainpipe again in broad daylight, the officers made their way to the Campus Security Offices, but no one was there. They waited for a moment or two, as the office wasn't locked. When they heard the toilet flush, they glanced down the hall to see the uniformed guard step out, a well-thumbed magazine in his hand.

Sixty-two-year-old George Stafford looked surprised, and a little flustered when he saw the uniformed officers waiting for him. When he'd composed himself he headed straight to his desk, wiggled open his top right-hand drawer, slipped the magazine inside and locked it. He dropped the key inside his shirt pocket and fastened the button to secure it.

'I hear from Dani Miller that you were working last night,' Helen said, after making the perfunctory introductions.

'Aye, I was, and I'm still here which tells you what? I'm dedicated, or a bloody fool.'

'Why was that then?' asked Lisa.

'Young Terrier got called out on another mountain rescue mission, and I get to cover for him for my sins. Her indoors wasn't the least bit 'appy. No doubt I'll be in the doghouse when I get 'ome.'

'A rescue mission?' Helen sounded impressed. 'That sounds dangerous and exciting.' She turned to Lisa. 'I didn't hear about it on the news though, did you?'

Before Lisa could answer George butted in. 'That's exactly what her indoors says. But, I don't suppose they broadcast every rescue, do they?'

'Miss Miller informed us that you told her you'd have to be Spiderman to climb up to her window on the fifth floor,' said Helen.

He pulled a face at the officer's blank expression. 'Have you seen how high that window is? I mean, come on,' he scoffed.

'No matter what you think, it appears that someone *did* climb up the drainpipe and enter the room via an open window. We think that Miss Miller had a very lucky escape.'

Stafford looked genuinely shocked. 'Well, I'll eat my hat,' he said, as he opened his left-hand drawer and shuffled around to find the olive green, dog-eared incident log book. 'I better fill out a report pretty darn sharpish, otherwise I'll be getting my P45.'

Lisa's eyes narrowed with suspicion. 'That's the best you can do?'

Stafford rubbed his stubbly chin. 'Yes that's about it, I'm afraid.'

Helen's expression hardened. 'Could you perhaps check in that incident book of yours, and see if there have been any other recent incidents that we should know about?'

Stafford put on his glasses and ran his grubby finger down the dates of recorded incidents. When he came to the report of a peeping-tom, he stopped, and looked up. 'You have to realise that if some students are not getting the grades they want, then they have been known to tell porky-pies as an excuse for not being in the right frame of mind to study. I've seen it all in my time.'

Helen raised her eyebrows. 'I think that's a bit harsh. Surely the law of averages would suggest to you that some reports are genuine?'

'I know what you're saying, but I tell ya. This is how stupid it is. Last week a girl rang me, in floods of tears. She had heard breaking glass in the kitchenette of her ground floor accommodation, and her housemate was away for the night. I rushed around there.' George rubbed his chest. 'I thought I was having a heart attack, which turned out to be indigestion, but that's by-the-by, and what do I find but a cat that had entered through the window that she had left open for it, and it had only gone and knocked over the saucer of milk that she'd left on the windowsill. They'd named the stray cat. Lucky, they'd called it. She was bloody lucky I didn't wring her bloody neck. Pets are not allowed on campus.'

Stafford took his glasses off, and rubbed one blood-shot eye with his knuckle. 'What I'm saying is, not everything is always as it seems. You would not believe some of the wild-goose chases the students have sent me on.'

'I don't suppose you have the description of the peeping-tom written down?' asked Helen, her tone icy.

Stafford flicked over the page. 'White male, average height, slim build. Which just about sums up eighty per cent of the male students on the campus.'

'Description of clothing?' asked Lisa.

Stafford shook his head.

'What did you do about the peeping-tom?'

'Says 'ere that we stepped up our patrols for a few nights, and we found nothing. I guess that's what we did.'

'Did you go and visit Miss Miller in the early hours of this morning, to make sure she was okay? Give her some support and reassurance?'

Stafford pulled a face. 'Why would I? We've got to be very careful going into young ladies' rooms in the middle of the night y'know. All sorts of allegations could be made, if you get my drift. Anyway, in the end you turned up, and now t'job's sorted.'

Helen's eyes grew wide. 'Is it?'

Stafford looked bewildered. 'What do you mean?'

'The police take incidents like this very seriously, especially our Detective Inspector, Charley Mann, head of Peel Street CID.'

-

Driving back to Peel Street Police Station Helen and Lisa discussed Mr Stafford, and the role of the security guard at the university.

'I wonder what he meant by stepping up patrols?' said Lisa.

'Perhaps they looked out of the window, or walked to the door. He doesn't exactly fill me with confidence, does he you?'

Helen shook her head. 'Jobsworth comes to mind.' She frowned.

'What's up?' asked Lisa.

Helen turned her head briefly towards her colleague who was sat in the passenger seat. 'I'm wondering how we record this incident in accordance with Home Office guidelines.'

'I guess burglary,' suggested Lisa.

'Burglary with intent to rape? He hasn't stolen anything, damaged anything, raped her, or inflicted any harm.'

'He was naked… Do you think it was his intention to rape her, or do you think it was just a student prank?'

'If so then should we record it as a nuisance incident – naked intruder, on campus.'

Helen pulled a face. 'I reckon we should send a report through to CID, for the attention and guidance of Detective Inspector Charley Mann and see what she advises.'

Lisa nodded. 'I agree. The last thing she'd want, I'm sure, is for something like this to be dismissed. That's not going to help any of us understand what's happening on our patch, or the people we are dealing with.'

'True,' said Lisa, reaching for her phone and starting to type on the keypad.

Charley's response to the officers was waiting for them when they got back into the office, and they were pleased with what she said.

Thank you for consulting, she wrote. *The offence of burglary is defined by section 9 of the Theft Act 1968 which now reads:*

(1) A person is guilty of burglary if –

[(a) he or she enters any building or part of a building as a

trespasser and with intent to commit any such offence as is mentioned in subsection (2) below; or]{.classed_para para_class=no_indent_top_space_half}

[(b) having entered any building or part of a building as a

trespasser he steals or attempts to steal anything in the building or that part of it or inflicts or attempts to inflict on any person therein any grievous bodily harm.]{.classed_para para_class=no_indent_top_space_half}

[(2) The offences referred to in subsection (1)(a) above are offences

> of stealing anything in the building or part of a building in question, of inflicting on any person therein any grievous bodily harm ... therein, and of doing unlawful damage to the building or anything therein.]{.classed_para para_class=no_indent_top_space}

[(3) A person guilty of burglary shall on conviction on indictment be

> liable to imprisonment for a term not exceeding −]{.classed_para para_class=no_indent_top_space}

[(a) where the offence was committed in respect of a building or part

> of a building which is a dwelling, fourteen years;]{.classed_para para_class=no_indent_top_space_half}

(b) in any other case, ten years.

   [(4) References in subsections (1) and (2) above to a building, and

> the reference in subsection (3) above to a building which is a dwelling, shall apply also to an inhabited vehicle or vessel, and shall apply to any such vehicle or vessel at times when the person having a habitation in it is not there as well as at times when he is.]{.classed_para para_class=no_indent_top_space}

Burglary with intent to rape:

[Section 9 (2) originally referred to the offence of raping any woman

in the building or part of the building in question. The words 'raping any person' were substituted for the words 'raping any woman' on 3 November 1994. This was consequential on the changes to the definition of rape made by the Criminal Justice and Public Order Act 1994. The words 'or raping any person' were in turn repealed on 1 May 2004. The offence of burglary with intent to rape is replaced by the offence of trespassing with intent to commit a sexual offence, contrary to section 63 of the Sexual Offences Act 2003.]{.classed_para para_class=no_indent_top_space_half}

Chapter 1

'This girl, Dani Miller, has been very lucky on this occasion,' said Charley. 'The next person might not be so fortunate. I want you to work with Helen Weir and Lisa Bayliss, liaise with the university, the security guards and the Students' Union, and see if they've been informed of any other suspicious incidents that have occurred around the campus recently. I'm hopeful that other people may come forward, in confidence, when they hear about Dani's experience.' Charley pulled a face. 'I know, it might take time, and time is of the essence…'

'At least we'll know if we're dealing with an isolated incident, or whether there's a pattern of events developing, that is becoming increasingly worse as the offender grows in confidence,' said DC Annie Glover thoughtfully.

Charley nodded. 'Exactly. I want an update in fourteen days, but for now, I'll leave it in your very capable hands.'

-

The time on Charley's clock showed 5.10 am. Gale force winds and heavy rain overnight had interrupted her sleep. The bedroom was cold. Outside it was now still and extremely quiet. It was too early for the central heating to kick in. However, a warm fuzzy feeling washed over her when she realised it was Sunday.

With three soft pillows to her back, and the duvet wrapped around her, Charley sat up in bed, sipping coffee from her favourite mug. It was a present from her best friend, and colleague, Kristine, who had bought her the gift when she was on secondment in London, just before Eddie's sudden death. She thought about him now. She had found justice for his murder, and that was something to focus on. She was getting better at finding the positives in a situation and banishing the negativity that sometimes plagued her. Being in charge of Peel Street CID, in her home town helped. She liked her job, all things considered, even if she was pleased it was her weekend off.

Snuggling into the duvet, she groaned with relief when the taste of the liquid caffeine washed over her tastebuds. Enjoying the smell as much as the taste, she soon found her body responding to it.

'Why,' she sighed heavily, as she rested her head back on the pillow and closed her eyes, 'does the first coffee of the day taste so good?'

Charley looked beyond her window at the first victims of dawn. The stars that were visible between the clouds winked out one by one, and she counted them as they faded into nothingness. Daybreak was her time, her quiet solitude when she gathered her peace, and turned her soul to nature's song at the beautiful sunrise that had begun to appear over the horizon.

Despite the rain that had noisily lashed, thrashed and splattered her window overnight, she never thought of closing the curtains, preferring to look out, as she did, across the rolling Marsden moors, whatever the weather. It was the little things that pleased her, and it made her happy that she lived alone with nobody to think of but herself.

She took another sip of coffee. As the rain battered down on the roof, she found herself thinking about the torrid nights, such as the last that she had walked the beat in uniform. She had often questioned her sanity. After all, who in their right mind would wander around the dark, deserted city centre streets, alone, in the middle of the night, in all weather conditions?

The rain started up again. In her mind's eye she imagined looking down at the water flowing over the toecaps of her shiny shoes. Running over the cobbled street, it flowed along the gutters and gurgled down the drains, which appeared to be unable to cope with the heavy rain. She shivered at the thought of the rain running down her neck. People often said that 'rain' was the best police officer, because it kept people indoors. That was true, for a number of reasons, but it didn't make being out on the streets in the rain any more enjoyable. She pulled the duvet further up her body.

Selfishly she took a moment to enjoy the feeling of being able to sprawl out alone in her big, warm bed. Men were off her agenda for the foreseeable future. The question of Charley's past, and her only long-term relationship, was still commented on by others, especially the dinosaurs she worked with, but these days she refused to be drawn. The fact that her childhood sweetheart and local newspaper reporter Danny-Ray had ended up serving a life sentence for murder when she was the investigator was not one of her finest moments. To say what he had done had left her reeling, and feeling betrayed was an understatement. Never again, she vowed, would she trust someone so wholeheartedly.

She pushed her memories of that particular case from her mind and closed her eyes once more. Then her bubble was burst by the unmistakable ringtone of her work mobile phone.

'Hello, this is Charley Mann,' she said quietly. Her voice sounded hoarse to her ears, because she hadn't spoken to anyone yet, that morning.

'That you, boss?' said old-timer Detective Constable Wilkie Connor, practically office-bound after being mowed down by the journalist-cum-murderer, Danny Ray, which had left him with life-changing injuries.

Charley smiled to herself. 'I hope so,' she said.

'The body of a partially clothed female has been discovered on the outskirts of the town centre,' he said, quick and to the point.

Without pause, Charley swung her legs over the side of the bed. The rush of adrenaline made her heart rate increase. Running her fingers through her tangled hair, she listened intently.

'Your attendance is urgently requested.'

Chapter 2

The fact that Charley Mann wore no make-up, and habitually slicked her hair back into a bun at the nape of her neck for work, saved her considerable time when getting out of her bed to attend a scene.

Connie Seabourne, the press officer, updated her as she got ready for work. 'The female has been found under the sidings arches on Viaduct Street. Found by a postman on his way to work. Reports suggest that a large stone has been dropped directly onto the victim's head,' she said.

Charley saw her grimace at the grisly news, in her dressing table mirror, but was pleased to hear that apart from the victim having been pronounced dead by attending paramedics in the first instance, the body had remained in situ, and instructions given for the area to remain sealed until her attendance.

Forty-five minutes after Wilkie Connor's initial call, the Detective Inspector found herself driving along Northgate and noticed the long railway viaduct straight ahead. In this part of the town, she had been told by her grandparents, farmers themselves, that the inhabitants of the small town of yesteryear came along a quiet lane to the vast open fields with their ploughs and oxen, to prepare their strips and to sow and eventually reap their harvests of oats, peas and beans.

Viaduct Street had changed very little since she was a child, Charley noted on arrival. The rock-faced stone construction of forty-four arches built between 1845 and 1847, had duly stood the test of time, faithfully supporting the main railway line from Huddersfield along the lower Colne Valley.

Suddenly the ground where she stood began to shake. Charley stood stoically, and steeled herself for what was to come. Stone dust floated down onto her coat. She closed her eyes, and instantly she was taken back to her childhood. Her elders had watched on, and waited for her to run the first time. She was as frightened then as she was now of the bridge above collapsing, as the train rattled and roared above her. However, like most things in life, she had come to realise, the perception was often far more worrying than the actual event.

'How often does that happen?' said a wide-eyed Annie Glover, who had crept up behind her, unheard above the noise.

'Oh, about every fifteen minutes,' said Charley.

Annie checked the ground beneath her feet, and the animals grazing in the surrounding fields. 'I don't think my nerves would stand living here,' she said.

'No, mine neither, especially after a train derailed and slid off that parapet,' Charley said, pointing to the archway above, with a stone-cold look on her face.

Annie cowered. 'O.M.G!' Charley heard her say under her breath.

Patrol Sergeant Peters, walked lazily towards the pair. Before he spoke he gulped down the remains of a takeaway coffee. 'Ma'am,' he said, lifting his chin towards Charley in anticipation of his instructions.

'Close the road back as far as the traffic lights on the high street,' she told him. 'Including any footpaths that lead into the area.'

'Including ginnels and snickets?'

Charley nodded. 'Especially the ginnels and the snickets. The sterility of the area is of paramount importance.'

Watching Peters direct his available troops, Charley was immediately struck by the paucity of patrol staff. Sadly, no matter how desperate she was for extra hands, there was no magic wand available to conjure up more staff from Peel Street nick.

'First job, telephone HQ and ask for extra resources,' she said to Annie.

Detective Sergeant Mike Blake had arrived, and he and Annie Glover followed in the Detective Inspector's wake.

The familiar feeling of adrenaline pumping through Charley's veins kept her on high alert as she walked towards the inner scene. There were so many things to consider and to do after the discovery of a body, that her busy mind chased each one of the well-trodden processes around her head. There was no second chance to secure evidence, so it was extremely important that nothing was overlooked in the next few hours.

Charley's instructions continued to roll off her tongue, like the lyrics from a well-known song. A murder scene was her comfort zone. Having learnt from the best as a detective on major incidents, she had also suffered at the hands of misogynistic predecessors, and the equality of opportunity meant it had been a continuous struggle to achieve the rank of Detective Inspector. On the positive side, and Charley always looked for the positives, her experience, both good and challenging had helped her develop a leadership style based on empathy, encouragement and compassion. On promotion to detective sergeant, and upon her immediate secondment to London, she vowed to learn things that would help her police her own town more efficiently and effectively, when she returned. However, in the big city her positivity had been tested. An only child, her mother and father had died, and on her return from her mother's funeral she found herself plummeted into the investigation into one of Britain's most notorious killers – a colleague being subjected to a violent death, at the hands of cannibalistic murderer Titus Deaver. Both affected Charley deeply, but the fact that the conclusion at court of the latter prompted her secondment coming to an end, and her return to West Yorkshire, brought about a relief like no other. She now found herself at the cutting edge as the senior officer, the knowledge and skills acquired whilst away meant she relished every opportunity presented to her – more determined than ever to succeed where others had been found lacking.

'It doesn't matter how many rolls of tape you use!' she shouted to a pair of uniformed special constables fumbling with the 'DO NOT CROSS POLICE' tape. 'Make sure you protect the outer scene,' she said. 'Or I'll have your guts for garters,' she added, as she took long strides across the uneven, sometimes boggy terrain.

Working on the discovery of the body was Neal Rylatt, the on-call duty CSI Supervisor. He was already in the process of screening off the body at the inner scene from prying eyes, when Charley caught up with him. 'I don't want any cameras, mobiles or drone pictures appearing on the internet,' she said.

The well-seasoned CSI nodded, and continued on regardless, doing the job he did well.

Chapter 3

Charley soaked up the sight of the body like her mind was blotting paper. Her focus such, that everything else around was lost to her.

The victim lay on her back, the upper torso naked. Her denim trousers were rolled down around her ankles, stopped from going further by a pair of new-looking white trainers, upon her feet.

The large boulder that covered her head was the size of a football, in a position that hid her face from the investigators.

The officers stood in stunned silence for a moment. Charley's eyes flitted about restlessly.

The tension was broken by Annie's voice. 'Ouch, I bet that hurt. Could one person lift that rock?' she said pointing to the large offending object.

'I'll tell you when Neal's finished, and we try to remove it,' said Mike with a grimace, as he turned to look at Neal who was focused on photographing the scene.

With a final nod from the CSI supervisor, and the 360-degree footage taken, Mike stepped forwards to help Neal lift the boulder from her face. 'Ready,' Neal said as the men faced each other. It took a lot of effort to remove the boulder, to lay it back on the ground with as little movement as possible, to protect any evidence that the boulder may have been hiding from them.

Hands on his hips, getting back his breath, Mike turned to Annie. 'The answer to your earlier question is, it definitely takes two to lift the rock,' he said between gasps.

Annie's face morphed into a look of distaste at the gruesome sight. Her face crumpled. 'Oh my God,' she said turning away for an instant. 'I guess that rules out the possibility of anyone identifying her?' she said turning to Charley whose face was void of any emotion. 'How does that not make you puke?' Annie turned away.

The stillness of Charley's bent head revealed nothing but concentration. 'Because, if I ran away so would you,' she said. 'The mask of the detective is one that is perfected in time, sometimes we need it more often than others.' Charley leaned in closer to the mutilated face. 'An ID is going to be tough, though that's exactly what her murderer thought too. But, it won't stop us finding out the truth. Think of a crime scene as a puzzle. Some, like this, are more taxing than others, that's all,' said Charley, getting to her feet, and taking a step backwards to allow the men some space. 'I'm wondering if her killer has displayed her body like this deliberately, for someone to find?' pondered Charley, as she watched the men go down on their haunches.

'Or was it a random act of anger?' said Mike.

There was little skin left on the victim's face. Blood-splattered, broken cheek bones protruded, and her features were badly distorted.

There was no mistaking the glint in Charley's eye at the revelation that the girl's short, neatly cropped hair was a vivid fuchsia pink.

'What the murderers didn't realise was that there is no mistaking that their victim would stand out in a crowd. Hopefully, it will make the last sightings of her memorable to someone, for us.'

Slowly, Charley crouched down beside her, pushing her head forwards to within inches of the victim's face. She scanned the bruises on her naked body from head to toe, and back again, two or three times, until she was satisfied she had missed nothing. There were no visible operation scars, no tattoos that would help with her identification. 'Who's done this to you, and why?' she whispered to the corpse.

As she carefully pushed a blood-soaked strand of hair to the side of the victim's ruined face with a gloved hand, intense bruising became visible. She looked up at her team questioningly. 'It appears the bruising is more to the front of her neck…'

She turned back to the body and pointed out two reasonably clear footmark impressions around the exposed abdomen area. 'Interesting,' she said, thoughtfully, struggling to take her eyes off the marks. 'Neal, can you do the necessary…' she said pointing.

Before the SIO had finished there were multiple clicking noises emerging from the CSI's camera.

Mike dropped to his haunches beside her. 'See the partial sole impressions on her bare skin? They're different sizes,' he said. His eyes looked up towards Neal, who nodded in agreement.

'There are definitely two people involved you think?' said Annie.

'Absolutely,' said Neal.

Charley spoke out the myriad thoughts that were milling around inside her head, whilst she maintained the professional, strategic approach.

'Has she been stamped on, or walked over? Bruising means it would likely be before death, while her blood was still flowing…'

'I guess we will find out more when we get her to the mortuary,' said Mike.

Charley stood, and looked around at the faces of her team. With the Home Office pathologist unable to attend, there was an examination to be conducted at the scene. 'Right, what do we know about our unidentified woman?'

Annie pushed aside her thick, blonde fringe. Educated by nuns, the slightly younger police officer had far less life, and police experience. DC Glover had achieved her training, and

24

performed her probation in a small, quiet town in the south of England before her transfer to Peel Street. Her lack of experience however, was made up for by her eagerness to learn, and her likability factor meant she was a pleasure to have as part of the team. As always Annie was the first to offer her opinion. 'The obvious thought would be that she has been the subject of a sexual assault. She's also taken one hell of a beating. I can't see any personal possessions, or jewellery on her, or anything else discarded around her. Could it be that she has also been robbed?'

'Anything is a possibility,' said Charley. 'However?'

Annie lowered her eyes. 'We must rely on evidence to explain what's taken place, not assumptions.'

'Correct,' said Charley.

'Rigor mortis has set in, so she's been dead for a few hours,' said Mike.

Charley nodded. 'Shall we turn her over?'

Annie bent down to help Neal turn the body over, with gloved hands. The massive dent had crushed the corpse's head into an ovoid shape. Annie stayed down on her haunches, Charley joined her.

Charley's gaze travelled down the body. 'Minor grazes, and bruising to her back and buttocks. All these are consistent with her being dragged to her resting place.' The Detective Inspector's eyes moved beyond the body to the grass verge beyond the kerb where drag marks confirmed her thought pattern. 'Why would they move her such a short distance?' she muttered. Her voice rose. 'I'm surprised that her shoes haven't come off.'

Mike stood above the corpse, eyes wide, his hands sat on his hips. 'Could it be that they were fastened tightly, which would also account for the bottom half of her clothing not being removed,' said Mike.

'Possibly,' said Charley watching Neal strategically shuffling a body bag to the dead woman's side.

'And, now back again,' Charley said, helping the others to roll her back into the bag this time. It felt like such a momentous moment when the body was sealed within, and hopefully evidence with it.

With the ground beneath Charley's feet trembling, and the noises that told her there was an imminent arrival of another train overhead, a thought came to her, and she searched around for a cup or a bowl, something that if the victim had been begging at the train station, she could have used as a receptacle for coins, but, there was nothing.

She reflected that for some homeless people, shop doorways were their only shelter. She felt sorry for them. Unbeknown to others, she had often bought a homeless person a hot drink, given them a bar of chocolate, or a bottle of water, and on occasions, she had removed her gloves and socks, and had given them to the homeless person to help stave off the cold.

In the twenty-first century, people should not be living on the streets – it was inhumane.

'I hear the postman that discovered the body suggested to the officer who obtained his first account, that he thought he had seen her before, and that perhaps she may be a homeless person who could usually be seen begging outside the Medway Bakery on the High Street,' said Mike.

'If she was homeless, wouldn't she have all her belongings with her?' said Annie.

'And if so, where are they?' asked Charley.

Chapter 4

Charley and Mike turned to follow the private ambulance with the body inside, along the gravel walkway, careful to sidestep the few puddles left by the previous night's downpour.

'The postman,' said Charley, turning to Mike. 'How do you think he was so sure it was the homeless woman who sat outside the bakery? You couldn't see her face, or her hair, for the boulder.'

The pair stopped for a moment, facing each other. 'Maybe he recognised her clothing, or there was a rogue strand of hair on show? You've got to admit that that pink colour is quite distinctive,' Mike scoffed.

'He needs questioning about it, nonetheless,' Charley said. The SIO paused, a thought having just popped into her head. 'Will you call in at the bakery on your way back to the station? Just get an idea as to whether the postie's assumptions could be right about seeing her before, sitting outside? That distinctive pink hair is, like you say, the perfect focus for appeals, and possible witnesses.'

Mike shrugged his shoulders, amiably. 'I guess it's as good a starting point as any. She could be very well-known around there.'

'If she is, I'll extend the search parameters to incorporate the area between the bakery and where she was discovered, for obvious reasons.'

Both stood silent, alone with their thoughts for a moment or two. They looked back to the wider scene. Neal had been joined by members of his team, suited and booted, who were presently examining, swabbing and photographing the boulder and the area surrounding it.

Mike nodded towards the gap in the nearby dry-stone wall which resembled a missing tooth in a row of perfect teeth. Her eyes followed his focus.

A thought raised her spirits. 'Whoever lifted it might have possibly left skin debris?'

'Maybe,' Mike said, as he discarded his body suit into the evidence bag provided for him, at the exit to the outer scene.

The DS continued to walk on with his hands in his trouser pockets. The breeze was brisk but refreshing, and it felt good to feel the cooling wind in his face.

Various tamper-proof bags, with labelled exhibits collected from the roadway sealed inside them, were being put into the back of the CSI van, ready for transportation to the property store, in the Incident Room. Sergeant Peters leaned against the van, parked next to Charley's car, eating something from a napkin.

Charley looked at her watch and back at Mike. 'Time's getting on, I'll see you back at the nick for a briefing,' she said. As she approached Sergeant Peters she raised her voice in order to be heard. 'The scene needs to be kept secure until after the searches are completed. I'll leave it in your capable hands to arrange perimeter security, and to pass my instructions on to whoever takes over from you at the end of the shift.' When she opened her car door, and sat inside, Charley looked up at Peters. Her tone changed to a menacing one which made him stand up straight. 'Nobody crosses the line without my permission, and I mean nobody. Understood?'

Peters stood straight and gave her a salute. 'Message received loud and clear, boss,' he mumbled through a mouthful of sausage roll.

Leaving the old access road to the railroad tracks, where the rest of the vehicles were parked, she thought back to the corpse. Seeing another human treated that way repulsed her, and truth be told it never got any easier to cope with, but, she couldn't and wouldn't show emotion in front of the team. Her feelings had to be suppressed, she had to remain professional for the sake of the victim. She was the boss, the Senior Investigative Officer on the enquiry, and therefore she had to lead by example. The eyes of the team were upon her for leadership, and that is what she must always show.

With deliberate effort, and a tear in her eye, she concentrated on the road ahead. Once again that day she thought of her team in London, whom she had left behind after the Titus Deaver trial, still finding their colleagues violent death hard to deal with, and she silently prayed for all victims of crime and those who were left to mourn. This latest corpse was someone's daughter, someone's friend.

The day was warming a little, and her apprehension gradually eased as she travelled and the sky brightened. She looked forward to meeting the Home Office pathologist at the post-mortem, and hearing his thoughts after his examination of the corpse. Whilst it was ideal, and seen to be good practice, to have the pathologist in attendance at a scene, Charley was a realist and knew that it wasn't always possible. The pathologists, like everyone else in the emergency services, were stretched to the limit.

Back at the station old faces and new waited, in anticipation for the briefing to start, and all eyes were on the SIO as she stood talking to Detective Ricky-Lee who was holding a see-through plastic exhibit bag in his raised hand.

'They've found a sleeping bag, a hundred and fifty yards from the body. It's dry, and the condition suggests it hasn't been there long,' he said.

Charley eyed his prized possession with interest. 'If it belonged to her, Forensic will be able to confirm it for us pretty quickly,' she said. 'Has it been unzipped, turned inside out and have you made sure that there is nothing stuffed inside that might assist us?'

Ricky-Lee's face told her otherwise.

'Do it,' she said. 'And then send it to Forensics.'

Charley was well aware that forensic capabilities and computer databases were at the forefront of the investigations, but the seasoned detective's gut-feeling would always be required to select items at a scene that they thought would bring them results.

With the body registered at the mortuary, Annie had returned to the office. A nod from the young detective constable on her return, told Charley all was as it should be.

Silence prevailed the instant Charley stood at the front of her team.

'A woman, likely between the ages of twenty-five and thirty-five, was found dead this morning at 04.47 on Viaduct Street. The victim was partially clothed, and her features destroyed with a boulder in what we can assume is an attempt to delay identification. Initial findings suggest the body was moved to its final resting place, and therefore cause of death is still unknown. We're waiting on the pathologist's report to confirm. The hands of the victim have been swabbed, nail scrapings taken, and clippings from all finger and thumbnails secured,' said Charley, to her captive audience. 'This allows the samples and her hands to be scanned quickly, and her fingerprints to be checked on the automatic fingerprint retrieval system. If she is known to us, identification will be swift. At this stage, identifying the victim is our priority.'

Conversely, if she wasn't known to the police, then her identification would have to be made by other means such as someone reporting her missing, followed by visual identification, which may however prove impossible in this case, and then DNA, or odontology.

'DC Connor has anyone fitting her description been reported missing? DS Blake, could we talk to locals in the vicinity of the crime scene and see if anyone recalls seeing our victim alive, and if so when?'

In the audience several pens began to write.

'None of this will impact on the pending post-mortem, or the intense searching of the scene and surrounding area.

However, a quick identification would help the progress of our investigation, and allow immediate lines of enquiry to be more focused. It may assist us in tracing her relatives, and also her attackers, giving us the added ability at that stage to secure evidence against those responsible quickly, before it's either lost, or destroyed.'

Charley felt empowered. Every decision that was made on an investigation was hers alone, and that was what Charley had been trained to do.

Questions ran around her head as she spoke, and she guessed she was not the only one wondering, 'What made this woman the target of such a brutal attack?'

–

Back at the scene Charley's instruction for a fingertip search of the area was ongoing by a POLSA team. Only time would tell if anything seized during the fingertip search, that appeared to be discarded, was of relevance.

Every single item, whether it be chewing gum, cigarette butts, ring pulls, would be recorded and retained, so that at a later date, they could be revealed to any future defence team, to comply with Data Protection laws, which was the devil in the detail of the police prosecution file.

Sitting in her office, Charley pondered over what she had witnessed at the scene. Her concentration was so deep, thinking about the finer details she had witnessed, that when a knock came at her door, she jumped. It was Mike.

'We've not had a hit in our fingerprint database yet, but five staff from the bakery confirm knowing a woman fitting the description of our victim,' he said enthusiastically. Charley invited him to sit down opposite her. 'Apparently, she has been sitting outside their business premises for long periods of time for some weeks.'

'Do we have a name?'

'Not yet.'

'Did you get any statements?'

'It was lunchtime. They were busy. I told them that someone would be back to take them later today.'

'Fine,' she said. 'Keep me updated.'

As Mike walked out with a spring in his step, Annie walked in with a mug of coffee.

'Sit down,' said Charley. 'Show me your hands.'

Annie frowned. 'My hands,' she said, splaying her hands on the desk.

Charley scrutinised her fingertips one by one. It was her turn to frown. 'Thought so,' she said.

'Thought what?' said Annie.

Charley showed Annie her hands. 'That your fingernails are in no better shape than mine.'

Annie looked puzzled. 'Come again?'

'Our homeless victim had lovely clean, manicured fingernails. Don't you think that's odd?'

Annie's eyes lit up. 'Did she really? I was too busy looking at her Prada, Project Earth reducing waste trainers. I'd die for some of them.'

'Why, are they in demand?'

'I don't know if they're in demand, but they're out of my budget.'

'How much?'

'Six hundred quid a time.'

Charley blew out a long breath. 'Perhaps she stole 'em?'

'Maybe, but now I come to think about it, what of her hair as well? It was neatly cut, she didn't have discoloured roots, it wasn't faded.' Annie was philosophical. 'Blood-soaked but not faded.'

Charley was thoughtful. 'Not what you'd expect had the victim been living on the streets, as is suggested.'

'She might have been made homeless only recently?' offered Annie. 'We shouldn't assume,' she said, getting up to leave Charley with a smile on her face. When she got to the door Charley called her back.

'Make sure the HOLMES team have the Divisional database for all the CCTV outlets in the town centre will you please, and we'll need to seize the recording devices. The ones closest to the body being an obvious priority for viewing.'

Mike appeared at the opposite side of Charley's office door, as if in a hurry. He indicated to Annie to step back.

'I've got an update for you,' he spoke excitedly. 'We have a positive result from her fingerprints.'

Chapter 5

'Cora Jones, born 1st Feb 1985,' said Mike. 'However, she changed her name to Cordelia Le Beau for some unknown reason…'

'That makes her thirty-four. What else do you know about her?'

Mike acknowledged the question with a swift flourish of his notebook and a grin. Just as quickly he resumed his sombre tone. 'I knew you'd ask me that. Truth is, not a lot. Cordelia, as she is now known, has previous convictions, including one for assault,' Mike consulted his notes. 'The victim was an elderly woman. The offence took place at a private care home where she was employed as a care worker. Apparently, according to our intel, she wasn't the only one prosecuted for the offence. It says here that she was responsible for assaulting an elderly resident causing actual bodily harm, and also was responsible for giving the lady a black eye. However, according to another report, in Ms Le Beau's defence, the elderly lady was known to be violent, and noted for being difficult to deal with.'

Charley frowned. 'That's no excuse.'

Mike paused for a moment as he flicked through the pages of information. 'That occurred back in 2016,' he said. 'Then, in 2017, she was arrested and charged with shoplifting. It says here that she stole a bottle of wine and other bits of foodstuff from a supermarket. Total value of the items taken amounted to sixty-three pounds. She denied the offence. The case ended up in the Magistrates' Court. She was found guilty, and was given one month's imprisonment suspended for one year. All her previous antecedent history is being downloaded to the HOLMES database as we speak.'

'Was she married? Single? Living with someone?' Charley asked.

'According to her record she was single. There's no mention of a partner, but of course that may have changed.'

Charley replied slowly, as if thinking about what she was going to say. 'Okay, so let's get a priority action raised to research her background, including her last known address. Let's find out as much as we can about her lifestyle. Find out how a person lived…'

Mike finished her sentence. '…and you'll find out how they died.'

Charley smiled. 'Exactly! I'll brief the team once all the officers from other divisions have arrived to join us.' She looked over his shoulder to the clock above her office door. 'That's probably not going to be happening until about two o'clock. Hopefully, the post-mortem will be over by then. It's scheduled for midday. If any officers arrive early from further afield, instead of having them hanging about, perhaps Wilkie could brief them with knowledge of the area. It'll save time later. I'm taking Ricky-Lee with me to the mortuary as exhibits officer, and I also want Annie to be there for experience. As my deputy, I want you to keep an eye on things here, and update me as and when. I think that's it for now.'

Mike ran his hands through his hair, and his forehead furrowed with worry. 'As you are probably aware, the media are chasing updates.'

Charley's jaw tightened. The pressure was on, and Cordelia's body was barely cold.

'Leave the media to Connie and I. Right, is there anything else I need to know?'

Mike shook his head. 'No boss, I think you've got it covered.'

–

Annie Glover talked about everything and anything, other than where they were heading, as though she was desperately trying to put off the inevitable, which was attending the post-mortem of Cora Jones. Charley humoured her, aware that everyone dealt with trauma in their own way.

'Standing on the shoulders of giants,' Annie whispered as they passed through the mortuary gates.

Charley glanced at her. 'What made you say that?'

Annie looked vacant. 'Oh, I was given a two-pound coin in my change this morning at the petrol station, and the quote is written around the edge. Funny I've never noticed it before.'

'It was Newton, wasn't it? What do you think he meant by that?' Charley asked, as she pulled straight into a parking space next to the main door.

'My guess is that if Newton had been able to discover more about the universe, it was because he was working in the light of discoveries made by fellow scientists.'

Charley turned off the car's engine. Annie turned to her boss. 'I suppose it's a bit like me and you.'

'What is?' asked Charley.

'The saying. Isaac Newton and his bosses. I learn to build on what you teach me from your experience, without my having to go through what you've been through.'

Charley grinned. 'I'll take that as a compliment shall I?' She took the keys out of the ignition. 'One thing you're always sure of here is parking space,' she said, reaching in the boot for her briefcase that lay on top of her horse-riding gear. Charley breathed in the smell of horses that reminded her of her first love.

'Who would want to hang about here?' said Annie, breaking Charley's reverie, as the younger detective inspected the building before her like a child queuing for the ghost train.

Inside, Cora Jones was laid out on a stainless-steel post-mortem table, covered by a white sheet. The viewing window protected them from the pungent odours Charley knew to be in the air in the room. The implementation of standard infec-tion control precautions meant that no more would she stand in her green plastic apron and gloves, shoulder to shoulder with the pathologist, inches away from the corpse, and in some respect it saddened her. It was important to her as an SIO, to know how a person had died, and try to see that for herself.

Annie groaned, brought her hands quickly to her mouth, then turned away for a minute.

A glance across at Annie showed Charley that her younger colleague was wringing her hands and it occurred to her that at post-mortems, Annie might think of her late brother Ashton, his suicide, and the much later trial and sentencing of the pedophile priests, his abusers.

Charley knew very little about Annie's background and her home life. With the help of Botox, she also hid her emotions well. Maybe she was more like Charley than Charley realised, the SIO considered. Annie kept her private life to herself. She didn't blame her. No one knew better than Charley that rumours and bad news spread around a police station faster than any intelligence.

'You okay?' Charley asked Annie.

Forcing herself to look again, briefly, then directly back to Charley, Annie nodded unconvincingly. 'Why does the sight of a dead body get to me more at the mortuary?'

'I don't know,' Charley said softly. 'Perhaps it's because your mind is occupied at the scene where as here others are doing the work and you're the voyeur. Being up close to a dead body is stressful and not everyone can cope. I've known seasoned detectives faint at a post-mortem. It's nothing to be ashamed of, but that's why I want you here, to get you to accept a post-mortem for what it is. The necessary examination for the investigator to understand how, and why, a person has died.'

Cordelia's leggings, pants and trainers could be seen in-situ, around her ankles, just as she had been discovered.

When the sheet was taken from the body, Charley's eyes once again, automatically scanned her, from head to toe and back again.

Charley could feel Annie turn towards the examination rather than let anyone see her face. Annie groaned at the sight of her head injuries.

Ricky-Lee entered the viewing room, and immediately started setting out the exhibit labels, and marker pens on the table, ready to receive the exhibits through the flap-type drawer from the adjacent examination room.

Annie leaned towards the glass. Curiosity and her training took over as Charley had hoped it would, and she saw her focus move from the woman's head to her hands, looking for possible defence wounds. 'She has no rings on her fingers, nor indentations where a ring might have been,' Annie noted.

The notion sounded romantic to Charley, but she had a point.

'The most recent intel tells us she's single. That might explain things.' Charley glanced in Annie's direction for a brief moment. The young detective constable remained nose to the glass, silently staring through the window at the body, apparently now more at ease with the view which was so close and personal.

The turning on of the microphone indicated that Butterworth was about to start his examination. Dressed in protective clothing he stretched his arms above his head, before twanging his plastic gloves into place, one finger at a time.

In cases like this, Professor Butterworth's job was to ascertain the cause of death. He would attempt to find out if Cora Jones had died from, amongst other things, asphyxia, exposure, or an injury to a vital organ. Concerning the manner of death, she may have been killed by strangulation, a gunshot, knife wound, a blunt instrument, or indeed the boulder that had been dropped on her head.

Swabs from the mouth, anus and vagina were taken, and subsequently from relevant parts of the skin where the professor thought there was the best chance of obtaining DNA. In this case from her breasts. Hair was pulled, and cut from her pubic hair, and the hair on her head. Blood and urine samples were next. Professor Butterworth was thorough.

Noting all Cordelia's visible external injuries, whether they were serious or slight, for the recording device, he scoured her body from head to toe before having her turned over to check her back. CSI Neal Rylatt took photographs at Butterworth's request. The corpse may have a hundred injuries, but only one killed her.

With the victim positioned on her back, the professor picked up a scalpel to make the first incision, and Annie retched involuntarily. There were no obvious, visual signs of sexual penetration such as tears, bruising or scratches to indicate any form of penetration. They were reliant on swabs taken to ascertain if sexual intercourse had taken place.

Chapter 6

Inside the viewing room the air was filled with anticipation; the mood a mixture of desperate hope that Professor Butterworth's findings would confirm things that the detectives already knew, but more importantly, find things that they didn't, which would ultimately aid the investigators on their journey to trace the offenders.

Old man Butterworth was slow, methodical, and thorough in his approach to dealing with the lifeless body, which Charley likened to a mannequin. It was her belief that although life had once existed within, the vessel for Cordelia's soul was no longer required. Charley was impatient, aware that the corpse before her was decomposing.

The incision the pathologist had made down the front of the body revealed a cavity, from which he took great care in removing the woman's internal organs one by one; examining them in detail he recorded their weight. 'I want tissue samples and bodily fluids for further examination,' Butterworth said to his assistant.

'What do they do with the tissue samples and bodily fluid after they've done with them?' whispered Annie.

'Providing they are small samples, they'll be disposed of in the same way as samples from living patients. However, if they take the skull, or one of the larger organs for further examination they are duty bound to return the remains to be buried with the body,' said Charley.

There was no time limit for the examination, it was too important to rush. Charley steeled herself for the well-versed gruesome procedures to come, and the thought of the anti-cipated incision to be made in the hair at the base of the head, which would permit the little skin left to be rolled from the face, and would allow Butterworth to flip the top of her skull so that her brain could be scooped out for its examination, brought about the SIO turning her mind to counting, her preferred occupation at times like this. She started counting how many hours she had spent at mortuaries in the past year, too many to remember she decided after a while, but she was certain that it was longer than any time she had spent on holiday. Grimacing, she knew she was right to look away as the thick soup-like substance that was her brain spilled onto the table. There was nothing Butterworth could do to stop it. The men at the table, stepped back, and from memory Charley involuntarily gipped at the foul-smelling substance. Like the train rumbling along the tracks earlier, it was locked in her memory.

'What's he doing?' asked Annie in a hushed tone.

'I guess he's looking for a bullet,' answered Charley.

Annie's voice went up an octave. 'Has she been shot?'

'I don't know. He doesn't know. He's just ruling things out that could have possibly killed her.'

Butterworth looked up, and for the first time he spoke. 'A blood clot. There's evidence of a haemorrhage. She was alive when the head wound was inflicted,' he said.

Charley was surprised by the revelation. 'So, she was moved as she was unconscious, before the boulder was dropped on her head,' she said.

Annie looked puzzled. 'That sounds a bit odd, don't you think?' She paused for a moment. 'What would you do if you doubted Butterworth's findings?'

Charley was the Senior Investigator but she relied on the expertise of other professionals to help her solve a case.

'I'd seek a second opinion. After all it is the responsibility of the Senior Officer in charge of the investigation to check and question facts and actions of those involved in an enquiry, whoever they are, or whatever their role.' Charley frowned. 'Why do you ask?'

Annie was sitting with her chin resting on her hands. 'I just wondered.'

Ricky-Lee was also sitting with his exhibits book open, pen at the ready, awaiting the handing over of samples, or packages from the pathologist.

Charley's mind turned back to Cordelia's lifestyle. Charley had previous experience of working with outreach workers in London. She never judged people. After all, a spell of bad luck, rendering someone jobless and homeless, could happen to anyone, at any time in their lives, whatever their profession. Charley caught Ricky-Lee's eye, and he held her stare for a moment, raising an eyebrow at the professor's findings. He looked tired. Charley made a mental note to check in with him later. The fact he was in recovery from a gambling addiction was never far from her mind.

She turned back to the post-mortem. Some homeless people she had known were desperate for a roof over their heads, and readily accepted help, whilst others declined the offer of shelter, but would accept food and drink. Charley wondered which category, if any, did Cordelia Le Beau fall into? She definitely wasn't like any rough sleepers Charley had come across.

Almost three hours later, Cordelia's clothing, bloods, swabs, tapings and scrapings were collectively bagged up in their tamper-proof bags and containers to ensure they remained sterile, tagged with the necessary exhibit labels, which were attached to each individual item, in the possession of exhibits officer Ricky-Lee Lewis, ready to be transported to the pathologist for signing.

Charley stood by, watching Butterworth's assistant putting the internal organs into a black plastic bin bag, and depositing it in the corpse's cavity before sewing the incision wound up with neat, large mailbag stitches.

Some pathologists gave a running commentary from the start to the finish of the examination, some told jokes for the duration, but it was only now that Butterworth spoke at length to her about his findings.

As he stretched his back, he looked up over his mask, at the detectives in the viewing room, and he leaned his belly against the stainless-steel table where the body of Cordelia Le Beau still lay.

'The post-mortem is, as you know, to ascertain the cause of death. I'm all done here, and this is what I have deduced from examining the cadaver.' Butterworth spoke not only for the detectives, but also the recording device from which he would take his notes later, to produce his written report. 'Cora Jones aka Cordelia Le Beau has bruises at the back of both her upper arms, consistent with her being forcibly grabbed, and dragged backwards. This suggestion is corroborated by dirt, and grass stains, along with superficial scrape marks to her back, buttocks and the heels of her footwear.' Butterworth paused, and looked down at the corpse. He looked tired. He was obviously thinking and choosing his words carefully. 'There are two footwear impressions on her torso which are readily visible. The patterns from the soles are from two different-sized pairs of shoes, and are quite distinctive. One shoe print is much smaller than the other, possibly a female or a child's footwear. Finding out who they belong to is your domain.' Butterworth took a deep breath before continuing. 'She may not have been conscious at the time that these superficial injuries were sustained, but she was still breathing.' Butterworth's tone changed. 'I am quite satisfied Cordelia Le Beau was killed by a blow to the head, which as we have seen, cracked open like an eggshell when bludgeoned.'

'What about the bruising to her neck?' asked Charley.

'There is no doubt the poor lass suffered a physical assault. If you look closely you will see fingerprints on her neck, indicative with her being grabbed around the throat. Someone tried to strangle her, but that didn't kill her, although they might have believed at the time it had.'

Charley questioned the point. 'So, the attacker could have thought that she was dead before they threw a boulder at her head?'

'Her breathing would have been extremely shallow whilst she was in an unconscious state, so yes, that's quite possible.'

Annie looked puzzled. 'Then why would you drop a boulder on her head…?'

'Maybe they were trying to cover up what they'd done, they didn't want to see her face. Or like our theory earlier, they wanted to make identification of the body as difficult as possible. Or they realised she was still alive and wanted to finish the job.'

Annie was aghast. 'They didn't have to stove her head in though did they?'

Chapter 7

Junction Cafe was not on a road junction, but in a lay-by, off the main road. The aroma of frying bacon that assailed Charley's nostrils caused her stomach to growl. There was no canteen at the station and so Charley and Annie had stopped en route.

'I'm bloody starving,' said Annie, when she returned to the car with two bacon sandwiches, yanked open the door, and flung herself into the passenger seat next to Charley. A shiver ran down her spine. There was a cold wind blowing outside, and there was no doubt that a storm was coming. Charley wiggled her fingers. 'Gimme mine,' she said.

Annie took a satisfying bite of the soft, white teacake. The juice from the tomato inside dribbled down her chin. Wiping the liquid with her finger, she chewed the food slowly, moaning contentedly.

'I read somewhere that stress can shut down your appetite,' she garbled, her mouth full of food.

'Really?' said Charley, chomping the crisp bacon, while all the time thinking of her next move in the enquiry.

'Yes. The nervous system sends out messages to the adrenal glands to tell the kidneys to pump the hormone epinephrine.' Annie paused for a moment to nibble on a piece of bread. 'That's adrenaline to you and me. Then epinephrine helps trigger the body's flight-or-fight response, which temporarily puts eating on hold. I guess my adrenaline has gone!'

Annie took another bite of the greasy, reinvigorating butty, looking very pleased with herself.

Still chewing, Charley screwed up her paper bag, and stuffed it in the pocket of her door. Without further ado she switched on the engine.

'The postman needs eliminating,' she said, looking in her side and rearview mirror, before steering the car away from the kerbside.

Annie glanced at her boss, a puzzled look on her face. She popped the last morsel of the food in her mouth and swallowed hard. 'Why? Do you think he might be involved?'

Without taking her eyes off the road ahead, and with a cocked eyebrow Charley replied. 'We never assume, do we?'

Unblinking, the younger detective's eyes were intent on her supervisor's face. 'You can't help but develop your own theories about what happened, and who is likely to have done it though, can you?'

Charley agreed. 'Developing theories is better than drawing conclusions as you're much more likely to overlook, or ignore, evidence that doesn't fit the conclusion.'

'Mmm... so, what's your advice then?'

'We doubt, and question, even what appears to be definitive and damning evidence, until the investigation is over. New evidence, at any point, could radically change the enquiry.'

'What will we do next?' Annie said, eagerly.

'We will see what the postman said to the officers who took his initial statement. Then, we'll speak to him.'

'The person who discovers the body doesn't want to speak to us. He's obviously suss right?'

'If he doesn't want to speak to us, then we look at him more closely.'

-

Ricky-Lee was sitting at his desk waiting for Charley when the women returned.

'Where did you two get to?' he asked.

'Why?' said Charley, shrugging off her coat as she scurried past him.

'I need to discuss the priority for submission of the exhibits to Forensic,' he called after her.

'Can it wait ten minutes?' she shouted from her office where she was booting up her computer. 'I want to read the postman's statement again.'

Annie raised her eyebrows at Ricky-Lee. 'How about making us all a nice cuppa coffee while you wait, eh?' she said, smugly. 'Don't you know the person who reports the discovery of a body sometimes turns out to be the killer?' The young detective held her colleague's gaze a little longer than necessary. She had a glint in her eye. Ricky-Lee could not suppress a smile. Sitting down at her desk, Annie saw Wilkie who sat across from her was engrossed, copying something from his computer screen to paper.

'Stop winding him up,' he snarled, without looking up.

The friendly banter continued and Annie stood up to follow Ricky-Lee into the kitchen. 'The boss let you drive her yet, after you nearly knocked down that kid running away from the university last month?' he called over his shoulder.

At the kitchen door he turned to see Annie, a false smile upon her face.

'I tell you that twat was up to no good. He was running away from something, or someone you mark my words. All will come out in the wash, as Winnie says.'

Charley could hear her colleague chatting out in the office and got up to close her door. She understood that Ricky-lee and Annie likely needed to let off some steam after the post-mortem, but she needed to concentrate. Postman Dennis Mugglestone reported that he had seen 'all sorts' over the years. From folk the worse for wear, going home from what they called 'a good night out', just as he was heading out to work, to the hungry and less fortunate stealing food from the bins. He'd alerted the police on many occasions, he said, for many different reasons, such as people pushing wheelbarrows full of what looked like stolen goods along the streets, and others dealing drugs. 'I've never come across a body 'afore,'

Dennis was reported as saying. It was noted by the detective speaking to him that in his opinion the postman was still in shock.

However genuine Mr Mugglestone appeared to be, Charley knew that murderers often thought that by reporting a crime, they could bluff their way out of being named as a suspect. How wrong they were though. Especially on Charley's watch. Only evidence to prove them innocent would see anyone eliminated from an enquiry of hers.

Evidence had previously shown the SIO that the CCTV around the town centre was of good quality. Daily, it identified to the police the whereabouts of wanted criminals, and secured evidence against others. Viewing the CCTV in the immediate area around the Medway Bakery was identified by Charley as top priority. She was aware that her patience would be tested as a result, keen as she was to find a suspect quickly. A cup-half-full woman, she was hopeful that on this enquiry the CCTV would produce footage of the victim, her murderer, or possible witnesses to the crime.

The intelligence cell in the Incident Room was instructed to concentrate on the background of the victim, and also any incidents that may have occurred within the area involving homeless people, recently, or around Cordelia's chosen patch. 'Had she been affecting sales at the bakery?' Charley wondered. 'If so, could that be a motive for her murder? Even if that was correct, would someone really go to the extent of such brutality?' She thought not, but as always she would keep an open mind. Each case taught Charley something about man's inhumanity, and humanity, to fellow man.

The SIO poised her pen over paper, ready to add more details to her ever-growing list for the briefing.

1. Locate/contact next of kin/family

2. Collate CCTV from the area

3. Chase the test results from the post-mortem

4. Talk to other rough sleepers/charities for the homeless, see if they knew the victim

5. Doorstep interviews of resident/shop owners/workers local to the murder, see if they heard anything

6. All staff at the bakery to be interviewed

7. Search by the POLSA team to include drains and litter bins in their hunt for evidence

DI Charley Mann would make no apologies to the town's commuters for any inconvenience caused by the road closures and restricted access because of the outer and inner cordons, stating that all enquiries were necessary. There were no guarantees that, at this moment in time, those responsible for killing Cordelia would not strike again. A killer was on the loose, in Huddersfield town.

Satisfied that her team were working to full capacity, it was time to reassure the public. Murder always struck fear into a community, especially when the killer hadn't been caught. She looked out of her window, there was always a positive to be found, she acknowledged, as she closed her eyes and tilted her face to welcome the sun on her skin.

Annie had noticed something at the scene that was also puzzling Charley. She knew that a lot of homeless people often carried all their worldly goods around with them, so where were her possessions? Had they been stolen, or were they yet to be found, having been dumped by her murderer? Or maybe kept as a trophy? For now, Cordelia Le Beau was not ticking Charley's investigative boxes as being homeless. Her hair was well kept, her fingernails manicured, her shoes worth a small fortune. It just didn't fit.

She had thought of Cordelia last night, in the dark and the rain, terrified, as death came closer and closer.

What was Cordelia's story for being on the street? Charley didn't yet have the answer to that. That was something else to add to the list.

When she opened her eyes Charley saw ferocious black clouds marching across the sky. She had seldom seen such ominous-looking clouds develop so fast. Her eyes dropped to the ground to see people running towards the station for cover, as large droplets of rain fell on them.

–

The journalists collated for the press conference were sitting, or standing because the room was full, waiting for Detective Inspector Charley Mann's arrival. She in turn, was ready and eager to share with them some of the known facts of the case. There was also information she would hold back from the media, for now, which would be drip-fed to the journalists, to keep the enquiry the lead story, with fresh information. It was also sometimes useful to have a piece of information up your sleeve that only the killer could know.

Charley sat behind the desk prepared for her and took a deep breath. She needed to speak calmly and clearly.

'Good afternoon ladies and gentlemen, and thank you for your attendance, and patience. Earlier today, the body of a woman was discovered beneath the arches on Viaduct Street, in the town centre of Huddersfield, by a postman on his way to work. As a result, a murder investigation has been commenced under my command. We do know the identity of the deceased, but I'm sure you will understand that we are unable to name her, until we are satisfied that any known relatives have been traced and notified. Once that is done I assure you, we will pass on the necessary details of the deceased immediately. Hopefully that will be later today.'

Charley took a moment to scan the room and the faces therein before she continued. It was at times like these that she half-expected to see her wayward ex's face, head above the rest owing to his size and stature. Her heart skipped a beat. She knew, however, that it would be a long time before Danny Ray was released from his incarceration for murder.

'The victim had been subjected to a severe beating. Her body was left partially clothed. Rape hasn't yet been ruled out,' she announced. 'The attack upon her was extremely brutal, and I am confident, at this stage, that more than one person was involved. Her green parka-type coat, and other clothing believed to be worn by her at the time of the attack, was found close by her body. It appears that she may have been dragged a short distance from where she was rendered unconscious, to the location where she was found dead. The horrible finale to this attack which inevitably killed her was that a large coping stone, believed to be from a nearby dry-stone wall, was dropped upon her head, making it almost impossible to identify her in the normal way.'

The eyes of the journalists jumped upwards briefly from their notebooks to look at her, after the revelation. She saw heads bow and shake. She noted the narrowed eyes of disgust, and muscles in jaws tighten with anger, as she ground her teeth harder.

'It has been suggested that the victim was someone who sat, on a regular basis, outside the Medway on the High Street, and was easily recognisable by her pink-coloured hair. It is possible that she is known well, by people who frequent the area. My appeal this afternoon is for anyone who may know this lady, or have seen her, even spoken to her recently outside the bakery, or elsewhere, or have any information about this abhorrent crime, not to hesitate, but to get in touch with us here, at the Incident Room, and it goes without saying that I want to reassure them that their information will be treated in the strictest of confidence.' Charley took another deep breath. 'Any questions? As you can imagine, we have a lot of enquiries to pursue, and I am needed elsewhere, so if you could make it quick I'd appreciate it.'

'Maud Daunt, *Daily Diary*. How old was she and was it a sex attack Detective Inspector?'

'The deceased was in her early thirties and owing to the circumstances that she was found in, we are by no means ruling out that a sex attack is a possibility at this time. However, as always we will be keeping an open mind, and await forensic results to confirm.'

'Sarah Tame, *Chronicle*. Was this woman living on the streets?'

'As you are aware, our ongoing enquiries are in their infancy, but the attendant circumstance suggest that she was. However, not everything is always as it seems…'

'Ruby Lew, *Daily Mirror*. Should people be worried that this is not an isolated incident?'

'I want to assure people that we are treating this as an isolated incident. There have not been any other reported incidents.'

'Was it a gang attack?'

'We have evidence which suggests that there was more than one person involved. However, we have no information whatsoever to suggest that this incident was gang related.'

The questions continued, and Charley moved to one-to-one television and radio interviews. Her intention was for this murder investigation to be on everyone's lips, the topic of people's conversations across the community, and elsewhere.

She wanted people to be as repulsed by the attack as she was, which hopefully would prompt them to call the Incident Room with information, no matter how trivial they thought that might be. Every piece of the jigsaw puzzle was necessary to build the bigger picture. With the media briefing over, Charley hot-footed it back to the Incident Room to brief her enquiry team. Slowly and clearly, she updated them on the post-mortem and identification of the victim.

'The post mortem results show us that we are looking for two suspects, according to the pathologists who examined the footmarks found upon her abdomen. Whilst I am relaying to you the facts, there are some inconsistencies with our victim being homeless. Such as, the expensive shoes she was wearing, her clean fingernails and styled hair. We don't know how long she has been homeless so this may be relevant, or not. Her state of undress implies that she may have been sexually assaulted. At this moment in time there's no evidence to suggest she was raped and therefore we must wait for the forensic results of the internal swabs taken at the post-mortem. I'd also like to know why she felt the need to change her name?'

She went on to tell the team what she expected from them, along with their tours of duty that they would be expected to work, until further notice.

Charley also told them that her door, and that of her deputy, Detective Sergeant Mike Blake, were always open to them, for any concerns or issues that they had in relation to the murder, or on personal issues.

When the briefing was over Mike sought her out in her office. She had her head bent over paperwork that Tattie had delivered from the internal mail run. 'We've just been given a recent address where Cordelia is known to have been living,' he said, eagerly.

Her tired eyes instantly found his. 'Let's do the necessary, and quickly,' she said.

Chapter 8

Cordelia Le Beau's previous convictions showed her last known address to be 4, Mill Lane.

Annie was in high spirits on the fourteen-minute drive to the given location. 'I read that Slaithwaite was named one of the coolest places to live,' she said. 'Which is of course, why I chose to live there.'

Indicating to turn left onto the Manchester Road DS Mike Blake briefly turned to look at Annie who was sitting next to him in the passenger seat of the CID car.

'You mean that's the only reason?'

The young detective thought about his question. She stared steadily at the dull landscape passing, seeing in the distance the outline of farm buildings, and the dark satanic mills that lined the canal. 'Well no, I also watched *Where the Heart Is*, and I thought how lovely it would be to be part of such a tight-knit village community.'

On seeing Mike shake his head in an unbelieving fashion, Annie briefly hunched her shoulders and gave him one of her carefree smiles. 'I'm very much looking forward to the Moonraking Festival in February. All that lantern-making, and storytelling,' she said enthusiastically.

'Do you know the official name for the natives of Slaithwaite is Moonrakers?'

Annie's eyes were wide. 'No, but now I'm intrigued as to how that came about.'

'Local smugglers, caught by the excise men, tried to explain the nocturnal activities as "raking the moon from the canal".'

Annie looked bemused. 'What were they really up to?'

'Fishing out smuggled brandy.'

'You're joking,' Annie laughed.

The change from the clean countryside, to dirty streets and black-walled houses where the mill workers once lived, in the shadow of the woollen mill, was dramatic. Mike slowed the car down at the road sign at the bottom of the cobbled hill that was Mill Lane, to enable him to locate number four in the line of terrace mill cottages. Job done, he turned the wheels directly towards the kerb, parked expertly on the steep hill between two small vehicles, and turned off the car engine. 'I kid you not,' he said.

For a moment the detectives sat in silence, heads turned in the same direction towards the quaint creeper-laden cottage. The former home of a mill worker, tucked away in the little hamlet was not what either had expected. But still they had one thing on their minds. What would, if anything, come to light within its walls?

'There's nothing to suggest that Cordelia still lived here,' said Mike.

'There's nothing to suggest she didn't,' said Annie.

Simultaneously they opened their doors. When Mike joined Annie on the uneven flagstoned pavement, the detective constable raised an eyebrow at her supervisor. 'Hopefully the occupiers, or the neighbours, will be able to assist us with our enquiries,' she said in a hushed tone.

Finding No. 4 secure at the front, and with no response to their knocking, Mike peered through the downstairs windowpane, looking for signs of life, or an obvious disturbance.

'What can you see?' whispered Annie, straining to see over his shoulder.

'It's furnished,' he said.

The pair walked around to the rear of the property by way of the ginnel at the side. A little meandering stream brought them to a path which lead them to the back door. Through the window, they saw unwashed pots on the kitchen drainer. Annie pointed to the rubbish bin, full to bursting.

There was no doubt that the house was lived in, but by whom?

Annie caught Mike's attention by way of a nudge of her elbow, when she saw the curtains next door, twitching.

A few minutes later Lady Eugenie Toms announced herself from her doorstep. She paused for a moment, glanced up and down the street, as if looking for someone, before hurrying towards the three-feet-high wall that separated the properties. She was dressed in brown lace-up shoes, a heavy tweed skirt and a dusky-pink woollen twin-set, with a string of pearls around her neck.

'Caught up with her at last?' she said, crossing her arms under her ample bosom. 'About time!'

Taken aback by the neighbour's forthright outburst, the officers were somewhat surprised to hear that the elderly lady was talking about Cordelia Le Beau, who, she informed them, lived alone at No. 4, and had done for over a year. The detectives exchanged a look.

'When was the last time you saw her?' Mike asked.

'Yesterday morning, I believe.'

'What was she doing?'

'How would I know? She got in her car and left.'

'Can you describe the car for us, please.'

'It's dark blue. I don't know what make, I'm not particularly interested in cars, you know.' She paused. 'It's a small car.'

Annie wrote this in her notebook. It could prove to be of major importance.

'Does she have any regular visitors to the house, or neighbours she's friendly with?' asked Mike.

'She's a bit of a hermit if truth be known. She lives alone. No, no one visits. She acts as if she likes to think herself invisible, but she's far from that,' she chortled. 'She might as well have a beacon on her head with that pink hair. I presume she's done something? That's why you're here?'

'Actually, Mrs Toms, your neighbour was found dead this morning. We're here as part of the murder investigation.'

Mrs Toms' demeanour changed quickly. She turned pale and swayed, as though she might fall. She reached out to grab the wall to steady herself.

Annie lurched forwards grabbing her arms. 'Are you okay?' she gasped.

The action prompted an instant recoil. 'I'll have you know I was a matron. It'll take more than news of a dead body to shake me,' she snapped.

Detective Sergeant Mike Blake watched the colour return to Eugenie's cheeks. 'I understand that finding out someone you know has been murdered is still a shock,' he said, softly. 'Now, why don't you take yourself inside, make a nice cup of tea and rest for a while. When you've had a chance to digest the news we will return and take a statement from you,' he said, handing her a card with his contact details. 'Can you explain what you meant just now when you said, "caught up with her at last"?'

Eugenie appeared flustered. 'Oh, you know, it's just a saying…'

'Okay. If you want to speak to us beforehand, you have my number,' he told her.

When Eugenie closed her door behind her, Mike was on the phone to Charley confirming Cordelia's address, and the sighting of her leaving her home the previous day in a dark blue car. In return he heard from Charley that the staff working at the Medway Cafe had been interviewed. All were consistent with their description of a woman that they had seen regularly, sitting outside the premises. Apparently her purpose was begging. The staff knew the woman by the name of Cordelia, however some said this unusually fanciful name struck them as being false for a Yorkshire speaking lass.

Charley also revealed that the proprietor of the Medway Cafe had been less charitable to Cordelia than the staff, who often took her warm drinks and food. He docked staff's wages for encouraging vermin, and several times the officers heard that he had been seen moving Cordelia on with the toecap of his size eleven boots. 'Food attracts vermin,' and 'vermin need eradicating,' he reportedly told his workers.

'Do you want me to call a locksmith out to allow us to gain entry into number four?' Mike asked Charley.

'No Mike. Let's get a uniform presence there and let them force entry, for all we know someone could be dead or injured inside, and remember that when you go inside it may be a crime scene.' Charley said. 'I'll get some additional staff there so we can do the initial search as quickly as possible.'

Within minutes of the detective sergeant putting his mobile phone in his pocket, he saw two uniformed officers walking towards him and Annie, armed with a door ram which very quickly gained them access.

At the door the officers were momentarily stopped in their tracks by the darkness within that made it difficult for them to see anything, and the poor lighting made little difference until their eyes adjusted to it. They found the interior of the quiet, cool cottage neat and tidy. No furniture appeared out of place, or disturbed. Purposefully, the pair visited every room for a visual check, to ensure that no one else was present, dead, injured or secreted before a more structured search began.

Annie was puzzled. 'Cordelia had a nice, comfortable home. Why sit on the streets?'

Mike shrugged his shoulders. 'I presume begging is lucrative.'

'Perhaps in a big city, but in Huddersfield?' Annie questioned. 'It doesn't make sense.'

'You have to realise that there is not always a satisfactory explanation for someone else's actions, and we have to accept that there is no logical answer to our questions either.'

In the second bedroom there were unworn clothes hanging on a rail, with the price tags attached. The more expensive items had security tags firmly secured. If the contents of the room were anything to go by, Cordelia was apparently also a shoplifter. In the same room they found a plastic bucket full of coins of various denominations.

Mike tossed his head towards the bucket. 'How much do you reckon?'

Annie considered his question. 'A hundred quid?'

'Try two, or three.'

'What're you thinking?' said Annie as she followed Mike down the narrow open staircase into the lounge.

'I'm thinking that if Eugenie Toms' information is correct, and Cordelia has a car, then we need to find the documents that relate to her vehicle. The sooner we get a registered number, the sooner we can circulate it.'

Annie scanned the furniture in the dining area. Her eyes fell on a writing bureau.

Vehicle documents within told them that Cordelia's car was a dark blue Mini Cooper, registered number AXY 750W. A quick call to the Incident Room, saw the number quickly placed on the Automatic Numberplate Recognition system, and circulated to all patrol units.

'*Owner's body discovered in a town centre street. A murder enquiry has been established, led by Detective Inspector Charley Mann. The location of this vehicle is sought as a matter of urgency, and the Incident Room should be contacted.*' This was the text being written in the Incident Room to accompany the 'flag' on the ANPR system.

'At least we know that if the vehicle passes an ANPR camera it'll be instantly checked against database records and flagged as of interest to the operation,' said Mike.

'Then, they'll be able to check historical data to see if the vehicle routinely travels a route.'

'I wonder if the car is still in the vicinity?'

Annie shrugged her shoulders. 'We'll soon find out.'

By late afternoon, the house search was well underway, background enquiries were being made in the Incident Room and police officers were out gathering information and taking statements where necessary, throughout the town. Charley relied on uniform support to assist with these initial checks along the high street, utilising a house-to-house pro-forma.

Cordelia's home was once again secured.

'Could the murderers have the car?' Charley spoke her thoughts to Annie when she and Mike returned to the office. 'Any patrol coming across the vehicle will be fully aware of what had happened to the owner, so they would naturally approach with caution and act accordingly when it was discovered.'

'What kind of a person would stoop to such depths to con good-natured people out of their hard-earned money?' Annie asked.

Wilkie Connor, sitting at his desk opposite Annie, was listening to the conversation. 'The same low-life who swipe charity boxes. Why are you surprised?'

Annie screwed up her face. 'You wouldn't think she'd make enough money targeting shoppers and commuters in Huddersfield to maintain a house and a car though, would you? I barely make ends meet, and I have a job.'

'Being a police officer is a vocation, not just a job, and that's what the government rely on when they freeze pay, and increments. Perhaps she does have a regular job, and she needs to beg to boost her income to afford her lifestyle.'

'I read something the other day that said eighty per cent of beggars are not homeless. It's we who think that by putting something in an empty cup, we are paying for food and shelter, when the most likely beneficiaries are the nearest off-licence, drug dealer, or the mysterious people seen dropping beggars off in the city centres, and then picking them up at the end of the day. Which is so sad for the genuine people in need.'

'You think she's got a pimp she's working for?'

'Maybe it's a social thing… perhaps she's just lonely?'

'It's no good guessing. What we need now is to gain every bit of intelligence there is about Cordelia Le Beau, and promptly,' said Charley.

Chapter 9

In a private interview room at Peel Street police station, nineteen-year-old Angelica D'Souza sat, ashen-faced and tearful, waiting anxiously to speak to the person in charge of the Cordelia Le Beau murder enquiry. She had told Martie, who was working at the enquiry desk that she was a single parent who worked at the Medway and that she insisted on confidentiality. He immediately seated her in an interview room then requested Charley's attendance. The reason she gave for wanting confidentiality was that she was in fear of losing her job if it became known that she had spoken to the police.

The trembling started in Angelica's feet and spread through her body. Dipping her head slightly she saw how tightly clenched her hands were in her lap, and found that no matter how much she tried she could not stop them from shaking. She knew that the tissue Martie had kindly given her so that she could wipe her tears was entwined in her fingers, and crumpled beyond recognition, but she did not dare to loosen her grip.

As soon as Charley walked into the room, she noticed that Angelica D'Souza was chewing her lip nervously. Anxiety flashed swiftly across the young woman's face, immediately followed by a flush of relief in her cheeks as she saw that it was a woman who had entered the room. As Charley walked towards her, Angelica managed a weak, albeit awkward smile. Charley smiled back. Her smile was reassuring to Angelica as were her words, when she sat down opposite her and immediately thanked her for coming to the police station to see her.

Charley informed Angelica that she was the person in charge of the murder, whom the young lady had specifically asked to speak to. She then assured her that anything she told her would be in strict confidence.

'What I've come to tell you might help, or there again it might be nothing, so I apologise in advance if I am wasting your time, but I felt compelled to come.'

'Go on,' said Charley, patiently.

'The reason I'm here...' Angelica swallowed hard. She paused, distracted. 'Anyone can end up on the streets can't they?'

Charley nodded in agreement. 'Absolutely.'

'Through no fault of his own, my uncle ended up homeless,' she said through trembling lips.

'Sadly, it happens all too often,' said Charley sympathetically.

'You see, I read tea leaves, and the day that Cordelia died she asked me to read her tea leaves.' Angelica's eyes filled with tears. 'All I could see was flowers. Lots of flowers. I thought it might be her birthday. I told her that she was going to get flowers...'

Charley put a hand over the young woman's across the desk. 'Take your time.'

'Over the past few weeks I have seen my manager, Mr Marsh, giving Cordelia a hard time. He shouts at her, swears at her, calls her horrible names, threatens her and I've even seen him throw a bucket of cold water at her.'

'What sort of words did he use to threaten her?'

Angelica looked up at the ceiling, squinting her red-rimmed eyes at the bright lights. Charley could see that it pained her to talk about it. 'He... he threatened to kill her.'

'Do you think he meant it?'

Angelica looked surprised at her question. 'I don't know. He gets angry very easily, and he specifically warned us not to encourage her, but...'

'What did he mean by encourage her, do you think?' Charley interrupted the young woman.

'Giving her warm drinks and food.' Angelica looked downcast. 'He docked my wages last week for the price of the mug of tea, and a warm sausage roll, but it was freezing cold, her lips were blue, and we were going to throw them away as we were closing up,' she told Charley, with feeling. 'She loves our old-fashioned tea, made with tea leaves.'

Charley frowned. 'Why do you think that he would let Cordelia get under his skin?'

'He says that she's not homeless. He says he's seen her driving a car, and that she has the nerve to park it nearby. He says she is a whore.' Angelica fell silent for a moment, with a pensive look on her face. 'I don't know what to believe. Why would she sit on the pavement begging, in all weathers, and sell her body for sex, unless she was desperate?'

'Did he mention what sort of car he had seen her driving?'

Angelica shook her head. 'Sorry, if he did, I don't remember.'

'Did he say where he'd seen her park the car? It would help us to locate it.'

Again she shook her head, more slowly this time. 'Sorry no, but he might have told the officers who spoke to him at the shop earlier.'

'What do you think about Cordelia, and her begging outside the bakery?' asked Charley.

'I guess, probably because of my uncle being homeless, that I identified with her as someone in need, and I tried to help in the way I know others helped my uncle, which helped him stay alive. I felt sorry for her, at least, I did…'

'Does that mean your feelings might have changed, why?'

'At first I felt guilty looking at her closely, because of what Mr Marsh said. However, what I did notice was that she didn't look as if she had been sleeping rough.'

'In what way?'

'Her nails were clean. Her skin was moisturised, her hair looked healthy; cut, coloured, neater than mine. Her clothes were crumpled but not dirty. Her condition was not in the least like some of the homeless people I have seen around the town.'

'What did you do about Mr Marsh's behaviour towards her?'

'I feel ashamed and angry with myself now telling you this but, I really need my job, so, rather than antagonise him further, I kept my head down, worked hard and tried my best to avoid Cordelia.'

'Is there anything else that you can think of which may help us with our enquiries?'

'No that's it.' For a second, the fear Charley had seen previously in the young woman's eyes reappeared. 'Please reassure me Mr Marsh won't get to know I've spoken to you? Whatever Cordelia was up to, she didn't deserve to die. I hope what I've told you helps in some small way to catch her killer.'

Charley shifted in her chair and stood. Angelica followed her lead. 'Don't worry, Mr Marsh will not be told you've been to see us. Thank you for coming in to share the information. Only time will tell if it is useful or not, but I think perhaps it is,' Charley said kindly.

Back in the Incident Room, Charley wanted to know what Mr Rodney Marsh, the manager of Medway Bakery, had disclosed to the officers initially interviewing him about what he had seen, and, more importantly, what he had done to Cordelia.

Twenty minutes later she was reading his statement in which he had not mentioned that he had seen Cordelia Le Beau driving a car, or that he had seen her parking up near the bakery.

Neither had he disclosed having any heated arguments with her, warning his staff not to encourage her, or docking their wages for giving her food and warm drinks.

'Had he something to hide?' wondered Charley.

'Mike,' she called to her deputy from her office door in the room being temporarily set up as an Incident Room. 'It's time for us to clear the ground beneath our feet where Mr Marsh is concerned.'

Chapter 10

Cordelia Le Beau wasn't the first, and neither would she be the last person to beg on the streets.

Begging was a recordable offence under Section 3 of the Vagrancy Act 1824, carrying with it a sizeable fine.

Charley had learnt a lot about begging on her secondment to London, where to try to tackle the increasing begging epidemic, anti-social behaviour orders were used to ban beggars from parts of the capital, and police handed out fines to people persistently asking passers-by for money. However, it didn't appear to have much impact on the serial offenders, or deter the illegal street beggars, some of whom were whole families, from flying into Britain, begging on the streets for a few days, then flying home.

The statistics that Charley had asked for revealed that, in Huddersfield, there were sixteen known beggars on their radar, and four fines had been handed out by the police the previous month, but it appeared that at that time the police had been criticised for targeting those in genuine need.

Studies proclaimed that more than 85 per cent of beggars ended up on the streets to raise cash to fund a drug or alcohol addiction.

Charley paused from her reading to scribble on her notepad: *Is there any evidence of drug or alcohol addiction/abuse in relation to Cordelia?*

There is no 'type' of beggar. Beggars were men, women, young people and old, living on the streets, in temporary housing, in hotels, accommodation for the homeless, or social housing, who may or may not be benefitting from social allowances, may be looking for work or excluded from the jobs market.

Evidence of Cordelia's way of life suggested that she had a perfectly good roof over her head, as did twenty-six others questioned in a survey of fifty beggars throughout the country, whilst only five were known to be sleeping rough, and sixteen were living with family or friends, sofa-surfing. In Cordelia's case she had an abundance of home comforts, and food in her cupboards, which puzzled the SIO as to why she would put her health and wellbeing at risk on the streets, in all kinds of weather, unless it was so lucrative that she didn't need to work for a living.

In university towns the latest research intimated that, owing to a lack of jobs that suited the student lifestyle, there was a worrying rise in the young people begging on the streets for financial support, as well as to fund alcohol, drug and substance abuse.

Huddersfield wasn't a big city, or even a particularly lucrative large market town, although to Charley it was a great town.

Charley stood, and paused for a moment at her office window, thoughtfully watching sleet pitter-patter against the windowpane and the two police officers in the yard below. Braving the inhospitable elements, with their heads bowed, being buffeted across the yard with their shoulders hunched, they got into the marked vehicle. She took a mouthful of cold coffee from her mug, winced at its bitterness, smoothed the material of her navy trousers, and headed out of her office directly towards the kitchen to make another.

The mood in the Incident Room was as grey as the heavy clouds heaped low in the sky, shrouding Huddersfield in a dense grey mist. The officers that had not purposefully headed for the door after the briefing to begin their separate enquiries, sat at their desks working quietly and diligently. She saw Mike heading towards her. He deliberately tugged at the cuffs of his shirt, and was straightening his tie when they met outside her door. Usually, Mike was more restrained, but it appeared the article in the newspaper he was holding had temporarily rendered him quite opinionated. 'She must have been making bloody good money, otherwise she wouldn't 'ave been begging,' he said, the moment he saw Charley. He waved a copy of the national, with the headline, 'Street beggar makes £500 a day despite having his own home,' under Charley's nose. 'Look 'ere.'

Annie's was the nearest desk and Charley leaned over to put her mug down, before taking the newspaper from him. The young detective stopped what she was doing to look at the pair, and Charley's eyes focused on the article.

'I don't mind admitting that beggars asking for money intimidate me,' said Annie, sitting back in her chair, and crossing her long legs.

'They're a bloody nuisance,' piped up DC Wilkie Connor who, dressed in casual clothes, cord trousers, an open-necked shirt and jumper, gave a big, long, wide yawn. His eyes, watery and tinged with red in the corners, gave Charley the telltale sign of the previous night's lack of sleep. She wondered how his wheelchair-bound, ailing wife Fran was, and made a mental note to ask him.

'It's hard to tell who is genuine and who isn't,' said DC Ricky-Lee, who was sitting at the desk next to the old-timer. In contrast the younger man was smartly dressed in a suit and a white shirt that showed off his all-year-round tan.

Charley raised her eyes to look at the stony-faced detectives looking back at her. 'The plight of those in desperate need is being overshadowed by those out to try to make some additional cash by conning the public. Driven by greed rather than necessity,' said Charley.

Annie frowned. 'Like Cordelia,' she said.

'Maybe,' said Charley. 'Or perhaps she didn't have any other income, lost her job, was between jobs, and begging, selling her body for sex, and shoplifting was a last resort, conceived by her as being a more acceptable option to provide her needs, rather than resorting to criminal activities such as drug dealing. However, the main question for me is did Cordelia's begging play a significant part in her murder, or was she the victim of an opportunist. If we knew that, then we would have a better indication of how to tackle this enquiry.'

'You mean was she targeted, or was she in the wrong place at the wrong time,' said Annie.

Charley nodded. 'Yes. Exactly.'

It had been less than an hour since its circulation when Charley received a phone call from the control room, to inform her that Cordelia's car had been discovered parked on West Street, less than half a mile from where her body had been discovered, and not only did the SIO get the confirmation of the location of the vehicle, but she was also told that the vehicle was secure. What she didn't expect was that a set of keys was said to have been found secreted on top of the driver's side front wheel.

'Do you think that was her routine?' said Mike when she told him. 'To leave her keys with the vehicle?'

'Well, I guess if she was purporting to be a beggar, she would be aware that she could be arrested and searched by the police, or robbed, and by hiding her keys no one would suspect she had a vehicle, or a home.'

'Could it be possible that someone else knew her secret and planted the keys, after they attacked her?' he said.

Charley shrugged her shoulders. 'What would they gain?'

'If the guilty person was arrested then they would not be found with her keys in their possession.'

Charley sat quietly at her desk pondering the latest information. It appeared that Mr Marsh was correct about what he told his staff he had seen. Mindful that CCTV had been unavailable to them at the murder scene, Charley added to her list: *CCTV availability in the immediate vicinity of car?* She rolled her pen through her fingers. This could confirm for them if Cordelia had parked the car, and left the keys at the location.

Whilst there were a lot of questions to be answered, and things to find out about Ms Cordelia Le Beau, there was one undeniable fact, and that was that the woman had been brutally murdered.

Thoughts to record popped into her head and Charley wrote them down. *Could the fact that Cordelia had been deceiving people be a motive for her murder?* Charley didn't think so. Although she had to concede that people were killed for a lot less.

Charley walked out of her office and over to Mike's desk. 'I want Cordelia's car taken away for examination,' she said. 'We can't assume it was her who parked it where it was found.'

Mike spoke matter-of-factly. 'I've been doing some research. We have had a spate of vehicle thefts in the area. Thieves known to be stealing cars and parking them up to soak for a few days, to see if the stolen car is being tracked, if not, they return to pick it up and move it on.'

Wilkie was listening in to the conversation. 'If someone had nicked it, they'd hardly leave the keys for someone to find and take it,' he added cynically, fully anticipating the response.

'I agree,' Charley interrupted, but recognising Mike's thought pattern the SIO looked around the room to ask. 'Any response from our appeal, a relative or a friend?'

Blank faces stared back at her.

'It appears Cordelia really was a loner, and bearing in mind that ninety per cent of victims know their attacker, I wonder if Cordelia knew hers?'

'We really need a hit on the CCTV. This is now our top priority. Overtime has been approved.' The team nodded and got to work.

'Do you think it's going to be money well spent?' asked Tattie, the middle-aged office manager whose hair appeared more frizzy than usual, sandy-coloured and wild.

'I hope so. I want these killers caught before they can hurt anyone else.' Because despite what she had said to the press, Charley was not convinced this was an isolated incident.

It was dark, and the team had been working eleven hours, when an anonymous telephone call was received in the Incident Room. The caller was a female, and she sounded as if she had been drinking. Shouting down the phone she called Cordelia a bitch, and told Detective Constable Wilkie Connor, who had taken the call, that Cordelia deserved to die. No other words were spoken, and instead of calling it a day, the fatigued and hungry team set about trying to trace the phone call's origin as a matter of urgency.

Most knew from experience that all sorts of cranks rang an incident room, but someone obviously had something against Cordelia Le Beau to waste their time ringing in.

Drawing parallels between her past, and this present case triggered a trip down memory lane. Charley was contemplating the eighteen months since she came home from a four-year secondment in London to her home town of Huddersfield, on promotion as the head of crime, when suddenly she noticed Winnie, handing out sandwiches to the team from her basket on wheels. She smiled, it seemed like she had never been away from her Yorkshire police family. This was not how she had envisaged it would be. It wasn't how it had been for her predecessor.

The bodies had been relentless since her return.

On a positive note, although work continued on the previous murders at Crownest, it was too soon for the related court case to be upon them just yet.

God bless the old lady, Charley thought as she saw the look on the grateful faces for the most welcome, delicious and homemade sustenance. With no canteens in police stations the only way to get food was to bring it in, or go out to a takeaway, and when a murder broke and the officers were working flat out, morale soon tanked with no food in bellies, and Winnie knew that.

Charley watched Winnie making the rounds and thought briefly of her father. The two had been childhood sweethearts, but Winnie had moved away as a teenager and on her return discovered Jack Mann married and his wife pregnant. What Charley would give to be able to talk to her dad about the things she had discovered since his death. Had he found it hard to love two women? Or had he the same skill at compartment-alising as Charley?

She wondered if her mother ever knew about his love for Winnie? Maybe she did, maybe that was why she was able to teach Charley patience, gratitude, unconditional love, and, most importantly, that nobody was perfect.

Her father had been a worker, fighter, a believer in old Yorkshire legends; latterly in Karma. He showed Charley how to respect others, taught her discipline, to stand up for the principle of right, no matter what the consequences, and that true strength came from compromising when necessary, and compassion. He preferred the boxing ring to working on the land, and taught Charley all he knew about packing a punch. Charley, on the other hand, loved spending time at the farm with the animals, listening to her granny's folktales, and of course then there was Danny Ray, the son of the neighbouring farmer, a little older than she, who became someone she grew to hero-worship.

Her face suddenly turned sour. How did she overlook the elements of Danny's character that overrode her instinct about him even at that early age?

As Winnie worked towards Charley's office, Charley looked up at her certificates hanging on her wall. Her meteor-itic rise through the Force to become head of CID in her home town at the age of twenty-nine, was her greatest achievement yet, albeit tinged with sadness that her first murder enquiry resulted in her arresting Danny Ray for the ultimate crime.

The fact that she had not guessed that someone so close could be a killer still weighed heavily on her mind.

Now she was surrounded by more experienced colleagues for whom she had the greatest respect, and as the size of her team grew dramatically when a job like a murder broke, it did not faze her. She was more than qualified to do the job. The fact that she had brought about the breakthrough in the capture of one of Britain's most wanted murderers, Titus Deaver, the cannibal killer, could not be denied by her most ardent adversary, who had no option but to support her obtaining her present role.

She had missed that her boyfriend was a murderer, but that did not undermine everything else she had achieved. She took a deep breath. She could do this job. She would catch this killer.

A woman had called into the Incident Room. Even if the lead went nowhere, it meant that people were reacting to the crime following the media coverage, and that was always a good thing.

When Winnie knocked at her door Charley smiled widely. People now had murder on their lips, and she had food.

Chapter 11

An investigation is about searching for the truth, a murder investigation is no different, eliminating people from the enquiry at every step and therefore paving the way to the culprits.

Murder is the greatest test for the detective.

Despite the lateness of the hour, the police station was buzzing. There was anticipation in the air as the 2 to 10 pm shift was coming to an end and the night shift were getting ready to take up the baton. No one could ever say that a police officer's work was predictable. In fact, each call requiring attention was varied and able to be adapted as required.

Charley popped into the mailroom as she was passing, and picked up the few papers that had been deposited in her pigeon-hole during the afternoon. One of the positive effects or outcomes of such a large enquiry, according to the stats from HQ, was the reduction in the local crime rate, mainly owing to the influx of officers brought into the division, but however grateful Charley was for that, she was also aware that the attack on a lone female would require an increased visual level of uniformed officers on the streets. She knew, from experience, that women wouldn't feel safe until Cordelia's killers were caught.

Enquiries remained ongoing into tracing the anonymous caller to the Incident Room. Acknowledging that there was nothing more that she could do today, Charley switched off her office light, closed her door and bid the others good-night. Her parting instruction was that if there was any news she should be contacted immediately. Tucked under her arm was the intelligence file on Cordelia Le Beau – her bedtime reading. She knew sleep would evade her for some time yet, but the hours before sleep would be spent wisely, as she intended to read all about the woman's past, to gain a better understanding of what type of person Cordelia had been, prior to visiting her house with Annie tomorrow.

The town hall clock struck ten o'clock when she drove her car through the big gates of the station yard. She felt jittery, no doubt the after-effects of the adrenaline in her body after the recent rush.

Heading towards home, the Detective Inspector's tyres squealed on the tarmac, as she drove round the ring road of the wet, well-lit and relatively quiet market town. However the tranquility was brief. Blaring sirens shattered the usually serene, rural silence Charley was accustomed to at that hour whilst driving on Valley Road. A traffic patrol car, lights flashing and siren wailing, rocketed towards the A62. This was closely followed minutes later by an ambulance similarly announcing its presence. Her first thoughts, as she pulled into the kerb to allow them to pass, was that someone was going to have a busy night, and selfishly she said a silent prayer that her mobile phone would remain silent.

With no sudden call coming in requesting her presence, whatever the incident maybe, Charley continued to drive steadily home. Dark and gloomy fields spread around her, hemming her in on every side. It unnerved her to think what emergency she might come across ahead, so much so that when she parked up on her street she exhaled, the tension visibly easing from her shoulders. Looking along the street, she could see just one house in darkness. She told herself that she ought to know better than to leave all her lights off and let would-be criminals know there was no one at home, when she had timer switches for her lamps. She made a mental note to activate them.

Exiting the car to face a blustery northwesterly, Charley pulled up her hood, put her head down and sucked in the wind as she walked the well-trodden path to her front door where, with trembling cold fingers, she fumbled around in her pocket for her keys. In her mind's eye her home was beckoning with memories of her formative years, the promise of a cheery hello, a roaring fire, a warm meal, and a mug of hot chocolate, but instead of these niceties when she flung open the door, the hallway was pitch-black, eerily quiet, freezing cold, and rather than the wholesome smell of cooking pervading the air, it smelt of mildew and old footwear. The reality made her heart sink, leadened her limbs and slowed her spirit. Immediately she clicked on the switch that illuminated the staircase, the light revealing her pasty-face in the hallway mirror, and the red-rimmed eyes of exhaustion. Kicking off her shoes Charley dragged her heavy feet up the stairs. She was close to tears with a sudden sadness brought on by the grief she had not dealt with on her mother's and father's deaths. Too exhausted to close her curtains, she threw her bag on the floor behind the door, the file on the bed, removed a few of her clothes and crawled between the cool, cotton sheets. Cordelia's file lay within arm's reach, but it was a while before she began to read it, to try to shift the despondency she was feeling.

First impressions suggested Ms Le Beau, aka Cora Jones, was someone who did what she wanted, when she wanted, how she wanted, and took from others without conscience.

Charley was still far from sleep when she finished reading its contents, but she did feel the orderly process of a murder enquiry gradually reforming peace in her mind. She closed the file.

As she lay in the dark, she concentrated on the regular sound of her ticking clock, by her ear on her bedside table, and the swaying of the ghost-like image of the tree outside upon her wall, both of which, she recalled, soothed her as a child, creating a symphony of droning monotony. Before long she felt drowsy. The drowsiness soon descended into sleep and dreams, but in her dreams all she could see was herself flying blind through a midnight sky.

At five-fifteen, Charley rose, got dressed and went down into the kitchen looking for something to eat.

When she opened the fridge, a sour smell greeted her. Her first thought when she identified the milk as the culprit, was that she wouldn't tell Annie, not after enlightening her about Granny's Yorkshire folklore, and the Hobgoblin. The small, hairy, mischievous little man who, in return for a jug of milk or food would typically do small tasks around the house, like dusting and ironing, so it was said, but, as the folklore went, the Hobgoblin could be easily annoyed, and when he was, he was known to mix the wheat and chaff, extinguish the fire, and turn the milk sour. Smiling to herself, she flushed the rest of the milk down the sink, picked up a half-eaten bar of chocolate, and headed for the door, in work mode.

After the morning briefing Charley's thoughts moved from one thing to another, like a stone skipping across water. With Annie in the passenger seat, as they travelled together to Cordelia's home, she instructed the young detective.

'Remind me to check we've got the external and internal footage of the house ready to show at the next briefing,' Charley said.

'Already done!' Annie looked pleased with herself.

'Great, thanks.'

The purpose of the house visit was to gather information from Cordelia's home that would give them a pen-picture of her movements; hopefully enough to create a timeline for the last few days of her life. Some people kept diaries, others showed appointments on a calendar. The more technical used their mobile phones, laptops or tablets to record their activities.

'Where do you think Cordelia would keep her diary?'

'Probably in her head.'

Charley turned to Annie and scowled. 'That's a bit negative…'

Annie protested. 'I'm not,' she contradicted. 'We've not exactly been overrun with people wanting to help us with the enquiry have we? Let's face it, those that have come forward would have us believe that she sat outside the Medway begging every day.'

'That's true and maybe she did,' agreed Charley ruefully.

The SIO hoped that seeing how Cordelia lived would lead her to finding out how she had died. Was it plausible as was believed, that she had no relatives, and no one she called a friend? In Charley's experience, everyone had someone.

The detectives entered the house by the back door.

Cordelia's home was small, neat and well-organised, providing all the comforts one could ask for. All was still and intensely quiet, so much so that Charley felt sure that if the proverbial pin were to drop, she would hear it. The SIO stood perfectly still for a moment or two in each room, and scanned her environment. This purposeful act enabled her to absorb the surroundings. Charley sniffed. There was a hint of lavender in the air, perhaps the essential oil had been added to the polish used to create the high shine on the rich mahogany wood of the furniture. Cordelia was, it appeared, house-proud.

The next two hours were spent searching Cordelia's personal property, some of the correspondence that the detectives came across was in the name of Cora Jones, however there were others in the name of Heidi Bodie, Candy Kane, Emily Delaney, Anna Harris. It appeared that Cordelia Le Beau had several aliases.

Annie raised a questioning eyebrow. 'Why on earth would a beggar need so many different names?'

'A person can use whatever name they wish, however, legal documents issued, such as drivers' licences require proof, such as a birth certificate and may require a legal change of name if the alias is used,' said Charley.

'All of which appear to be missing, so as yet we don't actually know for sure, the name she was given at birth?'

'True, and it is important that we know what name she started life with.'

Certificates, showed that Cordelia had obtained three A-levels at college, in the name of Cora Jones, but there was no sign that she had gone to university. There were many diplomas in business studies, all with distinctions. She was, it appeared, nobody's fool.

'Have you come across any bank, credit card or mobile phone statements?' Charley asked, after not having discovered them herself.

Annie shook her head. 'No, but I guess she could have chosen to have them sent online?' When she realised that Cordelia could have as many online accounts in as many names, if not more, her jaw dropped. 'That's going to cause the techies a pretty bad headache.'

Charley looked about her. 'You're not kidding. Have you seen a computer?'

Annie showed her her bottom lip. 'Nope, I haven't.'

The SIO looked thoughtful. 'I realise we have had to delay to get her car to HQ on a low loader before searching the car. Do you know if they found a mobile phone, or a purse in Cordelia's car?'

Annie pulled a face. 'There's no invoices or receipts here to help track her recent movements either.'

'That's buggered part of the financial investigation into her background which would've revealed to us her financial status then. Although if she owns this property, that'll be a good source of intelligence.'

Charley's mobile phone rang. It was Wilkie updating her on the arrival at HQ garage of Cordelia's car, and to inform her that internal and external examinations had begun.

'Ask them to check for a mobile phone or a purse will you asap, and if anything of importance is found I want to know immediately. Make sure we have a photograph of the vehicle, which we can use in the future if necessary to revitalise the media interest. We might also use it to try to obtain information about possible sightings in the area. If there are any pay-and-display tickets in the vehicle have them bagged and tagged, the dates may tally with information, or give us information as to where she was on specific days. We don't know what evidence will be significant in the future.

'I'm satisfied about one thing,' Charley said as she turned at the back door before opening it.

'What's that?' said the younger woman.

'This house is not a crime scene.'

Everything had its place in the house, which told Charley that Cordelia was an organised person who perhaps enjoyed routine, and so with what appeared to be a lack of family, or friends, did this give them a clue as to why she was seen begging outside the Medway? Had begging become a way for social interaction without commitment because she was lonely?

—

At eight o'clock that evening the debrief began in the Incident Room, which was now up and running. The debrief was an opportunity to collate, share and discuss everything the team members had discovered so far during the initial stages of the investigation.

The room was full, and the atmosphere expectant. Charley's assumptions were right. The energy within was tangible. There was nothing like a murder enquiry to increase the adrenalin levels. Every officer present was aware that the next person they spoke to was the possible murderer. Everyone wanted to be that person who felt the murderer's collar.

Charley gave a brief résumé outlining what they knew.

'Cordelia Le Beau had several aliases, all these will need to be checked out. She was, it is thought, thirty-four years of age when she was brutally murdered. We have not as yet found her birth certificate, or any type of formal identification. She lived alone in a terrace house at 4, Mill Lane, in a quiet area of Slaithwaite. The car she drove was a mini, which we have recovered in the town centre, and is being examined. It was parked up not far from where she was found. We haven't come across any relatives or partners. We know from her neighbour that she had left her home the morning before her body was discovered.'

After a brief pause to let people digest what she had told them, she continued.

'We know her body was discovered by Dennis Mugglestone, a postman. We also know that at least two people were involved in the attack upon her. The owner of the Medway had seen her driving a car and suspected her deception. According to a witness, he also said that Cordelia was a whore, but there is nothing to suggest that as far as we can tell. He shared this information with his staff. Recently, he threatened her to move from outside his premises, and initially, for whatever reason, he failed to disclose this information to the officers who spoke to him. Therefore, it will be a priority for us to see Mr Marsh tomorrow morning, when perhaps he will explain why.

'I want pictures of Mr Mugglestone, Mr Marsh and his staff available to us, so that the CCTV operators can identify them. We also need their shoe sizes, and hopefully the prints we are having developed, showing the pattern and size of the shoes worn by those that stamped on Cordelia, will be available for matching purposes soon.

'Cordelia Le Beau's house was clean, and tidy,' Charley told them. 'There was a distinct lack of photographs about the place, and nothing to suggest a partner; ready meals for one in the fridge and a lone toothbrush in the bathroom. However, we know that people can be very inventive when they want to hide things. The house is not a crime scene. I'm of the mind that the killer may not even know where she lived. The clothes she was wearing when she was found indicate that they were her work clothes, just like you and I have. Annie made a comment to me that she had never seen a tidier wardrobe, and let me tell you, there was nothing in that wardrobe that would be suitable for begging. I was thinking we would find old, worn, crumpled, warm clothing, scruffy items, including hats, scarves, gloves. Instead what we found were smart, designer numbers, including evening wear. So at the moment we need to keep an open mind as to the motive for this brutal killing.'

Detective Constable Ricky-Lee told those present that along with CSI, he had searched her car. 'The keys we already know have been found resting on the wheel of the driver's side. Inside, we recovered a handbag, which contained her purse and a mobile phone. The phone was password protected. The purse contained two ten-pound notes. Apart from these two items there was nothing. Her car, like her home, is clean and tidy.'

'Have you generated an enquiry about her mobile phone with her service provider?' asked Charley.

'I have,' he said.

'Any sign of a laptop in the car?'

'No, ma'am.'

Mike Blake was on his feet. 'The known CCTV in the area has been collated, and where possible collected. There are a couple of call-backs to be done, and viewing will start in earnest early doors tomorrow by an identified team of four.'

Charley consulted her notes. 'Any update regarding the female caller, believed to be drunk, who called the Incident Room last night?' she asked.

'No, nothing yet.'

'All the staff at the bakery appear to have seen Cordelia at some time or other, but like I said earlier, the boss didn't tell us everything he knew, which is a mistake on his part if he thinks that we will stop there. You don't lie to a murder enquiry. He must be naive, or stupid,' added Charley. 'Tomorrow is another day, so I'll bid you goodnight. Thanks for your efforts today, and I'll see you all bright and early in the morning.'

Charley walked towards her office, and Mike followed. Before they left, they had to have a discussion with regard to their joint approach at the interview with Mr Rodney Marsh.

'I think we should invite him into the station to interview him, don't you?' said Mike.

Charley raised an eyebrow at her detective sergeant. 'That all sounds innocent enough. However, we both know that we will have actually misrepresented the nature and purpose of the discussion to disarm him, and reduce his resistance.' Her tone held a teasing note to which Mike reciprocated.

'The soundproofed room with armless, straight-backed chairs, thereby removing any sensory stimulation and distractions. By physically and socially distancing him, we can begin to subtly exert pressure on him to talk.'

'Soften him up using flattery, and build a rapport, ask benign questions and engage him in pleasant small talk, you're good at that.'

Mike almost laughed. 'What're you trying to say?'

Charley smiled at her detective sergeant. Office banter showed her a happy team.

Mike stood, closed his notebook with a snap, and prepared to leave. 'And, if he is happy to mess us about, then I am more than happy to reciprocate,' he said in a more professional manner.

Charley raised her eyebrows as she looked up from her desk at her detective sergeant. 'I have no doubt about that, and every confidence in you,' she replied.

Chapter 12

Early the next morning, DS Mike Blake and DC Wilkie Connor approached the Medway Bakery, whose shop had been customised to serve coffee and tea to customers who wished to consume the food baked on the premises. The purpose of their visit was to invite the owner, Rodney Marsh, down to Peel Street Police Station to answer a few questions.

There was an aroma of warm bread and baking floating in the air. Without a word, and moving with sharp, precise strides, Mike seized the door handle and pushed it wide enough to enter. Wilkie followed him over the threshold, sniffing the air appreciatively.

Marjory Lettice, the buxom, apple-cheeked shop assistant, stood with her back to the detectives, busying herself behind the counter. The bell alerted her to their presence. 'I'll be with you in two shakes of a lamb's tail,' she called out cheerily. When she turned, she appeared surprised to see two men in suits flash their warrant cards at her. Both had a look of concern on their faces at the disturbing guttural sound coming from the rear of the premises.

Tilting her head to one side Marjory paused, listening carefully. After a few moments she narrowed her eyes at the men, then started chuckling. 'Don't look so worried. I don't think he's murdered anyone today, yet,' she said with a chuckle.

With a straight face Mike stared questioningly at her.

'Ahhh… It's Rodney. He says it eases his chest. I know this to be true, because my father and his sailor pals made much the same noise whilst hoisting a sail,' she said, as she took them through to a passage where a sallow-looking Angelica D'Souza stood, forlorn, with her back to the wall like a scarecrow covered in flour, biting her lip. The air was hot and humid and filled with tension.

The sweating Rodney Marsh was swearing and cursing as he removed a burnt batch of bread from the oven. Another man tipped trays of ruined delicacies into the bin. Mr Marsh's face was like thunder.

Marjory stopped at the door, turned and spoke over her shoulder in a hushed voice. 'Although characteristically bakers are known to be misanthropic, morose and very unstable, so you never know...'

When Marsh looked up momentarily from stretching the dough with the heel of his hand, he saw the detectives' eyes upon him, but, rather than stop what he was doing, he continued to fold the dough, repeatedly rotating it through 90 degrees, aggressively patting and folding it in turn.

It was apparent to the detectives that they would have to make a move if he were to engage with them. Taking their warrant cards out, they vocally introduced themselves, but still his focus remained on knocking back the dough and punching it down, as if *it* was his arch-enemy and not the person who had burnt the products. A few moments later, Marsh began to knead the dough gently. Wilkie took a step towards him. 'My father was a baker, and he used to say that if a man kneaded dough whilst in a bad temper he put bad temper in the bread, and that bad temper goes into the person who eats it.'

Folding the sides of the dough into the centre with the hand of someone who could clearly do it in his sleep, Rodney Marsh finally made eye contact with Wilkie. 'I don't know where you source your information, but it's obviously not from the right place.' Then he looked back down at the dough on the large wooden table. After a few moments he stopped to pat it and enlightened Wilkie Connor further. 'For your information the more firmly the dough is kneaded, the better the bread.'

Taking advantage of having caught Rodney's attention Mike Blake interrupted. 'We'd like you to accompany us to the station to answer a few questions.'

Marsh stopped, and scowled at him. 'You're having a laugh? Can't you see I'm busy?'

'Perhaps if you'd been honest with us from the outset Mr Marsh, a visit to the station wouldn't be necessary, but as it is we would like you to come with us,' Mike Blake said firmly.

Marsh set his lips momentarily. 'What if I refuse?'

'Then you'll be arrested on suspicion of murder and taken to the cells, where you will wait until we are ready to interview you.' Mike's voice was harsh.

'Much easier and quicker if you come along with us voluntarily,' added Wilkie levelly.

The baker was silent, reflecting that the request was not negotiable. He smacked his hands together, casting flour in all directions. 'I'll be having a word with your boss,' he said angrily whilst he undid his apron. He threw it down on the table, muttering under his breath something which they couldn't make out.

Mike moved impatiently. 'That's right y'will, because I know she wants a word with you too.' The detective sergeant's eyes found the coat hooks behind the door in the bake room. He looked at him sternly. 'Come on, what are you waiting for? The sooner we get to the station to further matters, the better all round.'

Hands plunged deep into his coat pockets, and eyebrows dragged downwards, Rodney Marsh followed the detectives out of the bakery, into the shop.

'Keep an eye on things will you,' he said to Marjory, jerking his head in the direction of Angelica. 'Don't let them fuck up the next batch. M'lad will be back from his rounds soon.'

Sitting in the rear of the CID car, Rodney Marsh's face resembled a death mask. At that moment, the young butcher's boy, and the baker's lad, hired to deliver their wares, both rode their bikes onto the pavement at precisely the same time.

Marsh shouted to his son, 'It'll be okay,' but all he could do was stare. Mike was struck by the stark contrast between the hardy, ruddy-cheeked butcher's boy and the haggard, sallow baker's boy, as he pulled away from the kerb and drove off.

Twenty minutes later the three entered the dingy, window-less interview room; Wilkie Connor flipped a switch and the lights flickered into action. When Marsh was seated, Detective Inspector Charley Mann entered the room and had a few words with Wilkie, who then left, shutting the heavy door behind him. She appeared to be as pleased to be there as he was, when she slid into the chair opposite him, next to Mike. The SIO introduced herself, before getting straight to the point.

'It concerns me that you think it's okay to lie, and withhold information from us, on a murder investigation Mr Marsh.' With eyes like steel, she held his gaze before continuing. 'On top of that, I hear that you were also reluctant to come into the station today.'

Marsh shuffled uneasily in his chair. 'I have a business to run, the last batch was burnt by incompetent staff. I'm here now aren't I?' he said angrily.

Charley's face showed no emotion. 'We have a murder to investigate. I'm sure your team are sufficiently trained and efficient enough to manage without you for a short while. Even professionals can occasionally produce burnt offerings.' The SIO inhaled deeply as she opened the dossier in front of her. 'Let's see if we can sort this out quickly shall we? I'm sure that would benefit us both.' She looked up at him from the papers. 'Firstly, tell me why you didn't share with the officers the fact that you had seen the murdered woman previously driving her car, parking it up, and walking to where she sits outside your premises pretending to be a penniless beggar?'

'I didn't want to get involved, all right?' said Marsh testily. 'The woman was a cheat and a liar, and I told her so. End of.'

He stopped, but there seemed to be more left unsaid in his eyes. The silence grew thicker.

'Are you sure that is the end? We heard about your intense dislike of her.'

A faint blush rose in his cheeks and hung there for a moment. 'I didn't like her, no. She was a con-artist, who had a hard heart and a smooth tongue. I saw her attach herself every day to people who had little to give, and without conscience she took what they had.' Marsh shrugged his shoulders. 'If that's how she wanted to live her life, fine, but I didn't want her to do what she did right outside my premises, where I also caught my staff giving her freebies, and encouraging her, I mean how stupid can they be?'

Charley looked him straight in the eye. 'Did you tell her to go?'

He looked incredulous. 'Of course I did,' he said. Charley noticed his fist, resting on the table between them, tighten slightly. 'On numerous occasions, but that bloody woman just laughed in my face. Truth be told, she also cost me dearly in more ways than one. I've had to reprimand my staff, which in turn has caused bad feeling. I didn't want to, but what else could I do to stop them giving away my profits?' There was an awkward pause. He sat back, locked his hands over his stomach and gazed down at the floor between his legs, contemplating what had been said it seemed. The air hummed with tension. When he looked up at Charley a few moments later, his speech was rushed. 'You might as well know that I also threw a bucket of cold water over her, and before you ask, no, I'm not proud of it but she had approached my son, and his friend who appeared to be an age of her liking.'

'I guess that made her move?' said Charley, giving him a surprised look.

Marsh shook his head. 'No, she was as stubborn as a mule. She played to the crowd. It seemed people felt even more sorry for her, and I ended up being labelled as mean and heartless – it has lost me valuable customers, let me tell you.'

Rodney Marsh shuffled in his chair and wincing, stretched his legs. Years of working ceaselessly on his feet had taken their toll on his knees, leaving them weak and arthritic, but Charley couldn't help noticing that his loose-fitting, white T-shirt did nothing to conceal the size of the muscles on his shoulders and arms. There was no doubting his strength.

'It might come as a surprise to you that we already know about the dousing incident,' Charley said. She paused and frowned. 'She must have really got under your skin for you to assault her?'

Marsh shook his head, slowly. 'I'd never hit a woman,' he said meaningfully. 'I might rant and rave, usually for good reason, but I would never, ever assault a woman.'

'You don't think that throwing water over someone is an assault?'

Marsh grimaced. 'Okay, but you know what I mean, I didn't hurt her.'

'Can we say then that your plan to move her from outside your premises backfired.'

'Yes,' he said looking suitably ashamed.

'You'd have us believe that you just walked away after-wards?'

'Yes, I couldn't let her distract me any longer. I'd said my piece and you know the rest… I had work to do, and a business to run, just like I have today.'

Charley sat eyeing Rodney Marsh stonily. 'We hear that you threatened to kill her.'

Marsh pursed his lips and pulled his legs slowly in, gazing at her fixedly. There was a pause.

Charley went on. 'Look, I understand how busy you are, but what was stopping you sorting her out once you'd finished work? Is that what happened?' Charley slanted her eyes at Marsh.

'Nothing, but that isn't what happened. I threatened her, threw the cold water over her, but nothing more.' Marsh smiled icily.

Charley turned her head to look at Mike Blake, and back at Marsh. 'Surely you can see how it looks from where we're sitting; you threatened Cordelia, assaulted her and now she's dead. Tell me, why didn't you tell this to the officers who initially spoke to you? You'd have saved yourself a lot of grief if you'd admitted the truth. We are, after all, investigating a murder. Did you think that we wouldn't find out about your attitude and behaviour towards Cordelia?' she questioned.

Rodney Marsh shook his head. His face softened. 'Look, like I said before. I didn't want to get involved,' he said quietly, looking at the detectives sitting opposite him in turn. 'That's God's honest truth.' Marsh inhaled deeply, leant back in his chair, put his large hands covered with skin calluses behind his head, and tilted his head to the ceiling.

Charley could not help but wince at the burn scars on his arms. Before breathing out slowly through pursed lips, he looked down to reveal eyes filled with tears.

'My brother was self-employed when he was the main witness to a multiple murder investigation, and warned that he would be required for court to give evidence. As it happened he'd just finished two months' jury service when he was called up. In the end he couldn't work for nearly four months, hanging around in court as he did for days, weeks on end. Someone else came along and took his customers. It ruined him, he had a breakdown, and he has never been the same again because he can't provide for his family. I can't risk losing my business. I can't let that happen to me. My business is my life, and it relies on my being on site six days a week. Perhaps this is a wake-up call for me to train my staff to cope without me, but ours is a family business and I was waiting for my children to learn the trade in the hope that they would continue in the future.' Marsh swallowed hard. 'I don't deny that I'm glad that woman won't be sitting outside my premises anymore, but neither do I wish her dead.'

'Perhaps you just didn't mean to kill her,' said Mike, matter-of-factly.

Panic flashed across Marsh's face, then he briefly closed his eyes. He took a handkerchief out and mopped his face.

'I swear. Please believe me. I'm not the person you're looking for. I'm sorry, I know now that I should have told the police officers everything at the outset. I wasn't trying to be awkward. Cordelia Le Beau, if that is her real name, wasn't good for business, but I also knew she wasn't homeless, or as innocent as she purported to be. However, I could have, indeed should have, put a sign in the window telling the public what I knew, and have done with it. I didn't, and I've learnt a valuable lesson.'

The SIO studied Marsh and nodded composedly. She closed the dossier in front of her. 'All right,' she said briefly. 'Is there anything else you'd like to share with us before you go, because as we continue our investigations into Cordelia's murder, I don't want to see you again unless I need some fresh bread.'

'No,' Marsh said quietly, shaking his head. 'Can I go back to work now before they burn the shop down?'

Charley nodded.

The DS took him to obtain his DNA, shoe size and the pattern of his footwear before seeing him out.

Half an hour had passed when Mike walked into Charley's office and sat down opposite her. Charley looked up from the heap of paperwork she was signing. To the left of her was a pile of newspapers, files, and the morning post still waiting for her to open it, to the right a blank computer screen. The printer was spewing out her requested data.

'His story makes sense. He seemed genuine, I thought.'

Mike screwed up his nose. 'Yeah.'

'But we got confirmation of what Angelica told me. He threatened the victim.'

His jaw set hard. 'Yeah. He had motive, he knew the victim, knew her routine. Even though he doesn't strike me as a killer, we can't eliminate him.'

'No,' she sighed heavily. 'Our suspect list will keep building until we get hard evidence.'

'Plus, of course, it looks like there were two people involved.'

Charley nodded. 'That reminds me, have we narrowed down the patterns from the assailant's footwear on Cordelia's body to a specific brand, or a type of shoe?' For a minute or two she lost herself in speculations.

'Not that I'm aware of.'

'Chase forensics, would you? Fingers crossed the tread is unique to a brand.' She thought for a moment. 'Make sure we're checking the footwear of everyone brought into the station, even those in relation to other cases. There's a chance our killer will be drawn to the investigation, wanting to be in the middle of things. It wouldn't be unheard of for the killer to come into the precinct under some false pretence.'

Mike nodded and got to his feet. 'Will do, boss, leave it with me.'

Charley turned to her computer, waiting in anticipation as she worked, for a call from officers viewing the CCTV they had secured, hoping for the words, 'Boss, come look at this...'

Suddenly Charley's printer came to a halt, and for a moment all was silent. She lifted the documents from the printer and scanned the pages. It was the information she had requested about the postman.

'Dennis Mugglestone,' she read, 'who thought he recognised the deceased.'

Charley felt impatiently around for a piece of paper and pen. Surely that must have been an assumption on his part. She was sure the victim's pink hair wasn't visible until the stone was removed. There was no way he could have seen her face. And her clothes were all but removed...

She wondered if they had got his footwear impressions from the shoes he was wearing at the time, as she scoured the page for the information. If both the postman and the baker did not fit the shoe prints, she could put them aside for now. Obviously, there was the possibility that someone came across the body and stood on it post-mortem and didn't contact the police.

The burning question that continued to go around and around inside Charley's mind was the motive; just precisely what was the motive? Was there one? Did someone hate Cordelia enough to obliterate her skull? Or was it a random act of extreme violence?

Charley sat at her desk reminding herself to remain open-minded until evidence identified the true facts of what had occurred. She was still waiting on DNA from a vaginal exam to see if they could identify the killer, so she added the question for an update to her list.

According to the footwear impressions page, the size of the footprints found on Cordelia's body, were size six and ten. It was definitely feasible that one could be a woman, and the other a man. Permutations swirled around her head and would continue to do so until she had answers.

Her list of unanswered questions was getting longer, and more urgent.

Her thoughts were suddenly interrupted.

'Boss, good news. We have a trace on the anonymous phone call,' DC Annie Glover announced, stepping into Charley's office.

'Really?' Charley smiled widely. 'That is good news. Arrange for someone to go and see who it is as a priority, and do the necessary, will you?'

Chapter 13

Leaving Charley at her desk reviewing the information they had so far, and considering the agenda for the next strategy meeting, DCs Annie Glover and Ricky-Lee Lewis set off to speak to the woman who made the abusive call to the Incident Room, who they now knew resided at 24, Alma Crescent, which happened to be in the middle of the notorious Byron Estate, one of the town's most deprived areas, built on the site of an old tram depot. Ricky-Lee said very little during the journey, but instead concentrated on the route he was taking through the maze to locate the house. Byron Estate had an unenviable reputation for gang violence, drug abuse and disorder, and Annie shuddered as she remembered the last time she had been here. She had spent a short time in uniform, after she had transferred from the south, and had been involved in an incident when two hundred youths had clashed with police following a drugs raid.

'This place,' she muttered, seeing the desolate landscape unfolding like the backdrop to a dystopian sci-fi film, with overflowing dog-shit bins and boarded-up houses. They passed a bus stop, a phone box and a pub, all covered from top to bottom in graffiti. They stood against the bleak scenery of semi-detached homes, and a cold grey sky. In the vicinity of where he knew Alma Crescent to be, Ricky-Lee navigated the car with due care and attention, a narrow road led to a cul-de-sac where cars parked bumper to bumper. Finally, he located No. 24. Immediately the CID car stopped it attracted several bike-riding youths, who began to circle it like wasps around a jam jar.

Doors locked, the pair appraised the mood and intention of the circling bike-riders, and although appearing idle, their eyes were constantly scanning the street both ways.

Ricky Lee nodded towards No. 24. 'What score would you give it for kerbside appeal?' he asked in a drawl.

'Zero. Sod's law that's the place we're looking for,' Annie said mournfully.

For a moment or two the pair sat in silence. The scene before her reminded Annie of a collection of paintings that she hadn't thought of for a number of years. Meanwhile Ricky-Lee was tapping his fingers on the steering wheel, whilst humming to a popular tune on the radio.

As quickly as the bike riders had appeared, they disappeared, dispersing in different directions.

Certain that the bikers had gone, Ricky-Lee turned to look at Annie questioningly. It wasn't like her to be quiet for so long. She broke the silence. 'I was just thinking... don't laugh... it's a bit like a painting out here.'

Ricky-Lee scoffed in surprise as he looked around the street. 'Right.'

'Not a pretty painting, obviously. I studied George Shaw at A Level, and he focused on the postwar Tile Hill housing estate. He said that exploring the neglected suburban surroundings of his childhood made him feel that "something out of the ordinary could happen at any time there, away from the supervision of adults".' Her voice quivered. 'It feels a bit like that here, don't you think?'

The car's mirrors gave Ricky-Lee a complete view of the street both ways.

'A bit, yeah, and I should know, being brought up in the inner-city.'

He reached into the back of the car for his suit jacket, looked into the rearview mirror, adjusted his tie and smoothed back his neatly cut hair. Unlike Annie, appearance was always at the forefront of the DC Lee's mind. Older than Annie by three years, with a failed long-term relationship behind him, his fake tan and the care he took with his appearance gave others the impression that he was self-centred, and this made him an easy target for his colleagues' teasing. But Annie couldn't imagine him without a tan.

Ricky-Lee dipped his head, made a face at her when he realised she was looking at him, and looked straight past her at the house. A huge leafless tree dominated the modest, over-grown front garden, which resembled a fly-tipping site rather than a cultivated plot.

The woman who lived at this address had had a few brushes with the law – drunken behaviour, theft, public nuisance – but there were no outstanding warrants for her arrest. It showed him that she had previous form, but presently she wasn't 'wanted'.

'Ready,' he asked Annie?

The detective nodded.

'Mind where you step. The piles of dog shit look like the size of mole hills,' he said in a protective way.

All of a sudden Annie felt glad that his gambling addiction that he'd developed during an undercover job seven years previously, and that had reared its ugly head three years ago, after which he lost his fiancée Beth and he'd decided to relo-cate to the north, hadn't managed to destroy his life. In fact instead, working at Peel Street, Charley had managed to get him the professional support he needed.

When Annie opened the car door, she was taken by the blue-grey tones that gave the house ahead of her a brooding quality. The closed curtains and sparseness of the setting created a scene from which all signs of domestic life were absent. Truth to tell, if Annie had had a choice, she would have given No. 24 a wide berth.

No sooner had they stepped onto the pavement when a fierce barking could be heard from inside the premises.

Annie rolled her eyes and groaned. 'Looks like we've got a welcoming committee. That's all we need.' Slowing her pace, she stepped behind Ricky-Lee. 'I'll be right behind you,' she said, tongue-in-cheek. 'You can be sure of that.'

Annie followed him through the broken rusty gate that leaned precariously against a pile of bricks, and up the long, flagged path with deliberate, unhurried steps. Ricky-Lee's eyes were focused on the door ahead, whilst Annie cast hers to the right, and to the left, and lastly behind her. Looking out for anyone who might have decided to follow them, and try to give them a nasty surprise. Finally, Ricky-Lee climbed the two steps to the door.

His knock was hard and determined against the wood edging the broken glass panel, held together with duct tape. They both became silent, watching and listening. The response was instant, and not surprising.

'Fuck off!' shouted a female voice from within, over the sound of the excited dog's barking. 'I'm not interested in anything you're flogging!'

Annie looked up at Ricky-Lee but passed no comment.

'It's the police,' Ricky Lee shouted back. 'We'd like a word.'

'You can fuck off as well!' came the instant reply.

Ricky Lee squared his shoulders and raised his voice further. 'We aren't going anywhere. We need to speak to you about the recent murder in town.'

The dogs barking ceased but the woman's voice was still persistent. 'I know nowt about any murder!'

Ricky-Lee's voice became more cajoling. 'Just open the door and speak to us then. You don't want uniform up 'ere to take your door off do you?'

By the sound of her voice, the woman inside appeared to have moved closer to the door. 'You can see that I could do with a new door,' she said, smugly. 'Look, I don't do drugs. Try four doors down, number thirty-two if that's what you're after, they're churning 'em out like the world's gonna end tomorrow.'

'Thanks for the tip off, but that's not why we're here. We need to speak to you.'

There was silence for a moment. Ricky Lee looked down to where Annie stood at the foot of the stone steps. There was a gathering tension, but his expression was both determined and reassuring. The sound of bolts being taken off broke their gaze, and the door began to creak open.

The large Japanese Akita's head squeezed through the gap, eager, impatient to escape its owner's grip on its thick, stud-encrusted collar.

The detectives flashed their warrant cards, but their introduction was muffled by the noise.

'Bronson, you twat!' the woman growled, swiping her free hand hard across the dog's head. The dog cowered and yelped out in pain. Annie winced.

Now both woman and dog stood before the detectives, filling the doorway. The dog slavered but sat, quiet and subservient at its owner's side.

'I'd invite you in but the house is a shit 'ole,' she said, her pale-coloured eyes glanced cautiously up and down the street.

Annie willed the woman to keep hold of the dog. 'Are you Kylie Matthews?' she asked.

Twenty-six years old, and twenty-six stone, Kylie Matthews stepped from foot to foot on the doorstep, growing bolder by the minute, or so it seemed. Something like a conceited smirk crossed her perfectly round pink face. She had an air of being smugly pleased with herself, though whether or not it was the novelty of the situation, or some deeper motive, was not clear. 'Fucking better be love, otherwise some other fucker has broken into my house and is impersonating me,' she mocked, in a deep rich tone of voice.

The tight, black sleeveless T-shirt that Kylie wore had stains down the front, her bulging black leggings sported an array of holes, and she wore nothing on her filthy feet.

Ricky-Lee tucked his warrant card back in his coat pocket. 'A phone call from this address was made to the murder Incident Room by a female…'

'I suppose you'll be wanting to ask me a lot of questions, then?' Kylie interrupted, with it seemed, an almost perverted anticipation.

'The caller said, and I quote, "Cordelia is a bitch, and she deserved to die." Was that you?'

Kylie tilted her big round head on one side. 'What if it were? Haven't you lot heard of freedom of speech?'

The sunlight that appeared from behind the clouds picked up the deep red marks between the folds of flesh under her chin.

'If it was you who made the call, we're just trying to find out why you said what you did.' Annie paused for effect. 'There isn't anyone else living here is there?'

Kylie hesitated, seeming to struggle against impulses. Finally she replied. 'No, there's no one else living here, just me and Bronson.'

'So it was you?'

Kylie winked an eye at Annie. 'You're pretty sharp you are, you should be in t'knife drawer.' Kylie laughed out loud.

Annie gave her a hard smile.

'Let's stop messing about shall we Kylie, unless you want locking up for wasting police time. Which in turn will result in Bronson being taken to the kennels.'

Kylie stroked Bronson's head and for a moment appeared to consider what had been said.

'Come on, help us out here, we're just trying to find out who battered a young woman to death,' intervened Ricky-Lee.

Considering her immediate response, it was clear to both detectives that they had spoken her language.

'All right! All right!' cried Kylie. 'Shall I tell you why? I did it because she hit Bronson for cocking his leg up. He's a pup for God's sake. She was sat on the pavement. What did she bloody expect?'

'What did you do, when she hit Bronson?' pushed Ricky-Lee.

Kylie's face turned red with anger. 'I should 'ave smacked her there and then, but I didn't because I knew that you lot would come and lock me up.'

Ricky-Lee considered what she had said, but it was Annie who spoke up. 'You're telling us that you made the phone call into the Incident Room because she once hit your dog?'

'That's what I said didn't I? Truth is I'd drunk the best part of a bottle of cider that night wi' mi' takeaway, and enjoyed a bit of weed too, courtesy of number thirty-two for keeping my gob shut about their enterprise.' Kylie scowled. 'I'm serious about them at number thirty-two y'know. If you come at night, their house is like Blackpool bloody illuminations. My drug-taking is purely medicinal and for personal use only, of course.'

'How did you know about the murder?'

'Saw it on the news. The telephone number come up on the screen. No law against ringing in with information is there? I must admit I didn't expect you on my doorstep like a couple of bloody Jehovah's Witnesses.'

'It's a murder enquiry Kylie.' Ricky Lee inhaled deeply. 'Did you know Cordelia Le Beau?'

Kylie shook her head. 'Nah, I've seen her sat outside the Medway, but I don't know her. Word is that she puts it about a bit, likes 'em young, but whatever floats your boat. I prefer 'em more distinguished like yourself detective.'

Annie suppressed a laugh. Ricky-Lee refused to be drawn but made it obvious that he wasn't about to hang about for more of the same from Kylie. Satisfied that she couldn't help the investigation, or assist them any further, the officers left, but not before Ricky-Lee told her, in no uncertain terms, that if she made another hoax call she would be locked up for wasting police time, and there would be no doubt that Bronson would be sent to the kennels.

On arrival back in the Incident Room, Annie stopped to speak to Helen Weir, one of the police officers viewing the CCTV. While the murder itself had happened in a blind spot, the cameras on the approach to and route away from the murder scene were being closely scrutinised. It was highly likely that the killer passed by at least one of the cameras in the vicinity. She was eager to see some of those caught on camera, leading up to the discovery of Cordelia's body.

Charley joined the pair.

'I've printed some stills that I've numbered for you. These run from midnight until the time that the body was discovered,' Helen told the SIO.

Charley slid into the chair next to Helen. 'Run me through what you've got,' she said eagerly.

'At 12.20, a man and woman linked arm-in-arm walked along the High Street. At 12.25 a lone male, coat hood up, dressed in jeans and wearing training shoes walked past at a swift pace. He kept his head down, and kept close to the buildings. Then at 12.40, a taxi drives along the High Street at speed. You can just make out that the taxi belongs to Zee Cabs. At 02.00 to 04.00 all is quiet.' Helen pressed a key on her computer. As she fast-forwarded the footage, Charley's stomach twisted with anticipation.

Helen slowed the footage down. 'The next thing is a couple of hours later when we see the postman.'

'Presumably he's on his way to work at the sorting office at that time?' said Annie.

Charley stood. 'That's great. Carry on the good work. We need to trace that couple, and that man. They could easily have witnessed something without realising what they were seeing. Can you give me the clearest still you have and I'll put out an appeal for the witnesses to come forward? I'll get Ricky-Lee to contact Zee's taxis and find out which cab would have been passing at that time of night.'

Helen nodded and turned back to the screen.

'Do you think one of them could be our killer?' Annie asked. 'That couple… they could fit with the two shoe prints…'

'I know...' Charley ran a hand across her eyes. 'What makes a person stand on a body? I've never come across anything like it before.'

Chapter 14

Crime Scene Investigator Supervisor Neal Rylatt sat opposite Detective Inspector Charley Mann, coolly looking over his papers, confident of his knowledge and ability in performing the specialist role with the police he'd been in for a number of years. His input for this strategy meeting was to utilise his experience to discuss the exhibits. Examination of every exhibit submitted came at a cost, and the budget was the SIO's responsibility. Neal would never understand how anyone could put a cost to catching a killer, although he knew that's how the system worked.

Picking up her pen, the SIO made notes as she listened to his suggestions for the next batch bound for forensic examination. Ultimately the decision was hers, but not to take his advice would be naive.

It was at times like these that she wished she had studied shorthand. Deciphering her scribble after the event was an art in itself, especially when it came to forensic and legal medical terminology. Eyes down, still writing, she instructed Neal, 'I want you to liaise with Forensics to see if there are any new findings that Eira is able to share with us, the discovery of fibres or foreign hairs for example, before we make any decisions, and at the same time ask her to assure us that our exhibits are being treated as a priority.'

When Charley looked up, she scanned the faces of the others around the table with a determined look on her face.

She was rewarded with a reassurance that Tattie had joined them. The office manager sat perfectly poised, lipstick perfect, between Mike and Ricky-Lee, taking minutes of the meeting.

Charley put down her pen, feeling relieved. 'As a priority, I also want us to be mindful of liaising with the local outreach teams, churches and any charities that you think of which may be able to assist us with our enquiries.'

She looked steadily into the faces of her colleagues, and on seeing a few puzzled expressions, she clarified her requirements by using her fingers to tick off the points. 'We're looking for the knowledge about, and numbers of, homeless people in the town, and their identities. Are there any reports of homeless people being abused, or assaulted recently. I would have expected them to have records of this readily available for safeguarding issues, amongst other reasons. One thing I learnt in London was that the homeless also tend to look out for each other, perhaps other street dwellers may also be able to help us with our enquiries. Of equal importance, did any of these organisations have dealings with Cordelia Le Beau, and if so, where and when did they last see her? Even if they didn't know her name, Cordelia was noticeable and memorable because of the colour of her hair.

'Also, check on any nuisance reports that may have been recorded, to see if there is any link to the enquiry. Let us speak to the workers at the retail outlets on the high street. The hairdressers, nail bars, coffee shops, restaurants, public houses, bars. I want Cordelia's death, and this investigation to be in everyone's conversations.'

Annie, amongst others, met Charley's eyes with gratitude for the clarification. Charley smiled.

Walking back to her office after the meeting, Charley noticed that the HOLMES computer operators were already at their desks, busily entering follow-up actions into the computer system. She stood for one moment, feeling grateful all of a sudden that the Home Office Large Major Enquiry System was one of the tools in her investigative toolbox, which collated information on serious crime reported from far-flung jurisdictions more quickly than any humans. Charley felt safe in the knowledge that the actions relevant to the enquiry would be immediately farmed out for the necessary priority enquiries by the team, no information was destroyed, and any inputted information could be retrieved at the press of a button.

'Had the police had HOLMES to make sense of the Yorkshire Ripper,' said Charley to Annie who had just joined her. 'Peter Sutcliffe would not have remained at large for five years.'

Annie gave the SIO a grim smile. 'What an evil man.' She shuddered. 'Thirteen women killed. I studied the case a little on my training. Wilma McCann, Emily Jackson, Irene Richardson, Patricia Atkinson, Jayne MacDonald, Jean Jordan, Yvonne Pearson, Helen Rytka here in Huddersfield, Vera Millward, Josephine Whitaker in Halifax, Barbara Leach, Marguerite Walls, Jacqueline Hill…'

Charley turned to her. 'I'm so proud of you.'

'You are?' Annie looked surprised.

'Yes!'

'Why?'

'Because you remembered the names of the victims, most people only remember the perpetrator, especially the notorious serial killers.'

Annie followed Charley into the office. She shrugged her shoulders nonchalantly, but it felt nice to know that she was proud of her. 'Remember I was schooled by nuns. Retaining facts was paramount. Anyway, you should know by now that I'm a bit weird about remembering details of things that are of interest to me.'

'Like my Granny's Yorkshire folklores?'

'Indeed,' Annie said.

Charley slid behind her desk, facing the door, and as she did so her smile grew wider.

Annie heard the telephone on Charley's desk ring twice before the SIO picked it up. She turned to close the door behind her and in doing so she saw Charley's eyebrows lift, then instantly fall.

Unbeknown to Annie, the person on the other end of the phone was Eira White. The forensic scientist told Charley that the swabs taken from Cordelia Le Beau showed that there was no evidence to suggest that sexual intercourse had taken place.

Charley put her elbow on the desk and her hand to her forehead. 'I still can't rule out the possibility that sex was the motive Eira,' she said gloomily as she studied the pictures of the murder scene. 'Her attackers could have been disturbed. If murder or robbery had been the intention why did they need to strip the body?'

'Perhaps the intentionally demeaning act was meant to be a belittling insult?'

'Mmm… You can't get more belittled than being dead I guess,' replied Charley, before thanking Eira and ending the call.

At two o'clock Helen knocked at the office door. The smell of freshly brewed coffee that Annie had brought with her for the women was especially welcome to the SIO, who hadn't had lunch.

'Please take a seat,' Charley said, acknowledging the three women as she pointed to the visitors' chairs at the opposite side of her desk.

Annie put the tray down, handed each a mug of coffee, then milk, sugar and a plate of Tattie's homemade cookies.

Charley sat back, and relished the warm drink and sweet confectionary. Meanwhile, Police Constable Helen Weir took the lead, giving the others a comprehensive outline of what they knew so far.

'As a result of enquiries being made into historical incidents of this nature on the campus, we found four female students, all of whom have a reputation for being hardworking and well-behaved, who told us the same story of waking during the night to find a stranger sitting on their beds, and with the exception of Dani, they confirmed he was fully clothed. Each individual description of the male, and the fact that he remained silent during their ordeal, was the same.'

Lisa interrupted eagerly. 'There could be others, but for whatever reason, no one else has come forward yet, despite several appeals for information.'

Charley ruminated a little before she spoke. 'It's my understanding that this guy has never physically touched any of the students?'

Lisa nodded her head in agreement.

'Hmmm, so he hasn't touched them or made sexual advances towards them, apart from being naked in the case of Dani Miller… It almost seems fanciful for such a prolific offender,' Charley mused. 'What does he do when they wake up?'

Helen's mind replayed the encounter with Dani. Immediately her lips curved in an unbelieving smile. 'When the students wake, and it's apparent that they have seen him, he stands and, in Dani's case he calmly got dressed, walked to the window, climbed out, and disappeared into the night.'

Lisa shivered with the memory. 'The windows are always the point of entry and exit, whatever floor the student accommodation happens to be on, which could be the first, or the fifth, the height doesn't seem to be a problem for him,' she said.

Charley's blue eyes narrowed at the observation. 'It is known that a criminal's modus operandi is comprised of learned behaviours that can evolve and develop, as they become more sophisticated and more confident, and it appears to me that in this instance, since he was naked during the most recent incident in Dani's room, that this is the situation here. He's gone a step further this time, and one thing I'm worried about is where this is going to end. Have you had any help, or contribution from security?' Charley asked in a low deliberate tone.

'Would you believe security is mainly focused on evidence gathering, reliant on CCTV of which hardly any of the cameras are in working order due to vandalism, and the students informing them of any issues, and I'll tell you why.

They have six employees, presently one is on long-term sick leave, one on a course, one on holiday, one position is vacant and the other two are trying to cover twenty-four hours, seven days a week and with two days off in that week, and one of those is a volunteer in the mountain rescue team,' said Helen.

Charley groaned outwardly, looking from one police officer to the other. 'CCTV cameras can't stop crimes happening, but they can help deter and identify perpetrators, so what are your thoughts?' Charley asked. 'I'm very conscious Lisa, that Helen has been seconded to work on our enquiry, so this leaves most of the footwork to you doesn't it?'

Lisa glanced sideways at Helen in a companionable way.

'It's okay. We're managing quite well between us, and one of our complainants thinks that they might be able to identify him if they saw him again, and so does Dani. I've contacted the Viper bureau to arrange for the witnesses to be given the opportunity to identify possible suspects, in a video identification viewing. However as you know, we'll only have success if he's recorded on the system.'

Charley tilted her head towards Lisa. 'Well, we know for sure that Viper will have a gallery of photographs of similar likeness to the witnesses' description, and that even though our suspect's identity is not known, they can be shown to our witnesses. As they say nothing ventured, nothing gained,' added Charley.

Annie nodded in agreement. 'Security has been made aware of the increased numbers of reports made to the police, and have been instructed to report anything of a similar nature to us immediately. I have been assured by the boss that they are briefing their staff, who have been given the description of the person that we would like to speak to in relation to the incidents, and posters are going up throughout the university as we speak.'

'Did we manage to get any footwear marks from the incident involving Dani?' asked Charley.

'Just a partial impression from a right foot, which we thought probably sufficient to do a comparison match if we have a suspect's footwear,' said Lisa.

'Could we check the footprint database to see if there's a match?' asked Charley.

'Already done, boss. There is nothing that links it to outstanding jobs,' Lisa replied.

Helen curled up her nose. 'We were disappointed that there were no marks of value lifted from the drainpipe.'

Charley released a slight breath, and adjusted her position on her chair. 'That's good work so far though,' she said in an encouraging way. 'Keep digging. It looks to me as if he is returning to his hunting ground where he had previous success. We'll get him.'

'He sounds like a creature of habit to me, and let's face it there are a lot of women in one location to choose from,' said Annie.

Charley inhaled deeply through her nose as she gave this some thought, then started to ask questions. 'He must spend a lot of time on campus watching his victims, to know exactly which flat is occupied by a lone woman. What worries me is that the control freak is getting bolder, and more confident as time goes on. What's the CCTV coverage like in the vicinity of any of these incidents, do we know?'

'That's something that we are liaising with security about at the moment, but they're dragging their feet – this is one of the cameras that are not working, and that has been disconnected.' Lisa swallowed a curse. 'You know the excuses from those who haven't the time to do what is in the job description.'

'Any difficulties, or if you don't get sufficient co-operation, let me know, and I'll get involved. Can you map the locations of the incidents, and see if we can locate a nucleus, if there is one. Do we have a common factor between his victims, such as appearance, are they on the same course, are they members of the same social groups etcetera?' said Charley.

'Does he break into the flats because the victims leave their windows ajar?' asked Annie.

'That's a good point, but how would he know that the occupant of the room is a female, without surveillance of his victim? He can only know this if he has seen them going into their flat, or been in their flat; or is it someone who has access to the residency records? We haven't had one male occupant disturbed at all, as far as I'm aware,' said Charley.

'No, you're right, and the blocks aren't separated by gender either,' added Helen.

'Could he be a student, or someone who works on campus, or just an opportunist wandering around the university grounds and buildings?' added Lisa.

'Let's develop a planned response, prepare an action plan, should another incident occur either on the complex, or nearby, and let's review what CCTV we can get hold of. I will have a word with the head of security. They need to step up the patrols whether they want to or not.' Charley stopped in her tracks as though a thought had just come to her. 'He's never spoken… I wonder if he's got a strong accent that might identify him, or a speech impediment of some kind.' Charley said.

Suddenly Mike Blake entered the room. Charley sharpened her focus on his large frame that filled her doorway. The three women turned to face him. 'Boss,' he said. 'We've just identified a young lad with the three girls on CCTV, on the night of Cordelia's death,' he said.

Charley's face lit up. 'Now that is music to my ears. One of our regulars?' Charley asked, jumping to her feet.

'Yes.'

The SIO followed by the others followed him into the Incident Room. 'Let's see if we can eliminate him, or put him in the frame,' she said.

'With pleasure, boss,' he said.

Chapter 15

By the grace of God, or the luck of the Devil, whichever way Charley looked at it, Maddox 'Maddog' Madoc Junior had reached the age of nineteen. His file suggested that this was no thanks to his upbringing. His mugshot showed deep, sunken, empty eyes, the windows to a dark soul, through circumstances and poverty. Well-known to the police, his father, grandfather and great-grandfather were all dead before their time owing to a life of crime. Each had spent nearly half their life behind bars, and Maddox was, it appeared, heading in the same direction, at full throttle.

'There's only one place he'll end up,' was the phrase on the lips of all the professionals who came into contact with him, from the headteacher who expelled him, to a long line of social, community and youth workers. Even the local community bobby noted that Maddox deemed it a treat to have a warm bed and breakfast, and that he welcomed the opportunity of being locked up, which is why he mostly took him home with a warning for minor offences. Maddox had grown up with no respect for authority, which was hardly a surprise, because he knew no better than to take by any means whatever he wanted, when he wanted, from whom he wanted. Young offenders' facilities, and latterly prison, were considered not to be a deterrent. These institutions were second homes to him, places where he could meet up with his mates, and meet new like-minded individuals who continued his tuition in criminal activity.

His mother, a sweet woman with bad taste in men, had a history of nervous breakdowns, spending much of her adult life appealing to everyone's better nature on behalf of her errant son, but even she had to eventually admit that he was a lost cause, and at times begged the police to arrest him, in the hope that a custodial sentence would somehow teach him right from wrong.

Stocky, loud-mouthed and known as a fighter around town, Maddox was well-known to the nightclub bouncers, security guards, and the landlords and landladies for one thing, and that was his tendency to get into trouble when drunk.

According to his police record, the last time Maddox was arrested was three weeks previously, on suspicion of robbery with violence and then bailed pending further enquiries. The victim, Charley read, was a young male, and the offence had occurred at a cashpoint machine in the town centre. When he snatched the victim's money, he also smashed the victim's head into the wall of the bank, before running from the scene of the crime. The team who had gone to his home address on that occasion had had to taser him in an attempt to restrain him. Only then were they able to handcuff and arrest him.

Although it was noted that he was intelligent. Maddox wasn't a clever thief, he relied on threatening behaviour and violent tactics to get what he wanted. It was also noted that his victims were always smaller and weaker, then, after coming into contact with him, fearful of reprisals should they speak out.

Charley closed the file and thought for a moment, looking absently out the window of her office. It could of course be pure coincidence that Maddox had appeared on their CCTV footage on the night of the murder. And then again, it could be a major lead. Maddox was now at the very least a person of interest to the case.

On the direct enquiry team today was Detective Constable Bill Whitehill, purposely selected for his experience and nego-tiating skills. He had built up a rapport with Maddox over a number of years, whilst dealing with both him and his father. It was hoped that the detective's attendance at Maddox's door would have a calming effect. Charley could hear Mike and Bill discussing their approach to the suspect through the open door of her office.

'Best to get uniform to cover the back door of Maddox's address,' said the shrewd, ruddy-faced DC Whitehill.

DS Blake gave him a surprised look. 'But we only want to speak to him at this stage,' he said. 'See what he knows.'

Bill eyed Mike closely, and a slightly pitiful smile of half-disbelief twisted his lips. 'That may be the case, but you obviously don't know Maddox. I'm telling 'ya, one whiff of the police at his door and he's not hanging about.'

Mike looked across the desk at DC Wilkie Connor working away at his computer terminal. 'Most people think that when we're investigating a murder, we'd get co-operation, but that couldn't be further from the truth could it?'

Bill shook his head slowly from side to side. 'Definitely not, it's odds-on that once we get to the Byron Estate we'll be verbally abused, spat at, or threatened with physical assault.'

'However, we don't have no-go areas on our patch, do we Bill?' asked Charley, walking out of her office and nodding at her officers.

Bill smiled kindly at the SIO. 'We certainly don't, ma'am! We are here to police and that's what we'll do.'

'Right, I want his shoe size, a shoe print, an alibi or lack thereof for the time of the murder, and the names of the three women he was with.'

'Yes, boss.'

'Find out if he knew the victim. I imagine they could have crossed paths in their line of work.'

—

The Madoc family council house loomed up in the rainy twilight as Mike steered the CID car cautiously around the corner of The Grove. The uniform car parked six feet behind. Immediately, curious youths congregated under the street lamps, observing the visitors. Not deterred by the weather, they were there for a reason, and seeing the police, they straightaway pulled out their mobile phones, no doubt warning the drug dealers that the police were on the estate, but the latter would not be intimidated.

'We can't expect support from the public in this area, if things kick off. In fact just the opposite,' said Mike.

'I recommend you park the car where we can keep an eye on it, if you don't want the tyres slashing that is,' said Bill.

As if privy to the conversation, the group nearby could be seen sniggering.

Focused on the house, Mike saw that the windows were cloudy with grime. Tired, limp curtains were suspended from their fixing in crazed disarray. The fact that the curtains were drawn together in daylight hours was no surprise for a house on the Byron Estate, because here they were drawn to protect, or hide, what was inside from prying eyes.

Once out of the car, Mike gave a nod to the two uniformed officers, who headed directly for the rear of the property. A moment later he and Bill set off towards the front door, all the while scanning the area around the premises. Upon reaching the door, Mike knocked loudly.

All was quiet. Bill looked at Mike curiously when there was no response.

The DS repeated the knock, but this time he announced himself. As far as he was concerned Maddox was inside, he was going nowhere, and he wanted him to know it.

To Bill's surprise, Maddox, wearing nothing but scruffy, dirty tracksuit bottoms, answered the door. He was bare-chested and the officers were presented with his obviously steroid-induced muscular physique, undoubtedly acquired in the prison's gymnasium. He had a display of tattoos that spread from his neck to his waist. Bill recalled Maddox as a pale, weak, apathetic youngster, but he was no longer that.

'What?' said the pimply youth, leaning lazily against the door jamb, looking as if he hadn't washed in a long time. His somewhat relaxed response to their appearance was particularly surprising to Bill.

Bill looked past him at the faded, peeled-back flock wallpaper, and a pile of electrical tools thrown at the bottom of the staircase then into the dingy, dark hallway scattered with boxes and other miscellaneous debris. 'Just getting up, or going to bed?' asked Bill.

Maddox pulled his hand from down the front of his trousers and showed him his middle finger, and grinned, exposing a set of crooked, yellowing teeth.

Bill smirked. 'That's more like it,' he mumbled.

'We're investigating the murder of the woman with pink hair, who used to sit outside the Medway; you might have seen her when you've been out and about in town.'

Noticing the expression on his face, the officers were hopeful that he knew something of her before he spoke.

'Everybody knows the pink lady, but I'm no murderer,' he said to Bill, taking a half-smoked roll-up out of his pocket and lighting it with a lime green, cheap plastic lighter.

'We're speaking to everyone in town that night who has been identified on CCTV, and you are one of them, caught on camera with three young ladies,' said Mike.

Tight-lipped, Maddox nodded. 'You think so d'ya?'

'We know so,' said Bill firmly.

'Did you see the pink lady that night, or anyone else that you know who might be able to help us with our enquiries?' asked Mike.

Maddox shook his head. 'Nah, don't think so,' he went on with a guttural chuckle. 'We were all too bloody pissed.'

'We'll need to speak to your lady friends to see if they saw the woman in question. Do you have their contact details?' asked Mike.

'I'll tell 'em you want to speak to 'em, but I'm telling you now, they won't remember owt.'

The raising of an eyebrow, and a stern-looking face told Maddox that DC Whitehill was not messing. 'Make it a priority will you. This is a murder investigation we're dealing with,' he said.

Maddox raised his eyebrows, and at the same time the tone of his voice changed. 'Yeah, I get it DC Whitehill,' he said rubbing the side of his nose with a grubby finger.

'We'll need a statement off you all about that night, so if you can come into the station together that would be great,' said Mike. 'Otherwise we'll keep calling back until you do, and I'm sure you don't want us around 'ere any more than we want to visit you.'

'Too fucking right I don't. People will start thinking I like ya.'

Bill raised his eyebrows, turned to look over his shoulder at the watching silent gathering beyond, and reached into his pocket from which he removed his wallet and held it high enough so they could see it. When he turned back to Maddox he winked an eye, 'Or a grass,' he said.

Maddox's face paled. 'You bastard,' he said with feeling, as the detectives turned and walked away, and the crowd looking on jeered. On the footpath beyond the garden they met with the uniformed officers who had been guarding the back door.

On seeing them, Maddox shouted. 'See you came prepared with back-up, you spineless tossers!'

Was that a tremble Bill detected in his voice?

Mike unlocked the car door and slipped into the driving seat. Blowing air out of his puffed cheeks, he breathed. 'Well, that was a response I didn't expect,' he said.

'There's got to be a first time for everything,' replied Bill, his voice soft, but keeping a steely face for the purpose of the youths. 'One thing we couldn't do, because he was barefoot, was get a look at his footwear.'

Mike leaned forwards to put the key in the lock and then started the car's engine. 'I'll highlight the fact on the action enquiry that his footwear impressions are still required, and check with the CCTV operators to see if his footwear is identifiable.'

'If I know Maddox he'll own a pair of expensive trainers,' remarked Bill. 'He's always had a thing about brands ever since he was knee-high,' he said.

–

Back at the Incident Room Charley was sitting reading through the latest intelligence bulletins, when she came across an incident report about someone walking their dog through an area known locally as Owler's Wood. The bulletin stated that the witness had been startled by a naked male youth running through the area. Charley knew that the wood wasn't that far from the university. Her interest was heightened. Immediately she forwarded the information to DC Annie Glover with a note.

'Do you think this could be connected to the naked intruder enquiry?'

Whilst it was on her mind, she requested the police dog patrol to exercise their dogs in the area when possible, and see if that helped to identify this individual, or prevent a recurrence.

Coming across a police dog, trained primarily to attack, would give whoever it was one hell of a shock. She smiled wickedly at the thought.

Looking up on hearing a commotion in the outer office, she saw Mike and Bill through her internal window. Her mind immediately returned to the murder of Cordelia Le Beau and she awaited their update at the debrief with eager anticipation.

Chapter 16

When Mike put the phone down he remained perfectly still, and the furrow between his eyebrows deepened. He wasn't conscious of Annie's return to her desk until her voice broke into his thoughts.

'You okay?' she said.

The detective sergeant looked at his watch before answering. 'Tell me, would you think it suspicious if Maddox, his girlfriend and her two friends were standing at the front desk waiting to speak to us, less than twenty-four hours since we asked them to pay us a visit?'

Wilkie leaned back in his chair, turned to Mike sitting next to him, and stretched his arms above his head. Opening his mouth wide, he yawned loudly. 'Put it this way, I'll bare my arse on the Town Hall steps if it isn't,' he said.

Annie considered her reply. 'Let's just say I wouldn't have thought it was normal behaviour for him, or any of his acquaintances come to that, to comply with any request from the police.'

Mike moved as if to rise, casting his eyes over the big flat-topped conference table at the centre of the CID office, which was far larger than the average, general office. Thus enabling it to double-up as an incident room. Then he swiftly counted heads. 'I think there are enough of us to speak to them separately, all at the same time.' The DS squared his shoulders and cupped his hand at the side of his mouth before calling out. 'Anyone free to take a statement?'

Minutes later the officers answering his call followed him down the steps to the front office.

'We need their shoe prints, and an account of their movements on the night in question,' Mike instructed.

'Looks like it might actually work in our favour that we didn't take Maddox's shoe prints yesterday,' said Bill to Mike, as they walked briskly together down the corridor.

'How's that?' Mike replied.

'Because none of them will be expecting us to take them.' Bill reached forwards to twist the security lock on the door which enabled entrance to the front office.

The others formed a queue behind him ready to follow on. Winnie came through the door, the smell coming from the old lady's shopping trolley told them that their warm breakfast sandwiches had arrived. All heads turned to follow her down the corridor, the officers' mouths watering, knowing they would be cold when they eventually ate them.

'I don't know which is easier to digest, the thought of what the scrote might be up to, or him baring his backside on the Town Hall steps,' Annie whispered to DC Ricky-Lee, nodding her head in Wilkie's direction.

'What surprises me is that you think there's actually a choice?' chuckled the DC, just as the door was released and the mask of the detective slipped into place.

Over the next two hours, Tricia Carmichael, Maddox's girlfriend, Beth Green and Kirsty Webb were interviewed about their activities on the night in question, and statements taken.

'Surprisingly, they all co-operated well, in a fashion, but everyone sang from the same hymn sheet,' said Mike to Charley, two hours later.

'What did they have to say?'

'They went out early doors, got smashed, and went home. None of them admitted to seeing Cordelia that night, yet we do know from the CCTV footage that they walked close by and towards where Cordelia was seen that evening, which seems a bit strange.'

'How did they react to having their shoe prints taken?'

'The girls were surprised, even slightly intrigued that they were asked to give shoe prints. I think they were expecting fingerprints like they'd seen on the TV and at the movies, but it wasn't a problem for them. However, according to Bill, Maddox kicked off big time, even threatening to turn over the table and chairs in the interview room. That was until Bill reminded him that he would find that really difficult as the furniture was bolted to the floor.' Mike chuckled.

Charley raised her eyebrows. 'What happened then?'

'Apparently, Maddox called Bill every name under the sun during the procedure, with the odd death threat thrown in for good effect should he ruin his trainers. On a positive note, we have identified four people captured on CCTV. Only time will tell if their stories hold up when their shoe prints are checked.'

'Good. Has anyone contacted the taxi company and find out who was out in that area around that time?'

'Yes, and we have a cab driver outstanding as well as a young lad walking on his own, and a couple walking together who fall into the relevant timeframe.'

'We need to trace and eliminate them as a priority. Tell me, do you think Maddox could be our killer?'

Mike nodded his head. 'Both Bill and I had this conversation earlier, and we're equally of a mind that there's a possibility he's a violent individual. And he's co-operating with us, which is totally out of character for him; something doesn't add up.'

'Let's make sure their shoe prints are treated as a priority for checking against the prints lifted from the body.'

Mike's nod was more definite this time.

–

What Annie Glover saw on her mobile caused her to rush into Charley Mann's office, demanding her immediate attention.

'Boss, you really need to see this,' she said, slightly breathless as she thrust her mobile in Charley's face.

With a sudden leap of her heart, Charley's eyes darted from the computer screen to Annie's phone.

'It's a video that was uploaded last night onto the university students' website and that security monitor,' Annie said by way of an explanation.

Dead silence reigned for a moment or two as the recording began. A young girl lay on a bed, her face covered with a pillow, her pyjama bottoms and her knickers could be seen rolled down around her ankles. It was hard to see anything else but the dull grey gleam of the white bedroom furniture. Charley looked for any sign of life, but none was visible. Then came the sound of a muffled, menacing male voice. 'I'm in control now. What shall I do next?'

Charley found herself holding her breath as he repeated the question three times. His cruel taunting and threats sent her reeling with frustration and alarm, as in the next moment the live stream suddenly cut off, and the screen turned blank.

Charley's eyes looked up to find Annie's staring back at her.

'I've no doubt that this was filmed on campus, and where we know Dani was recently visited by a naked intruder in her room, also at night,' she said. 'Security sent the video to PC Lisa Bayliss, and immediately she received it she shared it with Helen and I. There doesn't appear to be any clue as to who the girl is, any indication which room this was taken in, or of the identity of the male.'

'Play it again, Annie,' Charley demanded. 'Presumably no report of an intruder?'

'No.'

'I'm assuming that they've taken the footage down from their website?'

'Yes, it was taken down straightaway, and it's not uploaded elsewhere, as far as we can tell.'

'Good. Do we know, or can we find out the mobile number that the footage was sent from?' Charley asked.

'I don't know, but I'll find out,' she said confidently.

'It could be the offender's, then again it could be the girl's…'

Charley paused for a moment. 'What we need is a check of all occupants in the halls of residence. The quickest way would be to sound the fire alarm, which would immediately evacuate the halls to the fire-drill checkpoints, at which time a roll-call would be taken of those who had evacuated the premises, leaving just a few rooms to check.'

Annie nodded in agreement, and Charley was silent for a few seconds, looking thoughtful and increasingly worried.

'To be honest, I don't like the similarities between how Cordelia's body was left displayed, and this present one. There's a possibility we're going to find a body.' Charley picked up the phone with some urgency. 'I'll get onto operational support to see if, and how quickly, they can have a team out to help us, and then I'll ring the university. Will you inform the fire brigade that a test is to be held? Then let's get people mobilised.'

When Annie tried to move her legs, her insides turned to jelly. However, past experience told her that she was strong when she needed to be, nevertheless she was glad that Charley was working alongside her. 'Do you think he might have killed her?'

Charley took a deep breath. 'I think it's possible. What concerns me is that even after all the appeals that Helen and Lisa have done, no one has come forward to report this incident. This person responsible could be the naked prowler, and he's escalated his sadistic activities in time.'

Charley's face was grave as she waited for the phone to be picked up at the other end. Her eyes found Annie's. 'He's in control of what's happening, that's for sure, and we need to counter that.'

–

'Fire station informed. PCs Helen Weir and Lisa Bayliss are en route,' Annie said, as she launched herself into Charley's passenger seat. The two were heading for the university.

'It won't be long before we have a numbered police presence on site,' Charley said, looking in her rearview mirror when she reached the traffic lights at the ring road, to see others on her tail.

On arrival at the university the staff and officers were quickly divided into groups to cover the fall-out from the fire alarm. The police were informed that lectures had been cancelled, and that the students had been instructed to return to their rooms at the halls of residence, hopefully without it alerting the offender that they were on to him.

'A no-show at roll-call is to be a priority for checking someone's room,' DS Mike Blake told his team.

DC Ricky-Lee came towards Charley in the car park of the university, dangling a set of keys. 'I've got the spare set,' he said, with a smile of accomplishment.

'I've got another quick job for you,' she replied. 'Show housekeeping the video. It's possible that someone might recognise something, possibly the decor or the furniture, and may be able to point us to a particular accommodation block if nothing else.'

Once the fire alarm had been activated, the residents followed the instructions to line up in the designated areas, so that everyone present could be checked.

The results were that twelve occupants of the halls of residence were not accounted for, of which only four were female.

Charley caught sight of Mike walking hurriedly around the corner of the building where he'd been liaising with the administration staff. A moment later he was with them. 'I heard from security that we've got just four doors to knock on,' she said. At that moment, a gust of wind whistled through the residency complex, and around the central car park, causing Charley to move closer to Mike to hear what he had to say to her.

'I've just been told that three of the occupants have attended lectures earlier today, and can be accounted for, which leaves only one female to locate. Cath Crowther is nineteen years old. Her flat is number eleven, and in section blue, block F.'

This conversation helped Charley to figure out what to do next, as by a process of elimination, she believed that perhaps they had found the room they were looking for, but of more importance, where was Cath Crowther, and why was she not at her designated fire-drill checkpoint? There might be a genuine reason why, but Charley wasn't taking any chances and time was of the essence.

Using the master key Ricky-Lee had acquired made short work of getting into the building and entering the flat. On opening the door, the sound of the air-conditioning kicking in broke through Charley's thoughts. The noise coming from inside gave her a jolt of panic, and she instinctively stepped backwards into Annie, who took in a short intake of breath, not realising she had held it. A second later there was the click of the light switch at Mike's touch, and Charley stepped over the threshold. The sound instinctively made her turn in the direction it came from. However, immediately the light illuminated the room, and Charley instead began to absorb the sights in front of her. The bedding she'd seen on the live-feed footage, along with the position of the furniture, confirmed to her that there was no doubt that this was the room in which the filming had taken place, but where was the girl?

A shout from PC Helen Weir outside could be heard clearly inside. 'The window is insecure.' Her response to the find only brought more questions to mind.

'We need to get any CCTV available to us from the imme-diate area,' she said, lifting her gaze to Mike, knowing there was more to come. 'I want this room sealing as a crime scene.'

In the small security office with Annie and Mike, Charley stood next to Terrier, the security officer with halitosis. It was warm, and a tight squeeze for the three of them. She felt a little claustrophobic and nauseous, and all she could hear was the air the security officer forced from his lungs as they surveyed the CCTV images.

'I'm glad I fixed that,' Terrier said proudly.

The only other sound was from the TV in the reception hall.

At the sight of a hooded male that could be seen near block F at 11.36 Annie instantly recalled the incident not so long ago again, when a hooded male had run out of the university and into the path of her car. She was still embarrassed to know that her outburst had been heard by Charley back at the nick. 'I only just missed him, the fucking dickhead,' she'd said, sitting down in the office, and with trembling hands demanding a stiff drink.

The hooded man on the CCTV was wearing a luminous yellow waistcoat this time, and reflective strips, moving slowly, as if the wheelie bin he was pushing contained something heavy, they watched with bated breath as he pushed it away from the accommodation block, and out of sight.

'He's wearing gloves,' Annie mumbled.

'Don't all bin men?' questioned Mike.

'Shhh… Watch…' Charley waited patiently for a moment or two.

'What?' Mike asked.

Charley turned to see Mike looking puzzled. 'This bin man doesn't come back for any of the other bins. That's pretty telling don't you think? Play it again…'

–

Darkness threatened to fall early, and there looked to be a distinct possibility of a shower from the black, fast-moving clouds, which swept above the large number of officers who were gathered, awaiting the next instruction. The body dog had been requested, but Charley was told that it was an hour away, and every minute counted if they hoped to find Cath alive. Charley couldn't, and wouldn't, wait.

Neal Rylatt and his CSI team were busy working at Cath Crowther's flat. At the outside entrance of the complex

Charley told Neal, 'I want evidence,' in a voice that sounded desperate to his ears, in a tone he was used to from an SIO seeking a victim, or a perpetrator.

Turning on her heels she rang Wilkie Connor at the Incident Room with further instructions regarding Cath Crowther's background checks. 'Boyfriend? Ex-boyfriend? Family? Places she went regularly where she might have caught the murderer's eye?'

Suddenly, a magpie landed at her feet. Whether it was the shock, or her brain trying to contemplate the large bird stood staring at her, she felt unnerved by the sudden presence of a bird wreathed in superstition and legend. The old rhyme her Granny used to sing her ran round her head. 'One for sorrow...' She took a deep breath. She had to focus.

Mike crept up on her, and the bird flew off, its big strong wings flapping noisily as it left. All of a sudden she started shaking, and a dark shadow started to fall across her eyes. She lowered her head hoping to stave off a faint, because then she would be good to no one.

'I've instructed Wilkie to find out Cath's mobile number, her service provider. We could do with knowing whether it is switched on, when it was used, and where.'

She nodded in agreement, put her arm through Mike's and leaned heavily on him as they walked towards Annie at the recycling site. He turned to Charley, once or twice, and a glimmer of understanding flitted across his face. No one had had anything to eat or drink since work began.

'I understand that her parents don't live in West Yorkshire. Will you contact the nearest police station to despatch an officer, to request that they find out when they last had contact with their daughter.'

On reaching Annie, Charley let go of Mike's arm. 'Tell them, to reassure them, that everything that can be done is being done to find her.'

Annie was staring at the vast amount of green bins at the university's recycling site, and she despaired at the enormity of the task. Turning to Charley her face was crestfallen. 'Where do we start, they all look the same, and we don't even know if THE bin is still on campus.'

'We don't, but if there is a possibility that she's still alive, we have to search every one of them to be sure and quickly at that.'

Annie looked at her questioningly. 'You really think she's in one of those bins?'

'I don't know,' said Charley. 'However we can't assume that she isn't, and my gut feeling is that it's a distinct possibility.'

Ricky-Lee appeared around the corner of the building. 'I've good news Mr St Hilaire, the head of facilities at VAFY, told me that the bins have coloured stickers which correspond to the colours of the accommodation blocks, by the same coloured stickers on the lids.'

Charley looked up to the sky and said a silent 'thank you'. In her experience perpetrators trying to avoid capture, or sometimes for the thrill of notoriety of their crime, watch the police activity. Barely moving her lips in case she had a zoom camera pointed in her direction, she reminded Annie to be careful.

Annie followed her gaze. There was nothing the detective could do until everyone was in place as instructed. 'What're you looking up for?' she asked.

'I saw one magpie, and you know what Granny would have said. "Hello, Jack – how's your brother?"'

Annie shuddered as she crossed herself.

'"Devil, Devil, I defy thee!" I was schooled by nuns,' she said, just as the cry went up and the lifting of the lids began.

Charley saw the detached professionalism of the crime-scene technicians before her, as if seeing the scene from a movie. They performed their duties quickly, methodically and with urgency, and her heart was in her mouth, that was until she saw the hand of the search team shoot up in the air.

The starlings sitting on the telephone wires above chose that moment to take flight, and flew high and beyond the university buildings.

A glimmer of shock flitted across the tall, suited and booted officer approximately ten metres away from her. 'This lid, it's firmly shut, boss,' he shouted. The anticipation in his voice was tangible.

But the two inquisitive magpies on the roof didn't bat an eyelid. One for sorry two for joy...

Chapter 17

Despite being conscious of the necessity to limit the contamination of a possible crime scene, preservation of a life took priority.

Charley was surprised to hear that the wheelie-bin lid was sealed with some kind of adhesive. The SIO requested silence.

Anticipation grew amongst the team as the discovering officer began to force the lid with a jemmy. She shuddered as the stark alternatives crossed her mind. Very shortly she would find out one way or another if the missing girl was inside.

Charley watched the lid spring open as if it was in slow-motion. There was a resounding thud. The sudden noise sent vibrations through the site.

A piecing cry which rang through the night came from the officer at the bin.

'She's here!'

Charley's heartbeat kicked into top gear, spurred by a sense of hope at the shout. She moved swiftly forwards through the sea of officers in the process of searching the hundreds of bins, who stepped aside for her, their sharp intakes of breath accompanying her it seemed. When she reached the bin, no one spoke for several seconds, but she could imagine a hundred hearts beating just as fast as hers.

Annie was one step behind Charley.

Poking out of the container were a pair of human feet. Pyjama bottoms and knickers were visible around the ankles. The feet were bound with rope.

'Fucking hell,' Annie gasped.

Quickly the bin was turned on its side, and Charley urged the paramedics forwards. With painstaking care, the body of a girl was pulled free from a nest of rubbish. Having seen Cath Crowther's picture, there was no doubt in Charley's mind that this was her. The girl, who had been locked in her own private hell, was gagged by stockings, and was unresponsive.

Stooping low so she could see the young woman's face, the paramedic searched for a pulse that she feared would not be there.

Charley's attention was on the victim, as she was sure she saw her eyelid flicker at the same time as the paramedic turned to look up. 'We have a pulse,' the paramedic said with great urgency.

Airways cleared, an oxygen mask was placed over her nose and mouth.

Charley found herself chanting under her breath for Cath to keep fighting, whilst at the same time feeling a sense of relief that the task of finding her was over, and a sense of elation that she was alive – she had to survive.

Watching the paramedics work on Cath Crowther, because there was nothing else she could physically do, Charley looked for tell-tale signs on the body. There was bruising around her neck.

Annie was obviously of the same mind. 'I wonder if the attacker strangled her into unconsciousness, and thought she was dead?' she whispered to Charley.

Charley nodded. 'She would have been dead if she'd been there any longer,' she replied.

Cath Crowther was covered in a blanket, lifted onto a stretcher and carried to the nearby ambulance.

There was no time now for contemplation. However, there was a need for protocol to be adhered to. For continuity, Charley called for PCs Helen Weir and Lisa Bayliss to go with Cath in the ambulance, with instruction that it was imperative, on arrival at the hospital, for the victim's clothing to be preserved, if at all possible, for forensic examination, and for the medical staff to be made aware of the circumstances in which she was discovered.

'Her clothing could be a crucial link to who is responsible for the attack,' said Charley.

Once Charley heard the doors slam and the wail of the siren, she once again looked up to the skies, but this time to pray for Cath's life, and she thanked God that she hadn't left the search for her until daylight.

She was satisfied that Helen and Lisa had enough experience to be aware that, when Cath regained consciousness and was out of danger, anything she could tell them should be recorded by them, their being the officers in attendance. Then the next step in the investigation would be underway.

A hurried conversation with Mike Blake resulted in his ordering the manpower on site to seal off the area which extended from Cath Crowther's flat to the recycling site, where a small knot of curious people had gathered.

Charley contacted the police officer who was still with Cath Crowther's family, and he was able to inform her that Mr and Mrs Crowther were preparing to go to the hospital as a matter of urgency, in order to be at their daughter's side. Later, Charley would share with them the full details of the circumstances, but for now, everyone's concern was the preservation of the young victim's life.

'Cath Crowther's attacker would have had to move some bins around, to be able to place the one that she was in at the rear,' pondered Charley.

'The obvious reason is that he didn't want her to be discovered,' said Mike.

'Mmm… He would have hoped that she'd be crushed in the back of a recycling vehicle no doubt,' replied Charley, as more crime-scene workers began arriving, shouldering her aside.

Annie and Ricky-Lee joined the pair, eager for further instruction. 'I think everything is being done to trace and recover any evidence at the scene, we've taken every opportunity,' Charley told them.

Ricky-Lee produced his best full-on smile, flashing his white teeth for effect. 'According to Clinton St Hilaire, the head of facilities, we were damn lucky as the bins were due to be emptied early tomorrow morning,' he said.

'I wonder if the killer knew that?' Annie asked Charley.

'Let's say the more I learn, the more I'm confident that he has links to the university in some way.'

The two officers exchanged looks. 'That only gives us a few thousand suspects to eliminate,' said Annie.

Sandwiches and hot drinks, provided by the hastily summoned canteen staff were welcomed by everyone. Charley caught Mike's eye, and he winked at her. 'You did this? Thank you,' she said. Her lips had a tinge of blue. The night was drawing in fast, and it was getting increasingly cold. Charley held the warm mug cupped in her hands long after the hot drink had been consumed, her eyes unblinking as she remained focused on the scene. 'I'm really concerned about how our perpetrator has progressed so rapidly to murderous intent,' she said. 'He must have given the disposal of Cath's body a great deal of thought before the act, in the hope that he wouldn't be caught, and I can't help but think of the similarities between this and Dani's experience.'

As if she had just had a thought she jumped, and her eyes turned to look at Mike. 'Will you inform the Divisional Commander about the incident?'

The area around the bins had been subjected to hastily erected intense lighting, by a mobile unit specifically brought over from HQ. The light allowed the immediate area search to continue. Anything discovered that was felt to be of any significance would be photographed and seized as a potential exhibit.

'What would you be looking for Annie?' Charley asked.

'A discarded adhesive tube for one,' she replied.

Charley looked pleased with the younger woman's response. 'Do you think that the bin will tell us anything more?'

Annie shrugged her shoulders. 'I don't know, but if we don't try then we won't know will we?'

The search team, picking their way through the piles of rubbish on the ground where the bin was discovered made an early discovery. Working through a smell that would leave a lasting odour on all those in attendance, their eyes were focused downwards, as they examined visually, in situ, a shiny, silver-coloured zip-pull, from an unknown garment, and they called for Charley to look at it. Photographed and seized, only time would tell if this small piece of evidence would be relevant. Charley shuffled away from the scene, careful to not disturb anything, she looked at her feet which were covered in crime-scene covers taken from a Bootie Box. She saw that the bins had already revealed some unusual objects. Alongside the usual tins, plastic bottles and discarded fast-food containers, there were pieces of discarded clothing, a few keys, a suitcase, a mannequin's leg, an assortment of wigs, broken games, computer parts.

–

At Peel Street police station, the night team were just setting out in the marked cars and on foot at the beginning of their shift, when Charley and her team arrived back. However, the detectives' day was still not done.

Notebook and pen in hand, Charley sat in her warm office, her face animated, getting ready for the short debrief of her close team. Her sandwiches that Winnie had brought that morning were the only ones that survived, apart from Mike's because Wilkie Connor had made short work of the others, much to Annie and Ricky-Lee's annoyance, and he was not there to suffer the consequences having gone home. Charley paused deliberately at the conference table where the debrief was about to take place, and opened up her brown food bag, and Mike did likewise, to reveal cold bacon and sausage sand-wiches.

Annie threw off her coat and walked directly to the kitchen. 'I'll make a tea, shall I?' she said.

'Bring a knife, and the brown sauce so we can cut them in half to share,' Charley called after her.

Annie smiled to herself. That's just what she wanted to hear.

The team agreed that the killer took time to study his victims, and plan not just how he could get into their rooms, but also how he would get out. In this most recent crime he had felt calm and confident enough to do the live feed, before moving his victim from the flat to the bin, sealing the lid and dumping it back with the others, awaiting refuse collection. Did he believe he had actually killed her, because that was his intention?

The luminous waistcoat that he wore suggested to anyone seeing him that he was a workman. Therefore he wouldn't perhaps attract any undue attention.

'Do you think he works on campus in maintenance?' asked Annie.

'That's something that we can't overlook. I want the CCTV images that we do have from the university enhanced, so that we can see if there is anything else to be learned about the attacker.'

The disappointment of any real progress in the hunt for the attacker had coupled with the fatigue that Charley hadn't felt since the lead up to the capture of one of Britain's most wanted murderers, Titus Deaver, the cannibalistic killer, who had brutally slaughtered his victims including one of her colleagues. Charley knew that whatever the cost, as head of this enquiry, she had to make a concerted effort to display an outward show of hope, calm and assurance for the benefit of the team.

That night she sat on the window seat in her bedroom, arms folded, knees hunched up to her chin, looking out across the blackness of Marsden moors, and into a clear, starry sky thinking, meditating and pondering over the day.

The next morning, dark pouches under her eyes were evidence of her lack of sleep, and worry lines showed at the corner of her mouth and eyes. The stolen food bags the previous night had made tempers frayed at the office, and Ricky-Lee announced robustly his threat to 'get you back' to Wilkie Connor. This was an attitude which the younger of the two detectives wouldn't usually use towards his older colleague, an old-fashioned bobby who had, despite the demands of his wife, an invalid for whom he was sole carer, and his own recovery from his accident, succeeded in keeping up with the new technology. Wilkie Connor would be the first to say that he didn't have the breeding or social skills to talk his way up the ladder of success, but nevertheless, he was extremely good at his job.

Just when Charley was about to go out into the office and give them what for, Annie, who had remained at her desk with her head down, appeared at her door. 'Boss, I may have identified a link as to how he selects his victims. There's this aerobics class, once a week on campus… Helen and Lisa have checked with his other victims, and it appears that each of them have attended this Tuesday night class at some time or another over the past year.'

'Great work. So our man could be a voyeur who then stalks these young women.'

Annie's hair was tied up in a knot on the top of her head, showing that she had had no time to shower that morning. 'Just that. There is a walkway above, which leads into the changing rooms. Anyone can see them, without being seen. The gymnasium is also visible through a wall of windows which overlooks the sports fields.'

'He could then follow them back to their flats…' said Charley thoughtfully. 'When's the next class?'

'Next Tuesday night. Helen and Lisa are arranging observations, and looking at historical CCTV in the immediate vicinity. They have been instructed not to alert security though. Just in case it is one of their team who is responsible.'

'Good. Let's also use some of our own cameras so if the CCTV is out of action it won't matter, and we also don't alert anyone in asking them to get the CCTV fixed.'

Charley's phone rang. 'It's an update from the hospital regarding Cath Crowther,' the caller said.

The SIO closed her eyes briefly. *Let it be good news.*

Chapter 18

No matter how hard it was sometimes to end a debrief on a positive note for her team, Charley always tried. One of the most common phrases she used was one of her Grandad's old sayings, 'Tomorrow's another day.'

However, on this occasion the news that Cath Crowther was still alive and continued to fight was good enough motivation for everyone.

At home that night, Charley contemplated all she had witnessed that day; the enquiry was proving to be more complex than she had envisaged it would be at the start.

Sitting alone on the settee, quiet, in the dark, in front of the same fire that she had sat in front of with her parents as she was growing up, her mind retreated to the special place in her head, to the compartments where she kept her precious memories under lock and key, and she found comfort in them for an hour or two whilst she dozed intermittently.

'Smarter, cleverer men have tried to hoodwink me,' she mumbled, an hour later as she dragged her leaden legs up the stairs to bed. 'Whoever you are, whatever you do, you will not get the better of me!'

Charley woke early the next morning and flicked on her bedside light. Disorientated, she picked up her mobile phone and sleepily registered that it showed the time as 5.20. Her exercise routine, since she had returned from London, had mostly been riding Wilson, the ex-police horse owned by her best friend Kristine, but that had slowed almost to a halt lately. At one time she would have jumped out of bed intent on getting a hack in before she went to work when waking so early, but this time she dismissed the thought, turned over, and slept on until the alarm woke her at 6.30.

When Charley left the house the heavens opened, and within seconds the rainfall increased to a steady downpour. Once or twice she almost lost her footing on the cobbles as she walked to her car, and for once she was glad she wasn't out riding. Looking down she examined the smooth mud surface of the grass banking, and dodged the rainwater that continually seeped over the pathway from the field's surface, draining into the gutter that ran alongside the kerb. Her feet were soaked, the penalty for living in a semi-rural location, in the village of Marsden. With its peaks, canals, valleys and reservoirs, the Colne Valley had a wealth of outdoor delights and a rich industrial heritage.

Saturated by the time she reached the end of the row of terraces, she abandoned her umbrella, and threw it with haste into the boot of her car.

Charley's relief at the good news that greeted her was enough to lighten the dampest of spirits. Maddox's footwear, as well as that of Beth Green, a friend of his girlfriend, whom he had been seen with on CCTV the night before the discovery of Cordelia Le Beau's body, were proven to be a match.

Instinctively she knew it was just the information her fatigued team needed to hear.

At that precise moment the sun shed light upon the detectives through the window. 'As we suspected, it appears that their drunken night out wasn't as innocent as they would like us to believe, which would perhaps explain their co-operation,' commented Mike. Finishing off his coffee with a smack of his lips, he glanced up at the clock in Charley's office. 'However did we manage before CCTV?'

Charley loosened her hands which had been tightly clasped around her mug, and she looked relieved and calmer, somehow. 'I don't know, but what I do know is that it isn't a total deterrent.'

For a moment they sat in silence, and she contemplated the situation. 'What I don't understand is that the CCTV footage shows Maddox and the three girls together; granted they were off their faces, but obviously out together. Is it possible that two of the pack went their separate ways before they came across Cordelia?'

'Why?'

'Well, if stepping on the body was a deliberate act, I would have expected the shoe prints of all four to be present.'

Mike shrugged his shoulders. 'Who knows. If the four separated I'd have thought that it would have been Maddox and his girlfriend who paired off, and the others maybe shared a taxi?'

Spirits lifted after the finding of a victim alive, the entrance of Winnie into the Incident Room with a delivery of warm breakfast sandwiches was somewhat a treat for Charley and team, whose mood and determination had made them hungry in more ways than one.

'Call a briefing. I think they need to be made aware of this breakthrough sooner rather than later, don't you?' Charley said as she stepped out of her office.

Mike stood. 'Ten minutes?'

'Ten minutes,' she replied.

–

With the whisper of a breakthrough rippling through those present, Charley was pleased to note that all those in attendance at the briefing looked attentive as she greeted them. She informed them that four arrest teams were required to lock up the four murder suspects.

'Why are we arresting all four suspects? Because the CCTV footage tells us that all four were together on that fateful night. We don't know who was wearing the offending shoes at the time that Cordelia's body was trodden upon, nor do we know who did what. For example, did they encourage each other, and thereby their actions were a joint enterprise?' Charley took a moment to collate her thoughts. 'A priority from subsequent house searches will be to recover the shoes that the prints were taken from, and we need to revisit the CCTV footage to identify the clothing that the four were wearing that night. Where possible, we need to recover those items.'

'The last thing that we need is journalists, photographers or any other media asking questions, and second guessing what is happening before it gets underway,' she told Connie, the press officer.

DS Mike Blake picked up a black marker pen, and concentrated on the white board, upon which he broke down the police personnel available, and put them into teams each headed by a team leader who would be in charge of each group.

Charley pointed to the large picture of Cordelia which was attached to the second board, along with her physical description and that of her clothing. The information, in capital letters, had been written in the same black marker pen, but some words were in blue, highlighted and underlined in red. 'I want to emphasise that our victim's hair was this vivid pink colour, so if the suspects have been near Cordelia, it is possible there could be strands on their clothing,' said Charley.

When Mike took over from the SIO, she had time to consolidate her thoughts, and further theories. To her knowledge, the suspects had nothing to do with the university, which negated her earlier thoughts about the attacks being linked, but coincidences didn't sit well with detectives.

'Any questions?' Mike asked, which brought Charley instantly back from her reverie.

The end of the briefing was met with silence.

'Let's get this sorted, ladies and gents,' she said, with feeling, as the meeting broke up.

Within the hour, the teams were ready at their designated locations, and waiting impatiently for the signal to strike.

In Maddox's case, they were taking no chances; a door ram was used, and officers were in the house very quickly. As DC Bill Whitehill had predicted, quite correctly, Maddox kicked off violently, as expected on this occasion. Like a bullock that didn't want branding, he was seconds away from being tasered for the second time in his criminal career, when he was eventually subdued and handcuffed by Bill.

What was unexpected was that his girlfriend was present, and until Maddox was removed from the premises to the awaiting transport, she screamed, and she screamed loudly. However, with Maddox out of the way, Tricia Carmichael calmed down very quickly, and was allowed to dress before being handcuffed, and led out of the premises to another vehicle for transportation to the cells.

The search of the house began, without interruption.

Beth Green was arrested from her place of work, a nail bar in the town centre. She seemed to go into shock when being told that she was being arrested for murder, and was led away in handcuffs. Her boss, far from impressed with the unwanted attention to her business, sacked her on the spot.

Beth was taken directly to the cells, and officers went to her home address to do the searches.

Kirsty Webb was located and arrested at home; where she was sitting eating breakfast with her mother. Officers told her why she was being arrested, but unlike the others, officers searched her room whilst she was present, with the repeated shouting from her mother in the background.

'If you have done what they are saying, then you are no daughter of mine,' Mrs Webb told her.

Back at the police station, Charley felt a mild irritability which sleep deprivation often brought. She needed air. Turning, she opened the small window, and relished the waft of cold air for a moment or two, until her attention was drawn to some of the team returning, some with prisoners, others with evidence bags. The elation of the early morning calls on the suspects, and subsequent searches, coupled with real progress, felt like a weight had been lifted off her shoulders. Although she was well aware that this was not yet over, her team had managed to round up all their suspects, some of whom were presently in the custody suite being booked in, or already languishing in a police cell. Placed intentionally in separate areas where they could not communicate with, or see each other, they awaited their respective legal advisors' attendance, and the rest of the team continued searching.

The words, 'Boss, we've had double success and have seized the relevant trainers, and Beth Green's shoes, that are believed to be the ones that left the marks on Cordelia's body,' brought a smile to Charley's face. Charley's fears that they would have been disposed of were unfounded, and she couldn't be more pleased.

Bill's eyes were smiling when she looked up at him standing at the office door. 'Didn't I tell you Maddox had a thing about his trainers?' he said, just as Charley's phone rang. Bill turned to join the others who had returned, pumped up with success, and rowdy with it.

Eira White at Forensic told Charley that human skin particles had been found on the stone that had been dropped on Cordelia's head, and from those minute fragments she had managed to extract DNA, which, although there wasn't a match on the system, could be considered for any future suspects.

Charley immediately informed Eira of the main suspect's details, Maddox's previous convictions for violence, and updated her on his arrest, and the outcome of the searches so far.

'The footwear and clothing seized will be on their way to you before the end of the day,' said Charley.

'Maddox's footwear will go for further detailed examin-ation, and I'll get to work immediately on highlighting the points which make them an exact match with the marks on the body.'

'Thank you,' said Charley with deep gratitude. 'That means that we can use the information in the interviews.'

'Do you think any of them will roll over and tell you what happened?' asked Eira.

'I've no idea,' Charley confided, 'but I have every intention of keeping the team on standby to carry out any urgent enquiries which will assist with building a case against them, whilst we have them detained.'

'I guess the race against the custody clock has started then? Twenty-four hours, is no time at all.'

'Tell me about it, eight hours' sleep, tea breaks, food breaks, rest breaks, toilet breaks, and time spent with solicitors are all in the prisoners' favour.' Charley's laugh was one of sarcasm.

Two hours later pre-disclosure had taken place with the detainees' legal representatives, and Charley was having a pre-interview meeting with the officers involved.

'How'd it go,' said Charley, an hour later, seeing the long, downcast faces of Bill and Mike, their disappointment evident after their first 'no comment' interview with Maddox.

'You need to ask?' Bill said.

Charley watched the interview with Maddox's girlfriend on screen in the office. She heard Tricia Carmichael say much the same, but her body language was not that of someone arrested for murder, but rather of a young woman who had taken a fancy to one of her interviewers, Ricky-Lee. 'That could work to our advantage,' Charley noted.

By contrast, Beth Green and Kirsty Webb talked profusely to their interviewing officers. They told them which pubs they had visited, how much they had drunk, which was 'an excessive amount by anyone's standards', according to Helen Weir and Lisa Bayliss. They told them where they had gone afterwards, and how they had eventually got home.

During the next round of interviews, the four would each be asked about the fact that some of the footwear seized was a positive forensic match to the marks on Cordelia's body. Charley, like the rest of the team, awaited each of their responses to the damning evidence.

At the debrief the information was shared.

'Beth Green apologised for not telling the truth in the first interview, and whilst crying throughout this interview, she told us that, in their inebriated state, they had all walked past where Cordelia was lying, said that they thought that Cordelia was off her head on Spice or something similar, and continued by telling us that her pants were round her ankles, and her top had been removed. She said that they had laughed at her before the realisation hit them that she could be dead. Beth expressed regret that they hadn't got help for the victim, but could offer no explanation other than they were all very drunk as to why not. Apparently, Maddox had walked over Cordelia to see if she moved, and when she didn't he encouraged Beth to do the same. She admitted that it was a stupid thing to have done, but in her defence, she tells us that she was very drunk. She denied murdering anyone, and told us that that was God's honest truth.'

'When you asked her about the stone that had been dropped on Cordelia's head, what was her response?' asked Charley.

'No hesitation. Immediate and total denial,' said Lisa.

Helen nodded her head in agreement. 'She also stated that there was no stone on her head when they saw her, and repeated emphatically to us that they didn't kill her.'

'Why didn't they call an ambulance, if she was unconscious? Didn't they have any concerns that she was half-naked?'

'Beth told us that Cordelia was also on the game. Apparently well-known as a prostitute.'

Charley raised her eyebrows. 'Anyone else said this in interview?'

The SIO's question resulted in shaking heads, and both mumbling no.

'Do you think that she's genuine?'

Helen and Lisa were in agreement. 'Absolutely.'

Suddenly Charley felt the first sensation of a stone falling to the pit of her stomach.

'Could this really be the truth?' Charley asked.

Kirsty Webb in her first interview corroborated what Beth Green had said, adding that although herself and Tricia Carmichael had been encouraged by the others to walk over the pink-haired lady, they hadn't.

Most important to Charley was that both Beth and Kirsty were emphatic about the fact that Cordelia's head was uncovered.

Chapter 19

Morning came at last. Charley had slept fitfully, excited at the prospect of hearing what the ones arrested on suspicion of murder said in their subsequent interviews.

The dilemma for Charley was, were this group of four the murderers? She could put them at the scene, and it had been established that two of the four had trodden on Cordelia, that much was not denied, but there was no evidence that they had anything to do with the stone being dropped on the victim's head. It had been established that it was this stone which had killed her.

Armed with a list of questions, the teams set off to conduct the interviews, each with a spring in their step.

However, as the day progressed and the separate portions of information were combined, Charley began to fit together the pieces of the jigsaw which slowly but surely began to mirror the day, diluting what progress on the enquiry she thought they had made.

Tricia Carmichael was less emotional and more pragmatic in her second interview. She told Ricky-Lee and Annie Glover that she was used to seeing people lying in doorways, and off their heads on drink or drugs. She was a woman of the world. However, it hadn't registered with her that the pink-haired lady could actually be dead. And, she likely wasn't dead because there was no stone on her head.

Last but not least Maddox, encouraged by Bill after he had spent a night in the cells, finally broke his silence, and corroborated what the women had said in his statement.

'Did you kill Cordelia Le Beau?' Mike asked him.

At the very least both he and Beth Green were guilty of an assault. Being inebriated was not a defence, merely a mitigating factor.

'No,' he said categorically, with not a hint of body language to suggest to Bill, who had interviewed Maddox many times during his boyhood and as an adult, that he was not telling him the truth.

The fact that the four hadn't given Cordelia the help that may have saved her life, didn't make them killers.

Charley discussed the criminality of the four detained with Mike, and then with Jacki Stanley at the Crown Prosecution Service.

'The limit for police bail is twenty-eight days,' said Jacki, to Charley.

'Twenty-one days is sufficient,' Charley reassured her.

It was agreed that after interview all four would be given police bail to return to Peel Street Police Station in three weeks' time. Which meant that they could live at home, and go about their normal duties whilst investigations continued. A failure to comply would mean they risked being arrested and brought before the Magistrates' Court, which might then decide to remand them in custody.

During the day, incoming telephone calls into the Incident Room consisted mainly of attempted hoaxes, and mischief makers. Each call prompted an action to be undertaken by an officer, and had to be investigated.

'Up to now they have been perpetrated by members of the public getting their kicks from wasting police time,' Wilkie informed Charley who had asked him about the information received after the appeals in the press, as she was passing his desk on her way to make coffee.

In preparation for her debrief, Charley re-read the notes of those interviews that they had managed to conduct.

'I want an update from Forensic with regards to the DNA on the stone,' she told Mike. 'Maddox is a big lad and probably has enough muscle to lift the stone by himself,' she said.

'Ah, but did he? That's the burning question?'

'We will have to let the evidence speak for itself. If it's positive we don't have to wait for him to return on bail to the police station, we can re-arrest with new evidence, and charge him then with murder.'

While the SIO waited for the results to come in from Forensic, she picked at the cheese salad sandwich which Winnie had collected on the sandwich run, even though she had previously brushed aside the fact that she needed to eat. Her stomach was now in knots. Heavy black stratus clouds had been replaced by high cirrus wisps, and reflected her inner turmoil. Everything hinged on the results of the DNA from fragments of skin found on the stone; damning evidence along with what they already knew, if it was a match for anyone who had been arrested. She had formed an idea of how things would pan out should that be the case, and her excitement and impatience mounted minute by minute.

The results were in, and in less time than it took for her to look up from her sandwich at her computer screen, and register what she read, Mike was entering her office. He had a piece of paper in his hand.

'The DNA, it's not a match,' she said, monotone.

He looked enquiringly at the SIO. 'For our four?'

'For anyone on the national database.'

'Which would suggest that the murderer is of previous good character.'

'Yes, either that or he's never been caught before.' She rankled at the thought.

'Could it be possible that our four disturbed the murderer that night?'

Charley opened her drawer. 'Maybe,' she said. Finding what she was looking for, she extracted a pen and a notepad and started to write. 'They're on bail at the moment so there is no need for a knee-jerk reaction. I want to be sure about the next course of action. The last thing we want to do is charge someone with murder who was not responsible, but on the other side of the coin, neither do I want anyone to escape justice.' She pushed the notepad to the side, and took the paper that Mike offered to her.

'It's an update from the hospital,' he said, by way of an explanation. 'They're pleased with Cath Crowther's progress. It is hoped she will make a full recovery, and they are about to move her out of ICU to a general ward.'

'I've no doubt she will make a full physical recovery, but she's likely to require counselling for some considerable time.'

'Any further finds of interest in the search of the wheelie bins?'

'Yes, apparently they've recovered an empty adhesive tube and a gun applicator from the top of one of the bins. Both items, I am told, appear new.'

Charley pursed her lips and added a note to the list on her notepad. 'I wonder if they contain the same adhesive from the bin lid in which Cath was found?'

'Our next step is to see if the items were purchased locally, and if so, does the store have CCTV which might assist us in identifying her abductor?'

Charley's smile reached her eyes. 'Good work. Unbeknown to some, just because there have been arrests made, it doesn't mean that that's the end of the case,' she said.

The SIO looked studious.

'Penny for them?' Mike said.

'It concerns me that if the adhesive is found to be a match, it shows that he has been planning this. He has purposely sought out the adhesive and an applicator for when he required them, not *if*. It also tells me that he wasn't only thinking about abducting Cath Crowther.'

'You think he intended to kill her from the outset?' asked Mike.

'I do, and not only that, I for one think that he thought he had done so when he disposed of her body. He must be caught and stopped before he can strike again.'

Chapter 20

The next day the Incident Room was up and running early, before daylight properly manifested itself. A strong breeze blew across the backyard, as if the weather was eager to help. However, with it came the questions about the enquiry expenditure. The Divisional Commander, Chief Superintendent Bobbie Stokes asked Charley to stay behind after the morning meeting. He spoke to her in an authoritative paternal tone. The tone always made her hackles rise.

'I am aware that at this stage in the enquiry, developments motivate and inspire the workforce, and in light of new-found information overtime is not an option. But, by the nature of our profession, to which the responsibility of rank is added, this also means that decisions have to be made about a future course of action, which may be impeded by our peers owing to budget restrictions, at both Force and Divisional level,' he said.

The Divisional Commander saw Charley's jaw tighten. She was smiling but it wasn't a pleasant smile.

'The enquiry is moving at pace,' she said firmly, and purposefully. Her voice was controlled. Inside, the anger was rising. Her skin tingled as though she was covered in a prickly rash. 'And, I won't let finances get in the way of catching a murderer. If there are cost-effective lines of enquiry to be made then you can be assured that I'll make them, but whatever is necessary, I want it made known to the powers that be that I am, and always will be, fully accountable for everything. My officers were working with due diligence, providing value for money, and if anyone says otherwise...'

Bobbie held up the palm of his hand to her. 'Alright, I get the picture.'

The picture in her head was one of the hierarchy sat on their nine-to-five backsides, in the ivory tower, making decisions about things they knew nothing about because they had not walked the walk, or talked the talk in CID.

'I ask you one question, and you ask whoever is breathing down your neck. Who is the person in charge of the investigation?' She stood and raised an eyebrow at Stokes waiting for a reply. 'I will not allow myself to be shackled in any way,' she said before walking out of his office.

'At the morning briefing, Charley was told that the bed space at Huddersfield General Hospital remained at a premium, and the hospital medics had deemed Cath Crowther fit to be interviewed and, to the SIO's surprise, to leave, once necessary arrangements had been made for her welfare and safety.

Doctor Davidson, her GP, differed in his opinion, but he was told that there was nothing the medical profession could do for her at the hospital that would further benefit her, or warrant her taking up a bed in the already overcrowded general ward.

The hospital staff suggested that Cath write down her responses to the questions put to her. Talking required quite a lot of effort by the brave young woman, who could barely be heard.

Charley picked up the phone and spoke to her doctor. 'Once the bruising and swelling goes down I expect her vocal cords to return to normal, however that won't happen in the next few days,' he said.

'How does she feel about being discharged?' asked Charley.

'I should imagine she is anxious and scared.'

'I'm not surprised. Now the details of her abduction have been given to the media, I would expect that the information about her recovery will be in the public domain quite quickly, and her attacker will then be aware that she hasn't died, which we're sure was his intention.'

'I will be advising that she gets counselling,' he told Charley. 'Although, I am hoping she will take my advice and go home to stay with her parents a hundred miles away, to recuperate for a while.'

Specialist officers (STOs) who were trained in interviewing survivors of such attacks were called upon to speak to Cath, and Charley spent time with them to work out the interview strategy.

Then at noon, when sitting down with the others to eat, she turned her attention to a list of workers and maintenance people, past and present, that Wilkie Connor passed over the table to her: a database of over a hundred names. She knew by Wilkie's face that the task was a logistical mountain to climb, hampered by Tattie's collation of the budget for this, which was likely to be costly.

With the Divisional Commander's words of warning still ringing in her ears, Charley spoke her thoughts out loud.

'Could we narrow this down? Younger men? Those capable of scaling a drainpipe? Those with a connection to the victim?'

'We can discount women, although they are only a small percentage of this workforce,' Mike said almost apologetically.

Charley nodded her head exaggeratedly in appreciation of his input.

'How about we prioritise those presently on site?' added Annie. 'It's more likely that the perpetrator is someone currently working at the university, or having access to the facilities now.'

'I agree,' said Charley, 'then we can move on to recently left personnel if we have no joy. DNA will of course be requested during their questioning, whether or not they admit to knowing Cath Crowther.'

'The elimination factor being ultimately the DNA profile, and therefore mass screening, where possible, to be a way forwards?' Mike asked.

'Yes, and if we have to, we test every bloody man on campus,' she said more bloody-mindedly.

Wilkie smirked, and Charley's instincts were raw.

'I agree, it won't be an easy operation,' she conceded, 'but, I won't give up until he's found.'

'What next?' asked Annie.

Wilkie put his head in his hands. 'Make us a strong coffee,' he said.

'I'm going to liaise with Forensics, Eira sent a message to say that she can now confirm that the adhesive used on Cath's would-be coffin is the same as the discarded tube found in the bin,' Charley said, sounding more upbeat. She stood up and put the remains of her lunch in the bin before heading back to her office.

The two detectives exchanged glances.

Annie eased herself up from her chair, and stretched her back. 'You know what the boss is like when she gets the bit between her teeth,' she said to Wilkie, as she headed for the kitchen. 'Best, crack on.'

—

Charley's priority was to seek possible evidence available to her from the two adhesive exhibits. 'Where did they come from, and who bought them?' she said to the team later that afternoon.

Annie scrutinised the pictures of the exhibits. 'It's just occurred to me,' she said. 'The bastard might have taken time to seal the lid to stop people looking inside, but he didn't put enough on to stop the weight of her body sliding out when the bin was tipped upside down in the bin wagon.' Annie shuddered. Her eyes were wide in astonishment. 'She could have disappeared forever, couldn't she?'

'Quite easily,' said Charley.

'I wondered why he moved her from the flat?' said Ricky-Lee.

'Because a dead body would have brought police in numbers on to the campus which he didn't want, as it would have disrupted his predatory pattern,' said Charley.

Annie looked up. 'You think he has more planned?'

Charley raised her eyebrows, about to reply, when her phone rang. Expecting an update from Eira she rushed into the office, and in her haste almost knocked the receiver off its cradle.

'We've discovered a stain on Cath's bedsheet, which has been identified as semen, and we are processing it to obtain a DNA profile. Could your officers ask Ms Crowther if she has had any male friends staying over recently? If not we have a possible DNA profile for her attacker, which in turn will give us something positive to eliminate suspects, and once a profile has been obtained, we will automatically check it against the national database to see if the person has been previously recorded. If so, you'll have a name for the would-be killer very soon.'

The prospect made Charley's heart skip a beat. She rejoined the team.

'Some positive news. Forensics have been able to extract DNA from a semen stain on the victim's bed sheets.'

Annie thought about what she had said and grinned suddenly.

Cath said, 'we can't let ourselves get too excited. He might not be in the system. The stain could be from a boyfriend. As yet we still don't know who the predator is, or when he will strike again.' Charley looked at Annie and answered her earlier question. 'Because, yes, I do think he has more planned. This is not over.'

The next phase in the investigation was soon underway. Enquiries were prioritised at local stores that were known to stock the same adhesive as the perpetrator had used. More importantly, was there a way of finding out who had bought the adhesive, and when, or was that too much to ask? Meanwhile, at the campus gym, officers requested and obtained a list of members, and likely suspects.

In preparation for the debrief, Charley read through the information available to her for the actions completed that day, including the consensus of those who had come forward and who were willing to make a statement in the hope it may be helpful.

The SIO picked up the map that had been used to establish the static covert observation points to be used from external and internal vantage points on campus, to be covered after Tuesday night's class. The big question now being, would the offender turn up. If so, Charley was confident that they had covered all opportunities available to catch him.

The intended attached pro forma for the users of the gym was ready for her to sign off. With an animal's cunning, the questions were intended for replies that would alert the team to any scrap of information the attendees could possibly give them. However, the wording of the questions was fanciful, and not direct.

1. How often do you visit the gym?

2. Is it the same night every week?

3. Do you visit the gym on your own?

4. Are you a student at the university?

5. If so, do you live on the campus.

Charley scribbled on the form. 'Make it simple!' she wrote.

6. Have you been approached or been followed by anyone, coming to or from the class?

7. Has anyone been in your room uninvited?

8. Have you ever been followed by anyone?

9. Do you have any idea as to whom the predator might be?

She put her pen down, and rested her head in her hands. It was a waiting game. The trouble was, Charley wasn't in a patient mood, but she knew that only time would tell them whether the perpetrator would walk into the trap they had prepared for him. A thought brought a smile to her face. If he did, there was no doubt that they would shock him to the core, in the same way as he had shocked his victims.

–

On Tuesday, Charley remained in the control room, looking at the CCTV screens. Unable to keep still, she paced the floor, willing the would-be killer to come into sight, and listening closely for any messages that came over the airwaves, on the dedicated channel, sent by the officers at the strategic observation points. Although the adrenaline was pumping around her body she felt wan, and increasingly anxious to be able to give Cath some positive news.

The officers had been instructed to maintain radio silence until such time that they had anything to report, and presently the airwaves were silent.

Everyone had been in place for an hour before the aerobics class was started. Two officers at each point to ensure their safety and the safety of the people on campus. Each officer had been provided with a police baseball cap to immediately identify themselves as police officers. The officers were instructed to remain in place until a target was apprehended, or they were otherwise stood down.

A downside to their plan was that the turbulent weather was unforgiving, and the rain fell in torrents. Tattie had worked a split shift to enable her to go home and feed the cat. Her frizzy hair was still dripping when she entered the room and passed Charley an update from the officers speaking to Cath. 'She's adamant that no male friends had been in her room,' she said with a little nod and a knowing look. The office manager waited for a few moments whilst Charley absorbed the information.

Thoughts raced through Charley's head. Had Cath's attacker slipped up already, as Eira had suggested? What this confirmed to Charley was that, apart from his being a control freak, he had become sexually excited before, during or after his attempt on her life, and that scared the hell out of the SIO.

'Can you pass this information on to Forensic so that they're aware,' she said.

As Charley turned her focus back to the screens, her spirits were lifted to see all officers in the positions agreed, which allowed them to determine immediately when a suspect or someone acting suspiciously was spotted. The principle of an outside stake-out location, was to allow the arrest to take place in the grounds and not in the gym, and it reduced the likelihood of hostages being taken. This operation was costly but the analysis provided a strong indication that the gym class was an extremely likely location to arrest their perpetrator. Was this the break she had been waiting for?

The eagerness of all concerned was not matched by luck. The keen eyes of the observers missed nothing, but the suspect was a no-show, and the team were stood down. Some faces were downcast, making their disappointment clear. These officers had families themselves. However, all was not lost as enquires were made of those in attendance at the class.

A debrief awaited them back at the station.

Charley began upbeat. 'Nothing ventured, nothing gained. We will repeat tonight's approach for the next few weeks, on the off-chance that our man returns to his previous, possible hunting ground.' She thanked everyone involved for their efforts and ended the meeting. 'Remember, tomorrow is another day.'

In their role as Specially Trained Officers (STO's) Mike and Annie met with Cath for the first time, in hospital the next morning. The officers introduced themselves. Cath's mum and dad were sat at her beside. Her mother's face was wet with tears, her dad's contorted with anguish.

At their daughter's request to speak to the officers alone, Mrs Crowther stood and leant over the hospital bed. Her face softened in a motherly way before she carefully planted a butterfly kiss on her daughter's forehead; mindful of her bruising.

Mr Crowther followed his wife to the door where he put his hand on her shoulder. Together they turned. 'We will be in the canteen if you should need us,' he said, softly.

When Cath was sure that her parents had gone, her face crumpled. 'I wish I could take away their pain,' she sobbed.

Her voice was hoarse when she calmed a little, her muscles shaky. 'I told them I'm okay. I'm alive aren't I?'

Cath put a hand to her face, closed her eyes and breathed in deeply just as her throat closed and tears threatened again. The ache in her gut intensified until warm tears squeeze out from her eyelids and burned her eyes.

Annie reached out to comfort her. It seemed that the detective's closeness worked its magic to calm Cath's breathing though and she appeared to relax. Sniffing, Cath opened her eyes and wiped the wetness from her cheeks.

Strands of hair fell from her loose knot on the top of her head.

'Mum says that my hair smells weird. I told her that it's the shampoo that the hospital have given me to wash it with,' she said. Her eyes wandered to the striped, fleece pyjamas that her parents had bought for her, and she tugged with pinched fingers, at the bottoms. 'I made a joke about them, they're not really my style. Little do they know that beneath them, I have scratches, fingernail impressions in my skin, bandages and plasters. My vagina is sore, no doubt with all the prodding… And, I can't get rid of the feeling of emptiness… I'm so afraid.' Tears poured in earnest.

Sat in the chairs that Mr and Mrs Crowther had vacated, Mike and Annie listened silent, compassionate and reassuring.

The room was south facing. It was warm and humid, but the officers could understand her reluctance to open the window that looked out onto the dense woodland, in the hospital grounds that could hide another intruder.

Annie noted that Cath was curling her toes under the bedcovers. It was obvious she was in pain. She was nervous, irritated, angry. Who could blame her?

'We understand that you may not be able to answer all our questions,' said Mike, softly. 'However, the more you can tell us, the better our chance of identifying the suspect.'

Annie continued to speak in the same vein. 'If you're comfortable with talking about what happened we have some questions to ask you. What happened? Where did it happen? When did it happen? Who did this to you?'

The detective saw the look of being overwhelmed in the girl's eyes and she understood. 'How about we start with you telling us what happened, shall we?' Annie said.

Cath took a sip of water. A tired smile tugged at her lips. 'I'll do my best,' she replied, in a rasping voice. She coughed and swallowed hard before she continued.

'My first thought when I woke up to find a naked stranger sat at the bottom of my bed was that I was going to be raped. I sat up and was about to scream when he reached out, grabbed me by the throat and with one powerful thrust, threw me back into my pillows before filling my mouth with a light, nylon material that gagged me. At that point I thought that I was going to die. I could hardly breathe and I couldn't scream, although I tried.' Cath reached for a glass of water on her bedside table and took a sip. When she replaced it she accidentally knocked her bruised wrist and winced. She paused.

Annie winced too, ready to soothe her, but Cath talked through her pain.

'I recall how swiftly he tied my hands, and covered my head, with rough, sacking material. It smelt strongly of cheap washing-up liquid. Two powerful hands then clasped my neck…' she swallowed hard. '…to choke me.' Cath took a gasp of breath which made her cough. 'I couldn't breathe,' she gasped. The memory of how she felt at the time was as raw as her visible wounds.

Annie found it hard to hide her shock when Cath uncovered her severely bruised neck, which looked like a tight, dark, mottled scarf.

'Being strangled was the last thing I remember before becoming unconscious,' she said.

'And, when you came round in the hospital…' asked Annie tentatively.

Cath's voice was becoming barely audible. She was obviously finding it increasingly difficult to speak. Bravely she pushed on.

'I felt terrified, and in severe pain. I was told that I had been found in a wheelie bin, potentially penetrated sexually by a stranger, and that I should get retested for HIV, because results didn't always show up immediately. I was also told that I will be discharged as soon as possible, so that I can get back to my normal life.' Cath leaned forwards and looked down at Annie's bag that lay at the side of her chair. 'Have you brought my knickers and pyjama bottoms that I was wearing? They told me when they took them that I was only allowed to keep my necklace.'

'I'm sorry,' said Annie. 'I'm afraid that we will have to keep them for a while yet…'

Cath looked annoyed with herself. 'Of course,' she replied. 'What was I thinking?'

'Were you aware that you were filmed, or that the footage was shared on social media?' asked Mike.

Cath shook her head.

'You describe your assailant as a stranger. Do you think that you would be able to identify him again?'

She nodded as emphatically as her wounds would allow. 'His face, those staring eyes, as black and as hard as granite, will be imprinted on my mind for the rest of my life,' she said in a whisper.

Cath's eyes caught the movement in the corridor outside. Through the window they could see that Mr and Mrs Crowther had returned. With a little forced smile and a wave to her daughter Mrs Crowther sat down outside, to wait. Seeing his daughter's pale, puffy face, and red eyes, Mr Crowther tapped at the door.

'I think she might have had enough for today, don't you?' he said.

'Yes, you're right,' said Mike closing his notepad. The detective sergeant found Cath's eyes. 'We'll come back later, if that's okay with you?'

'Or maybe we will see you at home,' said Annie. 'If your discharge is imminent.'

-

In the office Charley read Cath's statement which was enlightening, and much of what she read was not surprising, considering the perpetrator's escalating behaviour.

Tomorrow the specialist officers would be returning for another chat, in the hope that she had remembered more, and again they would make notes of what she was saying to them, which ultimately would be put into a written statement for a future prosecution file.

Despite there being no physical evidence connecting the two crimes, Charley couldn't shake the feeling that this predator had already escalated to murder, and that his victim had been Cordelia Le Beau. The MO was different, and the crime scenes were nothing alike, but the hatred of women was the same – the way both women had been stripped of their clothes and their bodies dealt with in such a dehumanising way...

Cath's description of the attacker was telling, and fit their suspect perfectly:

White male

Approx twenty years of age

Fair hair

Clean shaven

Physically fit

He didn't speak

The description, also identical to that given by Dani Miller, showed Charley how lucky Dani had been. She had screamed. Had that saved her life? Had the perpetrator learnt from that night that he must silence his next victim, which was why he grabbed Cath by the throat quickly, to stop her from screaming?

Eira's call just before lunchtime was not what Charley wanted to hear, but what the SIO had expected.

Once again, there was no hit on the national database linking the sample of DNA taken from the bedsheet.

'It appears that her attacker has no previous criminal record,' said Eira.

'That doesn't make him any less dangerous, does it? It just means that he is going to be harder to find.'

'Being invisible to us brings about confidence, but that said, it might make him less careful. He'll slip up, you mark my words,' said Eira. 'They always do.'

'He isn't about to stop until such time as he's caught though is he?' replied Charley.

'Hey, come on, that's not like you. Good job I've got some positive news for you isn't it?' she said.

'What is it?' Charley asked eagerly. 'Come on Eira, spill the beans!'

Chapter 21

Charley could hardly disguise the joy in her voice when she told her team that the crime stain discovered on Cath Crowther's bedding had now been examined, and identified as semen. Further examination gave them a DNA profile.

'That said, there is no match on the national database. The attacker is not recorded. Whilst it's disappointing,' she paused before delivering the next piece of news, because she hadn't yet processed the implications of what she had been told by Eira, 'the DNA is an exact match to another unidentified sample found on the stone from Cordelia Le Beau's murder scene, which we know had been dropped on her head by her killer. We now know that the attacker for both crimes is the same person, and we have the ability to positively eliminate suspects.'

Annie listened intently, her eyebrows furrowed with concentration. Her face brightened at the news, and her eyes found Charley's. 'That really does link the crime scenes,' she said.

Charley nodded in her direction. 'On the balance of probabilities, I think it is beyond reasonable doubt that our would-be killer in this case has killed before. We saw with our own eyes that both incapacitated victims were found with their underwear around the ankles, leaving them semi-naked.'

'This is a specific sexual act in itself, which proves to me he has a calm trait of controlling behaviour in his character, which makes him need to display the bodies in this way,' said Mike.

Charley stood up and stepped to the side of the chalkboard, where she pointed to the description of the perpetrator, the link to his DNA profile, and the pictures of the victims who swore they could identify their attacker, before she continued. 'We know what he looks like. We know his preferred hunting ground. We have his DNA and we have witnesses who can identify our attacker. Whilst we have all this evidence, what we still don't have is him. He is likely to strike again. We need to apprehend him before he does.'

Turning on her heel she scanned the faces of those assembled. 'Who is he? Where is he?' she continued. 'Our elimination processes must be swift now we have the DNA profile, and carried out on a daily basis. No matter what it takes, we cannot allow this evil, sadistic perpetrator to attack and kill again,' she said, emotionally. Charley turned to Mike. 'Get photographs of the university staff fitting the basic description to show our victims to see if they are able to identify the killer for us.' She looked back to the team. 'Anything come out of the results for the questionnaire? Do we know if Cordelia was ever on campus? If not, how did she cross paths with her attacker?'

With nothing fruitful gained from the questionnaire, and no link to the university and Cordelia Le Beau, the frustration of her unsolved murder enquiry, coupled with the attempted murder of Cath Crowther, and the incidents involving Dani Miller and the others, was getting to them all.

The hunt so far had been relentless, and would continue to be so, the difference now being that they had substantial evidence.

The positive news she had shared from Eira, was the only good news of the day, however. After a meeting at HQ attended by Chief Superintendent Bobbie Stokes, and other divisional commanders, Stokes called her up to his office.

'As you are aware, Charley,' he said, 'police resources are under continuing constraint like never before, and I've been asked to speak to you in relation to the procedure for returning the officers drafted onto your enquiry team from other divisions.'

'They want them back now? It's not happening, we've had a positive breakthrough today, and to make that count I need all the resources I have,' she said.

He nodded. 'If…'

'Not if; when I'm in a position to start releasing staff, then I'll do so.'

'…Or when, let me finish, new leads are established, or something conclusive turns up, such as you have him in custody or named, then we will have further conversations about staffing.'

Charley opened her mouth as if to protest, but Stokes held up his hand. 'My decision is final,' he said. 'You've probably got two, three weeks at the most before the next commanders' meeting.' The SIO knew, by the look on his face and his manner, that arguing with the head of the division would be a waste of both her time, and his.

Reluctantly, Stokes agreed that PCs Helen Weir and Lisa Bayliss could remain, 'If their inspectors are agreeable, and I will speak to them on your behalf, and that would be only until they are required back on their own rotas. It's the best I can do.'

As the days passed, tempers flared with little provocation needed. Accusations against members of the team, however small, were capable of escalating into personal rows. Trying to keep the team focused and motivated amongst such strong, determined, frustrated individuals was a daily battle for supervision, and Charley made a concentrated effort to maintain an outward show of unity and support, offering assurance when needed.

Cath Crowther was far less able to cope now, knowing the full facts of what had taken place. At one point, her feelings of anxiety rose to such a high level that she talked of suicide to her counsellor, who was sufficiently worried about her state of mind and safety to speak to Charley. In the end the young woman managed to find the strength to refuse to allow her attacker another victory by giving up her studies that she'd diligently worked at for over a year, and that had cost her dearly owing to personal sacrifices.

The usually outgoing, friendly young woman had disappeared, her concerned family and friends told the family liaison officers. Cath had become withdrawn, all her trust gone. Every male was a suspect to her. She slept briefly, and then only with the help of medication prescribed by Doctor Davidson.

Returning to her room on campus to complete her studies and achieving good grades despite her ordeal, was her main focus, but not what her parents wanted to hear so soon. Neither was it a decision that Charley agreed with, although she understood her reasoning that she couldn't let her attacker define her future.

Her parents begged the family liaison officer to get Charley to intervene, and persuade her to stay with them. However, there was no shifting Cath, and all Charley could do was make sure that the university was aware of her decision and offered the student support. Liaising with security, Charley suggested that they ensured the CCTV was fit for purpose, and she had locks on her windows. She spoke to the divisional crime prevention team to install a panic alarm in Cath's room, and made her promise that when she left her room that she did so in the company of a friend, or a fellow student. She wanted Cath to be confident that her attacker would not return, knowing he was still out there. They were, in truth, no nearer to finding him than they were on the days following the attempted murder. Even Charley had doubts that crossed her mind with increasing frequency, as it seemed that her cunning attacker was still able to evade capture.

Finally, the hoax calls, and others into the Incident Room started to dry up. It appeared to Charley that the public had accepted that he would not be found anytime soon, so had probably lost interest. The media also thinned out. They had nothing to feed on. The victims' faces no longer appeared on the front pages of the newspapers, not even the local press. Full-page reports about the crime became thumbnail pictures, with brief updates that Connie Seabourne, the police press officer, negotiated to try to keep the enquiry in the news, but even her efforts were wearing thin.

It seemed that the general public was learning to live with a murderer in their midst. It was a fact that women constituted the majority of persons at risk of harm by Cath's offender and they had informed officers of many ingenious ways which they had thought of to try to protect themselves. Which wasn't surprising as they felt increasingly vulnerable walking the streets.

However, Charley was aware, these attacks on young women weren't random.

As far as they knew he hadn't raped, or attempted to rape, his victims, but now they had the evidence that proved he had become sexually excited during the attacks, to the point of ejaculation. Was this because he knew how valuable a DNA profile was to the police, or was he inadequate, or simply unable to control himself?

The investigation continued to prioritise males who came into the investigation by one way or another; connected or not, they were subjected to a simple mouth swab test for comparison against the offender's DNA. The suspect database grew and grew, however, with samples going to the lab in batches of thirty, the innocent were quickly eliminated.

Enquiries had taken Ricky-Lee to Brook's DIY store, where it was confirmed that the adhesive and applicator gun used to seal the wheelie bin had been purchased, and the information he received that afternoon added weight to the evidence already accrued, and supplied further leads to investigate.

'The bar code tells me that the products were bought a week prior to the attack,' said the manager.

Charley's relief at Ricky-Lee's update was heightened by more pieces of information which the clerk at the small business retrieved from his ancient computer system, and this confirmed that the latest attack had been well planned.

'On the downside, they don't have CCTV, and the counter staff can't remember any particular person buying the products, which are often bought together.'

'Can they tell us if the buyer of the products paid cash, or did they use a credit card?' asked Charley.

'Cash.'

Charley's face instantly lit up at the thought of fingerprint retrieval, to become downcast a moment later.

'But the takings are banked on a weekly basis,' said Ricky-Lee.

Charley thought hard for a moment before relaying her next instruction. 'Seize any CCTV that concentrates on the street. With a transaction able to tell us a date when the products were bought, and presumably a time, there could be an opportunity to see the buyer leaving the store with the items. Whilst looking through CCTV footage is labour intensive, it may well prove invaluable to us in an attempt to identify a suspect.'

It was late afternoon, and Charley needed to liaise further with the Crown Prosecution Service before they went home.

Locating the information for the Cordelia Le Beau murder enquiry from her computer, she searched the screen for the information she required. She began to read. The pathologist's report told her what she already knew, that the cause of her death was the stone being dropped on her head, and until that occurred, although she was seriously injured, she had been alive. Mr Butterworth also said when it was likely when this was done. 'Did the killer make absolutely sure she was dead by this macabre act, or was the killer another person who came upon her injured body?' Charley considered.

Charley knew that Maddox and crew had been at the scene. They had admitted it in interview, and Maddox and Green's DNA profiles were not a match for DNA recovered from the skin on the stone. However Charley felt that they should still face charges of assault, after all the evidence suggested they had stamped on her whilst she had been lying on the ground, not simply walked over her, as they would have had the interviewing officers believe.

In respect of Tricia Carmichael and Pam Wilkinson, it was likely they wouldn't be processed with regards to the alleged assault. There was no evidence to suggest that, although they had been present, they had been involved in the assault, or encouraged their friends to do what they had done. If they had been, she would have had no hesitation in charging all four.

'We'd like a typed file prepared against all parties,' said Jacki Stanley, who picked up the phone when Charley rang CPS. 'After we receive it, a decision will be made. When we've read all the evidence we will decide if it is in the public interest to proceed, and against whom.'

'It's cut and dried, surely,' said Charley. 'I've got a killer to catch, and I don't want any unnecessary distractions.'

When they were running on full power, the days seemed to roll into one.

Charley ensured that liaison was being maintained with Forensic on a regular basis, to ensure the stream of sample submissions was proceeding smoothly, and, from speaking to Eira, she knew that they were working equally as hard on the examination and testing, and the major incident remained a priority for them.

When Charley returned home that night, she kicked her shoes off at the door, but instead of going straight upstairs to get changed out of her working clothes, she walked straight down the hallway and into the kitchen. She shivered, switched the thermostat to the 'ON' position and did the same with the kettle. She sighed deeply as she sat down on the sofa sipping the cup of tea, grateful for the warmth of the mug whilst the heating kicked in. She placed her mug on the coffee table and was just about to peel the tin foil from her Kit-Kat chocolate biscuit, when her mobile phone rang. Instinctively, she jumped from the chair to answer it. It was the inspector in the control room informing her about an incident that had occurred on the A62 Manchester Road, not far from the village of Slaithwaite where Annie lived. A girl had run straight out into the road from the school, and had been struck by a passing vehicle. The suggestion was that the driver had no opportunity to avoid her. Fortunately she wasn't seriously hurt, but she was being taken to hospital, to be treated for minor injuries and shock. Her parents had been informed.

Charley was puzzled. 'Why have you called me?'

'The girl was partially clothed, and told the emergency team at the scene that she was being chased by a man,' he said.

'Where was she running from?' Charley asked.

'Shrugs Park, where a man had suddenly appeared from inside a dark coppice, grabbed hold of her and dragged her towards nearby bushes. Fortunately she managed to break free when she scratched his face, and he loosened his grip.'

'Despatch CID to the scene, CSI to take nail scrapings, and STOs to liaise with family, and the victim at the hospital, if she's in any fit state to talk to us. I'm on my way.'

The small local park was cordoned off with police tape, and a search had begun to see if they could ascertain the exact location where the teenager had been grabbed. A sniffer dog and handler joined the small team, to help in the recovery of discarded clothing, before it got dark.

Miriam James was fifteen years of age. The bewilderment on her swollen face said it all. Her attacker had punched her, but the shock, and subsequent chase, enabled her to give the officers a good description of him; white male, athletic build, light-coloured hair, and clean-shaven.

Could this be the same person that Charley and her team were seeking? The person who had killed one woman, and attempted to kill another. The only time she would know that for sure, would be when the suspect was in the net. What it did tell her about him, if it was him, was that he was relentless and ruthless.

'First thoughts, boss,' said Ricky-Lee, who joined her at the scene.

'This feels more like an opportunist, which is contrary to what we know about our man, who makes plans. However, we can't exclude him for the attack,' she conceded.

The press appeal was over, advising women and girls not to walk alone if possible, and never in secluded areas until this man was caught.

'Is it the same man you're looking for in connection with Cordelia Le Beau's murder and Cath Crowther's attempted murder?' shouted a journalist, who stood at the outer cordon with a photographer.

'We can't rule him out,' Charley called back.

By God she wished she knew where he was.

Chapter 22

Charley had ordered the scrapings that had been taken from underneath Miriam's fingernails by CSI, and must be fast-tracked by Forensic, in the hope that if she had grabbed hold of him, as it was thought, in her attempt to free herself from his grasp, there may be particles of her attacker's skin and blood in them.

Mike Blake had his eye on the clock, which showed nine-thirty, and he was pleased to note that the office was empty, with all the dedicated personnel working overtime, making enquiries in and around the area of the attack on Manchester Road, the adjacent park, and surrounding neighbourhood.

Luck played a defining part in their finding items of clothing very quickly, which they believed to be Miriam's. The rays of Annie's torch, which had been shining into the hedgerow, briefly reflected light from something partly hidden.

Bounding up the stairs into the CID office, Annie Glover showed her find to Charley, admiring as she did so the jumper that she held up in a see-through evidence bag, along with a necklace attached by a thread. She sensed the exhibits would be of some value as corroborative evidence that would hope-fully add weight to their case, by supporting Miriam's account of events. The sleeve of her coat was tattered and torn from her efforts to retrieve her treasure from the hawthorn hedge with its nasty thorns, but it was partly because of those thorns that the jumper hadn't disappeared down the deep drainage ditch beyond. Charley looked down at the mud trail Annie had left behind her, the residue of the thick mud that had sucked at her shoes trodden into the carpet. Annie saw her looking. The two women stood in silence for a minute. Charley's thin lips were compressed in her determination not to laugh. 'I wouldn't want to be in your shoes when Winnie sees that mess in the morning,' she said.

Annie's mood changed from elation to frustration as she dropped to her knees. 'Oh no, I'm a dead man walking, aren't I?' she groaned dramatically.

'Dead woman,' Wilkie corrected her. The older detective looked up at Charley from where he was sitting at his desk. 'I've got a cracker for her next appraisal, ma'am. "This officer could be likened to a small puppy, she runs around excitedly, leaving little messes for other people to clean up!"'

Charley turned her back on the pair. Office banter was something that she greatly enjoyed, it was her proof, if she needed it, of a tightly bonded team.

As ever, Annie was quick to respond. 'How about, "One-celled organisms would outscore him in an IQ test?" for his,' she said nodding her head in Wilkie's direction.

–

It was mid-morning the next day when Eira notified Charley that they had managed to obtain a DNA profile from the nail scrapings. Before asking whether it was a match with the current murder, Charley took a deep breath. When she was told no, the relief in knowing that Cordelia's murderer hadn't attempted to strike again so soon, was unexpectedly overwhelming for her.

'We ran the sample through the national database though, and we've got a match,' Eira spoke with confidence.

'Do we know him?' replied Charley.

'More than likely, he's local. A twenty-four-year-old sex offender by the name of Jim (Jimmy) Waddington, convicted previously in connection with a series of indecent assaults on young girls.'

Charley rolled her eyes. 'When was he released? I don't remember seeing the paperwork.'

'Last week, with an electric monitoring device attached to his ankle.'

'He was tagged?' Charley's face brightened. 'That means that the data stored on his monitor should show us his movements, confirm he was at the scene at the time of the incident, and together with his DNA will give us a watertight case against him.'

—

Jimmy had never been the brightest bulb in the chandelier, or the sharpest tool in the box, but the local bobbies knew him well, and when two arrived at his door, he let them in, only to immediately kneel down on the lino floor, and to continue to do what his mother had previously instructed; put his muddy clothes into the washing machine.

'Do you wanna a brew?' the semi-naked man asked with a smile when he stood up studying his visitors. Jimmy prided himself on missing nothing where women were concerned.

The officers moved him to the side before he could turn the machine on. James looked enquiringly at his mother, who had just appeared through the kitchen door.

'What's going on?' she demanded, surprised to see the police officers in her kitchen pulling dirty washing out of her machine. She put herself between the officers and her son, growling like a dog protecting her pup. 'Tell me what's he supposed to have done now?'

Jimmy noted the interest that the female officer showed him. He looked down the length of her thin, fragile body and smirked, she wouldn't cause him any problem. He turned his attention to the much taller athletic-looking male sergeant, who was speaking to his mother. A man not much older than himself, a boss man, he must be clever, maybe of the two, he was the one he should be careful of, he figured.

Back in her office at the station, Charley was confident that she could leave this enquiry with the two police officers, but she was still on the look-out to secure additional evidence.

'Let me know when he's in the cells will you,' the SIO said, when they rang to update her, 'and by the way, will you check to see if he's got any visible scratch marks anywhere.'

Charley made herself a cup of tea and laced it with sugar. It was two o'clock in the afternoon, and a sugar rush was badly needed to help her focus on other pressing matters. She sipped the piping-hot drink carefully, whilst checking the massive DNA screening base at the university. Knowing that the killer was still out there, and for all she knew, he might already have his sights set on his next victim, turned her stomach. However, she felt comforted by what she was being told by the team leaders, and seeing the determination and energy of the team for herself, sure that nothing more could be done to try to catch the killer, and further reassured in her own ability to have the perpetrator caught before too long, as she was constantly reminded by the hierarchy that it was her responsibility alone to solve the case, no one else's.

Sitting and pondering the case, a thought filtered into her mind that the perpetrator would be aware of the police activity around the campus, and that he might very well be looking elsewhere for his victims. Then as quickly as it came it was dismissed, because Charley never worried about anything that was out of her control, only what she could control. Even if she thought it would be slightly more effective, she was unable to spread the workforce available to her any thinner than it was currently spread. All she could hope for was that the general public had taken heed of the police warnings in the media, and although the case had disappeared from the headlines, that they were still being extra vigilant.

'Tell me,' Charley asked Wilkie Connor, 'has anyone at the university been difficult to locate by the swab teams?'

She knew that the killer would keep away from any DNA screening for as long as he could. Would he be thinking he was on borrowed time, and therefore increase his addiction she wondered, or did he think they were not even close to catching him, and as he became more confident would he become lax in carrying out his evil deeds? Truth was, she knew, it was impossible to get inside the mind of a killer. Even if hiring a criminal profiling expert was a consideration, despite the extra cost to the enquiry, in her experience, they only confirmed what she already knew. They could only give their personal opinion based on similar cases.

Eventually, when the perpetrator was caught, she might get some answers, although she may never uncover why he had committed these dreadful crimes, but that didn't stop her asking.

Charley could hear the phone ringing in the outside office. It broke her reverie. She saw Annie answer it, and raise her eyebrows at Wilkie sitting opposite her. When she put down the phone she said a few words to her older colleague, and he looked up at her as he started to close down his computer.

Annie locked her drawer and stood, grabbed her coat from the back of her chair, picked up her bag and slung it over her shoulder. 'Boss!' she called as she walked towards Charley's door.

'Yes!' Charley replied, seeing her standing in her doorway.

'I'm going to see the boss of a window-cleaning company that has the contract for the university. Mr Robinson has requested that we speak to everyone on his team. Apparently, one of his workers hasn't been seen since the day Cath was discovered.'

Charley frowned. 'Did Mr Robinson give you a name?'

'No, I didn't get the chance to ask as he cut the call abruptly, saying he'd see me soon. I think someone might have entered the room, and I guessed he wanted to keep the conversation confidential for now.'

Charley disappeared into her office to collect her coat. 'Wait for me, I'm coming with you.'

-

At the university the detectives met with Mr Robinson. He was a softly spoken, smart, elderly gentleman who had inherited the family window-cleaning business from his father.

'I've fallen off more ladders than you've had hot dinners young 'un!' he told Charley when she introduced herself to him.

'I bet you can tell us a story or two about the things you've seen,' Annie chuckled, and Mr Robinson nodded.

'I no longer clean the windows myself,' he said, rubbing his aching knee joint as he sat down in his chair. He beckoned the others to sit too, and asked his secretary to bring them tea. 'However, I do have a team of younger people who do that for me. Six months ago I set on a new lad by the name of Russell Peters. He's twenty-six years old, and I have found him since to be what the professionals would call socially inadequate. He has a speech impediment, and because of it, I think, he is reluctant to join in with the others, although, I have the idea that he would like to. He gets embarrassed easily, and you know what work colleagues are like for taking the mickey?'

The two detectives shared a glance.

'More often than not, Russell works on his own, and he seems happy to do so. He's proved to be a good worker, good time keeper, never been off sick, but since the incident with Cath Crowther we've not seen head nor tail of him, which is totally out of character.'

'Why did you decide to phone today to tell us this Mr Robinson?' asked Charley.

Mr Robinson appeared taken aback by the question, and indicated to a piece of paper on his desk. 'I sent his foreman round to his flat this morning to do a welfare check, and according to him, Russell's immediate neighbours told him that he had gone on holiday. Which seemed mighty strange because he hadn't mentioned it to him.'

'What address have you got for Peters?' Charley asked.

Mr Robinson considered the file on his desk. 'Flat 14, Websters Towers.'

'Which is approximately two miles from the university,' said Charley.

Annie had her head down and she was taking notes.

'Do we know if he has transport?'

'Cycles everywhere, I'm told. He's physically fit, athletically built, has short, fair hair, and his nickname is Monkey because of the way he goes up and down ladders, with no fear of heights.'

'And, no one has seen him since the day Cath Crowther was discovered?'

'That's about it in a nutshell,' said Mr Robinson.

'Do you have a photograph of Russell Peters, Mr Robinson?' Charley asked.

Mr Robinson took a scanned picture from Peters' file and handed it to Charley. 'I've a copy of his ID badge if that helps?'

'Should we presume that, although Russell Peters rides a bike, he also has a driving licence?'

'Yes, he does,' replied Peters' boss.

–

Charley was eager to speak to Wilkie Connor the minute they got back to the office. 'Check Russell Peters out on the system,' she said.

Wilkie handed her a piece of paper. 'Annie forwarded his details, it's already done. Peters hasn't been swabbed for his DNA, and he is linked to just one minor incident, when he was reported for nuisance behaviour four years ago, and warned about the dangers of swinging from balcony to balcony at the high-rise flats where he lives.'

Charley could feel a little flutter in her stomach. 'The fact that he has no previous convictions ticks another box for us.'

Wilkie silently nodded.

Charley's pulse quickened, and the look on her face told Wilkie and Annie that instructions were imminent, and they weren't wrong.

The SIO looked at her watch and scowled. 'I have a budget meeting planned with the Divisional Commander at two o'clock. Write this information up on the database. I'd like you to make enquires at his flat, with his neighbours to see if we can locate him as soon as possible. I want Russell Peters treated as a priority.'

Chapter 23

Wilkie Connor and Annie Glover were on their way to Websters Towers within the hour. The flats were known locally as Fawlty Towers because they had never functioned properly, according to the original design, along with another five high-rise flats in the Huddersfield town centre named after local breweries.

Websters Towers stood one hundred and twenty feet high. All the brewery named flats had dual aspect windows and large south-facing balconies. With eleven floors, Websters Towers contained eighty-eight flats. 'Apparently, Peters climbed down that from top to bottom by swinging from one balcony to another? He must be wrong in t'head!' said Wilkie.

Standing facing the wall of windows at the entrance lobby, waiting to be allowed access by the caretaker, Annie strained her neck to see if she could see the top of the building. 'I heard from someone that these flats sway in the wind,' she said.

Wilkie tapped the toecap of his shoe on the concrete beneath his feet. 'Swaying is the least of your worries if you see cracks down here. If the foundations aren't solid, everyone's fucked!' At that very moment, a loud buzz indicated the door lock being released, and ever the gentleman, Wilkie stood to the side, gesturing for Annie to walk through the door first.

The sound of their footsteps echoed hollowly, bouncing off the walls and ceiling of the large empty concrete space. The detectives walked diagonally towards the lift, situated at the core of the building. Standing for a moment in silence in front of the lift door, they waited for it to arrive. 'I hope it's working. I don't fancy walking up the steps,' Annie said, impatiently. When the lift door opened they walked in. Annie pulled the sleeve of her jumper over her fingers, and punched the buttons for the third floor.

'What's that smell?' she said, turning up her nose as the door clunked shut.

Wilkie sniffed the air. 'Smells distinctly like urine to me.'

Annie turned to Wilkie. 'I thought they weren't allowed animals in the flats?'

Wilkie laughed. 'They're not.'

Annie's stomach heaved. 'Thanks for that,' she said, looking up at the cork-like ceiling panels covered with brown water stains. Her eyes travelled down the faux-suede walls covered with graffiti, and eventually to her feet, where the old brown carpeting, curling up at the outer edges, was littered with dirty, discarded and trampled takeaway boxes, cigarette butts, sweet papers and crisp packets. The odd cardboard drink container and a few cans were scattered amongst the grimy litter. The lift chugged up to the second floor, and stalled at the third. The lights flickered. There was a low groan from the shaft below. A thought flashed through Annie's mind, and her heart beat a little faster. 'What if we get stuck?' she said. Her eyes sought the emergency button, but they refused to focus and everything was a blur. She grabbed hold of Wilkie's arm, but before he could answer, the lift motor chugged into gear and the doors creaked open in concert with the loud, deep rumble, that continued to echo throughout the chamber. Wilkie shrugged off Annie's hand. 'Numpty,' he said, stepping out onto the landing. He nodded in the direction of the security camera's lens that was covered with a wad of chewing gum.

Two dark-blue doors faced them, No. 14 and No. 17. There was no answer to the detectives' knocking at number 14. After a moment or two, Wilkie bent down and opened the letter box, to be greeted by first one inquisitive fly, then another. He wafted them away with his hand.

'What're you looking for?' enquired Annie when he stood up straight.

'I wondered if there would be a bike in the hallway, seems a sensible place to keep it if he was in, but there isn't. It smells like something's died though. Take a whiff.' Wilkie leaned forwards as if to open the letter box for her. Annie recoiled. 'No thanks,' she said, batting away the flies that settled on her exposed skin, as she began to itch from their unwanted attention.

The continued knocking and the calling of Russell Peters' name at No.14 caused a young woman, with a crying child in her arms, to come to the door of No.17. 'If you're looking for the nutter who lives there, he told my fella he was going on a long holiday,' she told them. A tired looking, skinny lad, in baggy jogging bottoms, and with tattooed sleeves slunk up behind her.

'I'd try the hospital if I were you Kojak, they've probably sectioned him at last. Now if you don't mind, stop making so much noise, 'er indoors is trying to get the little 'un to sleep so that I can have a little shut-eye m'self,' he said, before pulling his partner inside by her upper arm, and slamming the door shut.

Annie raised her eyebrows, and pulled a face at Wilkie. 'What I'd give for an afternoon snooze,' she said on the end of a long sigh.

Wilkie indicated for her to knock on the door of No.15, and he knocked at No.16, but there was no response at either.

–

Returning to the Incident Room, the two detectives were just in time for the afternoon briefing, and therefore able to update the team on their unsuccessful attempt at locating Russell Peters at his home address. However, they learnt that after further investigation, Russell Peters' name did not appear on any other police databases, other than the nuisance incident they were already aware of, where he had been advised accordingly.

Charley quickly moved the discussion forwards. 'I'm mindful that we are focusing all our attention on locating Russell Peters, and although we need to find him, we also need further evidence to either be able to connect him with, or eliminate him from the enquiry when we do. I suggest we make further enquiries at his workplace. For example, we need to know when he gets paid, and how, and if possible obtain his bank account details, and his mobile phone number. If we have that then we can make enquiries with his mobile provider, and track his movements past and present via his bank account. We can also find out the names of his contacts, and these can be checked out to see if they know of his whereabouts. If we have his bank details we can check where his bank card was last used. All this information is going to help find out who Russell Peters is, and hopefully where he is. For now he is still a priority, and when we get his DNA that will put him either in, or out of the enquiry for us. What I don't like is the fact that no one has seen him since Cath Crowther was attacked. He's not been to work, or spoken to his employers, which we have been told is apparently out of character. He has managed to avoid giving his DNA because he hasn't been at work, and yet he was aware before he went missing that his team were asked to give samples, and finally, everything we know about Russell Peters makes him our prime suspect at this moment in time, so we urgently need to trace him.'

Charley turned to Wilkie and Annie. 'Are you absolutely certain that he wasn't at his flat?'

Chapter 24

The moment Annie mentioned to Charley the putrid smell emanating from Russell Peters' flat, and the blowflies, describing their bloated bodies, huge eyes and wide head, the SIO knew immediately what this could signify.

'No ifs or buts, I want to get inside that flat today,' the SIO stated firmly. 'If it has to be done covertly, then so be it. But if you speak to the caretaker, she should have a key we can use. Entry in this case should be simple. Now, let's get this done pronto!'

–

Once the flat door was opened, Charley stood for a moment in the hallway, in silence. The first thing she was alerted to, apart from the smell, the flies and the heat, was a mutilated body, lying face down in the corner of the lounge, in a pool of blood and vomit. Hurriedly, as she felt under attack from the flying metallic blue and green insects, she pulled at the drawstrings of her suit, tightening it around her face. Her bodysuit provided cover for her clothing, and prevented any contamination of the crime scene. Her immediate task was to open the first window that she came to, to allow the swirl of flies to escape.

There was an underlying muted atmosphere of only one thing – death.

Charley squared her shoulders, and taking care not to touch anything, she prowled across the room to where the body lay. Automatically, the experienced SIO registered the broader, immediate details as well. The lounge in the flat was small with an attached toilet, its door wide open. As well as a door to the balcony, there was a window at shoulder height, both facing the town centre, a wooden floor with scatter rugs, and doormats placed at strategic points. There were blood stains splatted over the walls, windows, and spreading over the floor in places. A coat lay neatly arranged close by.

Stooping low, so that she could see his face which was turned just slightly to the side, Charley hunched down, and studied it further. There was blackish-coloured fluid oozing out through his nostrils, and a few attendant flies that were not discouraged by her being up-close. Charley pointed this out. 'This blood from his nostril could be an early sign of infection, but it may also be a sign that an infection is clearing,' she spoke her thoughts out loud.

As she studied the face of the victim, it appeared that it constantly changed shape as the blowflies eagerly fought for space to deposit their eggs and, although it was horrible to witness, Charley knew that their deposits would aid Forensic in determining a time of death. Her eyes moved from his head to his body, where blood stains were present on parts of his clothing. Finally she forced herself back to her feet.

Wilkie Connor remained relatively motionless beside her, except to imitate a car's windscreen wiper blades set to maximum speed to bat the remaining flies away. Charley was hardly conscious of his being in the room, until his voice broke in on her thoughts.

'What're you thinking, boss?' he said after a few minutes.

'I'm thinking that there's no doubt he's dead,' she said. 'Get paramedics here for confirmation, and CSI pronto, and get the entrance taped off. It needs treating as a crime scene.'

Annie joined them from the toilet. 'There are a few stains of blood over the floor, walls and near the tap in the basin,' she said. 'Plus a bottle of cheap toilet cleaner with a craft knife deposited in the sink.'

Instinctively Charley looked towards Neal, and then back to Annie. 'When it's been photographed in situ, get them both in an evidence bag,' she instructed Annie.

'Has he topped himself, boss?'

'We'll find out soon enough Wilkie,' Charley replied.

When the body was turned on to its back, clean-cut wounds approximately 6.5 cm x 2.5 cm x tendon-deep, could be seen over the anterior aspect of both wrists.

At the arrival of CSI Neal Rylatt, with the tools of his profession, the occupants of Flat 17 were at their doorway, unbelieving, watching every move. One look from Neal, booted and suited, made them retreat into their hallway.

Charley instructed Annie to ask them to stay inside, and to tell uniform to stop anyone else coming onto the landing.

Inside, Neil Rylatt was now otherwise engaged in taking photographs of the scene and the body. Despite his being so animated, Charley knew he was being conscientious, diligent, and also cautious not to step in the blood.

'It wasn't a half-hearted attempt then,' said Charley to Neal as she nodded towards the deep cuts.

The frown between Neal's eyebrows deepened. 'From my experience I'd say if it is suicide then it's complex. He didn't plan to fail,' added Neal. 'Is it Peters?' he asked.

'It's his flat,' said Charley, bending down on one knee beside Neal, to look closer at the victim's bloody face. 'Russell Peters is not on our system, so there's no rush to take his fingerprints here, we might as well wait until they take them at the mortuary, when he's cleaned up, and then they'll check them as a matter of procedure.'

Mike entered the room and Charley turned to acknowledge him. She looked puzzled.

'I know that look. What's up?' he asked her.

'He's taken a hell of a beating. He couldn't have done that himself, could he?'

'Guess not, but that isn't to say that the beating isn't a factor in his taking his own life,' Mike replied.

'True,' she acknowledged.

Neal prepared to check the pockets of the corpse's clothing. Rigor mortis had set in. He tugged at the grimy denim jeans. 'How lucky are we boss, one ID card. The photo's terribly scratched but the name is clearly legible, Russell Peters,' he said, as he passed it to Annie who was holding an evidence bag open for him to pop it in.

Wilkie Connor gave Neal Rylatt a cursory glance. 'I don't suppose there's a suicide note too?'

'Sorry, not this time,' said Neal with a smile.

Mike shook his head. 'The Divisional Commander is going to love another body on his patch, isn't he?'

'Never assume,' came the chorus from Wilkie and Annie.

Charley smiled under her mask. 'Find me his wallet, mobile phone, his bike, and...' She stopped in her tracks. 'Where's the door key that should be in that door if it was locked from the inside?' The SIO nodded her head in the direction of the front door through which they had come. The response was a collective shrug of shoulders.

Annie bent down to take a closer look at the victim. 'He doesn't fit the description of the man we have been given to believe is the attacker, does he?'

'How'd you come to that conclusion? Even his own bloody mother couldn't recognise him, he's so battered and bruised,' said Wilkie.

'Where are the broad shoulders the witnesses mention? Even when this guy was alive, I doubt that anyone would describe him as having a good physique.'

'Trust you,' said Wilkie.

Mike, ignoring the two of them, was looking studious.

'What're you thinking Mike?' asked Charley.

'I'm thinking, wouldn't you want to be more comfy, in a bed, or in the bath, if you were going to slit your wrists? Not on a floor... not like this...'

Annie's eyes were wide. 'Exactly, and tell me how did that knife get into the sink in the toilet?' said Annie, nodding her head in the direction of the attached toilet.

'Swab him for his DNA Neal, and when you're finished let's get the body to the mortuary, and then we can have a good look around to see what else we can find here that'll maybe help us further with our enquiries,' Charley said.

Notification came from uniformed officers at ground level to say that the private ambulance had arrived to take the corpse to the mortuary.

Wilkie Connor appeared to be sizing up the corpse. Annie wondered what he could possibly find to smile about, and looked at him quizzically.

'I was just wondering if they're going to use the lift, because owing to rigor mortis setting in, he might not actually fit.'

The look on Annie's face told him that she too doubted they would manage it, and together they moved out of the way and into the kitchen. 'Rather them than us,' she whispered to her colleague.

Easily visible in the kitchen, they found a map of the university campus. The shifting of the body bag against the walls of the hallway told them that the body had been removed, and after collecting possible evidence, the team were preparing to leave with their finds safely bagged and tagged in sealed evidence bags, of which there were many of all shapes and sizes.

Charley looked pale. 'The stench is getting right up my nose. Let's get out of here, and I'll instruct that a uniformed officer remains on the door until we know exactly what we're dealing with.'

'I'll arrange with officers from the Incident Room to come and speak to the occupants of the other flats on the landing, to ascertain when they last saw Russell Peters, and take statements from them,' said Mike.

'Seize the internal and external CCTV in the public areas of the flats,' instructed Charley.

Wilkie looked questioningly at her.

'If there's nothing untoward, the Coroner's officer can deal with the matter as a sudden death, and as you've been in attendance you'll all need to give the Coroner's officer a statement. However, if it is suspicious we can at least have his DNA checked against our killer's, and either way it will convict or eliminate him.'

Mike pulled a face. 'The last thing we need is another suspicious death to deal with.'

Charley took a deep breath. 'It's still not sitting comfortably with me,' she said. 'His body position, it was staged, a bit like Cordelia's was staged. I know it's a tenuous connection… but, are they connected?'

'Look on the bright side,' said Mike. 'If it turns out he's our man, think of the money he'll have saved the public by not having a trial.'

Charley scowled. 'He'd also have escaped justice. Let's get the samples off as a priority Neal, and get some answers.'

When she got back to the office, Tattie informed her that a post-mortem had been arranged for the next morning, so Charley wouldn't have long to wait for the pathologist's findings.

'Boss,' Mike said, 'once our deceased is cleaned up, and if we don't find any relatives, do you think that Mr Robinson seems like the kind of person who would be up for ID'ing him for us?'

Charley nodded. 'Yes, I think he might be,' she said. 'Ask him.'

Chapter 25

The post-mortem began, with DS Mike Blake and DC Wilkie Connor the officers in attendance, whilst Charley took the morning briefing. Delegation was not one of Charley's strongest qualities, but as frustrating as it was for her not to be able to be at the post-mortem, she knew that even she couldn't physically be in two places at one time. The SIO was comforted by the fact that she could rely on her deputy, Mike Blake, to contact her immediately should any issues arise. Every so often, however, as she sat in the quiet of her office, working on her daily tasks that didn't simply disappear when another investigation was stacked on top of her already high caseload, her mind wandered to what she knew – from personal experience of attending many post-mortems over the years – was taking place at this moment in time.

She recalled visits to the mortuary, a putrid odour drifted under her nose, and travelled up her nostrils, forming the familiar taste in her mouth. The one she knew surrounded the dead. Rummaging in her coat pocket, she found a half-eaten packet of Polo mints that she carried for the horses, on those few occasions she got to ride these days. She popped one in her mouth, instantly flinching at the thought of plucking hair samples from the corpse, and cringed at the sound that the skull cap made when it was flipped open for the pathologist to get to the brain; the crack could only be likened to taking off the top of a boiled egg, something she hadn't eaten since her first PM.

She was impatient to hear from the detectives, but knew that the speed of a post-mortem depended solely on the time taken by the pathologist and, of course, what he found. Once in the theatre, time became irrelevant, it had to be done properly, and with respect.

Charley traversed the larger of the two offices to the kitchen, to make a drink. Annie Glover was already there, filling the kettle. She looked bleary-eyed but her face broke out into a smile to see Charley. 'Any news?' she asked, as she opened the cupboard to retrieve several mugs off the shelf. 'Drink?' she asked, turning to face the SIO.

Charley nodded. Annie's hand hovered over the coffee jar. 'Make mine a strong one will ya.' ·

'That bad,' Annie said, pouring the milk into several mugs.

Charley slid into a chair at the small kitchen table, put her elbows on the top, and her chin in the palm of her hand. Her eyes went up to the clock. Annie slid Charley's mug of coffee towards her, and she took a gulp.

'You okay?' Annie said.

'I'm fine. Don't ask me why, but I've just got this over-whelming feeling that there is going to be a twist coming our way, and it's not going to be a good turn of events.'

Annie scowled. 'That's not like you. I always remember that on my first day, you told me that I should always look for a positive, no matter how hard it may be to find, and I want you to know that, whatever happens, we're all behind you. We're a team aren't we?' Annie said supportively.

'That's very nice of you to say so. Yes, you're quite right,' Charley said, sliding her chair away from the table, and picking up her mug. 'Ignore me, I'm just tired. Let's get this briefing done, and look at what we've achieved so far.'

-

Briefing over, Charley sat in her office gathering her thoughts. The content had been mainly regarding administrative matters and budgets, as there was little news on the investigation front to share.

The telephone rang. The swab that had been taken by Neal Rylatt, from the body found in Russell Peters' flat, had been checked by Forensic, and it was not a DNA match for that recovered at the Cordelia Le Beau murder scene, nor was it a match to the attempted murder of Cath Crowther. Although Charley had had high hopes for a match, it wasn't meant to be.

'Now what, boss?' said Annie, when she told her the news.

Charley gave Annie a forced smile through tight lips. 'I'm going to give Mike a ring to update him, and see how things are going at the post-mortem,' she said.

Mr Butterworth, the pathologist, had been running late, but Mike informed Charley that they were just about to leave the mortuary. 'What was interesting, was that he found a torn strip of towelling pushed down the victim's throat. We need to go back to No. 14 to see if we can find some of the same material at the scene.'

'A piece of towelling stuffed down his throat? Does Butterworth say how he died?'

'He suggests it wasn't the beating that killed him, he believes that he was alive when the wounds and bruises were inflicted upon him. There is no doubt in his mind that he died from asphyxiation, certainly not suicide, and a twist, his murderer was making sure that he didn't recover. Butterworth suggests we check the label on the toilet cleaner that we found discarded in the toilet. He wagers a bet that it contains sulphuric acid as one of the ingredients that was put on the victim's wounds.'

'The evil bastard,' said Charley.

Annie Glover was hovering at Charley's door, something she always did if the SIO was otherwise engaged, and she wanted to speak to her. Annie saw the SIO scowl, then put her hand to her head.

'That's all we need right now, another murder,' she said loudly, before putting the phone down.

'It appears that the suicide theory has been turned on its head then?' Annie asked.

'Yep!' Charley breathed in deeply through her nose, and out slowly through her mouth. 'Mike and Wilkie are on their way back. Can you get hold of Neal and tell him we need him to go back to the flat with us when Mike and Wilkie return? Mike told me that Butterworth found a strip of towelling stuffed down the deceased's throat, so with that in mind, I want to see if we can find the remainder of the towel, and anything else that might now assist us further with our enquiries,' she said.

'Who would kill our would-be murderer, boss?'

'Well obviously someone did, and we need to find out who. His DNA profile isn't a match for the DNA found at other scenes. That bothers me, because to all intents and purposes with all the twists, turns and red-herrings that this enquiry has chucked at us, Russell Peters was our man. We'll have to wait until we get his fingerprints results in, because as far as we know, he's not on the national database.' Charley looked at her watch. 'In fact, I don't know what's taking the fingerprints results so long to come back to us. In the meantime, I've got the same gut-feeling as I did when we were told that Cordelia was homeless. There are some things that just don't add up here, and of course we also have another murder to solve, not a suicide as someone wanted us to believe when they set the scene.'

'Forensic will match up the fibres and the cloth from where it was torn for us, if we can find its origin at the flat,' said Annie.

'It's good evidence, but we already know that the cause of death is asphyxiation because the pathologist has told us so. We know that he was killed in the flat. However, we don't yet know for certain who our corpse is, we have an idea that it's Russell Peters, but we must never assume. If it is Russell Peters then we now know he didn't kill Cordelia Le Beau, or attempt to murder Cath Crowther. Have we got this all wrong? Either way, we need to find out who killed our guy at the mortuary.'

'When you put it like that, it sounds so very complicated. I'll go make us a nice cup of tea, shall I?' said Annie.

'And, I'll update the Divisional Commander,' said Charley, her voice full of dread. 'He's not going to be a happy bunny.'

However, as Annie passed her desk, her phone was ringing. After taking the call, she went straight back to stand at Charley's door.

'Now what? I thought you were going to make me a cuppa?' Charley said, placing the phone back on its cradle after speaking to Bobbie Stokes. 'Can you make it a brandy instead?'

'Neal was trying to get hold of you but he said your phone was engaged. The prints from the body at No. 14, Websters Towers are a positive match on the system for a Lincoln Heinz who's got previous – it's not Russell Peters. As far as Neal knows, he says, our man Russell Peters you'll be pleased to know, is still very much alive.'

Charley puffed out her cheeks and blew out long and hard. 'The crafty bastard, trying to wrong-foot us by putting his ID card in his victim's pocket to make us think it was him. We need to know everything we possibly can about this Lincoln Heinz. Get Ricky-Lee on it as a priority.'

'What puzzles me,' said Annie, 'is that surely Russell Peters would know that we would find out that it wasn't him sooner or later.'

'Ah, but he would also know that it would buy him some time.'

'Buy him time for what though?'

Charley paused and considered her reply. 'To get away, or to carry on?'

–

Lincoln Heinz had previous convictions for minor theft, burglary, being drunk and disorderly, and he was a druggie. What Charley didn't know, and Ricky-Lee couldn't tell her from the short time he had spent researching Heinz, was how he knew Russell Peters, and how he ended up dead in Peters' flat.

Charley walked from the car park, along the single footpath around the building, and headed towards the entrance lobby of Websters Towers, Annie and Mike following in silence. They had arranged to meet with Neal at the scene. His CSI van was parked on the roadway ahead, alongside a police car. It wasn't an unusual sight, at any given time there would be at least one patrol car in the area, their occupants more often than not making enquiries at Websters Towers, to use their standard phrasing.

Annie left the others in the lobby to go speak to the caretaker. 'I'll update her, and find out what details she has for him,' she told Charley.

'Better let her know that we won't be releasing his flat anytime soon, since it's now a murder scene,' said Charley as she called the lift down with the press of a button.

'Any news on Lincoln's home address?' Charley asked Mike, as the lift took them to the fourth floor. 'Once we know that, then we can have the CCTV checked on the route from his home to Russell Peters' address.'

Mike shook his head. 'Nothing yet. It's looking increasingly as if he may be homeless.'

Charley turned to Neal at the door of the flat. 'See if you can find a better photograph of Russell Peters will you, and anything else that you think might help us to trace him? It goes without saying that we also need to find the towel from which was ripped a piece to stuff down our victim's throat.'

It was decidedly cooler than the last time that they were inside No. 14.

'Where the hell is Peters?' Charley said, pushing the inner doors wide open with a gloved hand, and scanning each room, half-expecting him to be in one or the other. 'He's got a taste for murder, and he must know we are onto him, because if not, then why would he try to fake his own death?'

The protective clothing over the detective's clothes made it an uncomfortable, restricted search, but it was something that was necessary, and something that they were used to.

'We've got to find the evil bastard before he strikes again,' said Charley, 'because there's no doubt in my mind that he will continue killing until we have him behind bars. He's a danger to the community.'

'Unless he has moved on of course,' said Ricky-Lee.

'You've probably thought of this but could Peters be using Heinz's ID?' said Annie.

'You think he might be pretending to be Lincoln Heinz?' said Charley.

'Why not,' said Mike. 'He can't use his own details can he, because he would know we would be straight on to him.'

'True. We must ensure that Cath Crowther is being kept safe,' she said. 'The last thing we want him to do is have a second chance to end her life.'

'Why do you think he would do that?' asked Annie.

'Because he failed, and my guess is that from what we know of this psychopathic killer he won't want to fail.'

All was quiet for a moment or two as the team separated to search the flat. Within minutes a shout went up from the toilet, where Neal had discovered a strip of towelling. 'I'd say this is an exact match to the one we saw earlier in the day, being removed from the corpse's oesophagus at the mortuary. Wouldn't you Mike?'

'Where was it?' asked Charley.

'In the toilet cistern, by the radiator,' said Neal.

'I knew when you went in there you were getting warm.' Annie laughed.

Neal moaned loudly. 'I guess you're hoping we'll flush him out now,' he replied.

Mike remained serious. 'Or, we try to restrict his movements by giving his details to the media, stating his present whereabouts are being sought for elimination purposes,' he said to Charley.

'I don't think we've much choice but to do that now, do you?' she replied.

Chapter 26

Charley breakfasted on a thick slice of Marmite toast that Winnie had insisted that she ate, but out of her way in the kitchen, whilst the older woman cleaned her office early the next morning. She drew back the blinds and stood for a moment to watch the day begin properly. Her mind ran quickly through what she had just read, which explained, to some extent, why Lincoln Heinz had become the character he was: homeless, penniless, and now most probably dead.

The circumstances caused by his mother's drinking and gambling addictions, and a birth certificate that showed his father as unknown, meant that Lincoln was said by those who knew him to have 'dragged himself up'.

DC Ricky-Lee's enquiries had revealed that, in his early teens, Lincoln Heinz was the victim of one of several of his mother's boyfriends, a bare-knuckle fighter, and after a traumatic experience, was never the same again.

The relatively young boy, placed in care, was forever running away to live on the streets, where he felt safer than he did inside amongst strangers, when he wasn't otherwise under the supervision of Her Majesty's youth prison service.

Normally, Lincoln, described by the locals in his later years as a private and pleasant young man, kept himself to himself, but always said 'hello'! He would often be observed, noted and spoken to by the police, and the volunteers from the homeless charities, for sleeping in shop doorways, or sitting by the heating vents outside fast-food restaurants, capturing what warmth he could from their extractors.

Charley had gone on to read that Heinz had last been checked out by a uniform patrol in the town centre, three weeks previously, sitting outside McDonald's, begging for food.

The locals continued to say that there was no malice in Lincoln, and no one appeared to have a bad word to say about him, they rather asserted that he was a real character in the town, with not a bad bone in his body. He had become part of the street furniture.

At the time of the reported sighting of Lincoln, he had given the police officers his correct details, and told them that he had been sleeping rough for just over a week, having been released from prison, where he had been serving a short sentence for the non-payment of a fine.

Owing to the fact he had no fixed abode on his release, he had been given only a small amount of money to get by. Most of that having been spent on sharing his good fortune with other homeless people, and being bullied into giving up the rest, he was considering breaching his bail conditions so that he would be taken back inside, where at least he would get a warm shower, a hot meal and a warm prison cell in which to sleep. No one would employ Lincoln without a permanent address, and neither could he sign on to claim benefits. He was stuck between a rock and a hard place.

Daylight had fully manifested itself when Winnie entered the kitchen, to tell her she was moving on to clean the outer office. She busied herself clearing away Charley's dirty crockery, but when she came to shoo her out of the kitchen she found that Charley had tears in her eyes. 'It was good old-fashioned policing by the local officer, who spent time talking to Lincoln Heinz, and recording the information as intelligence that has given us the most recent updates about him,' Charley said to the older lady. 'How was the poor lad supposed to get off the streets without any money which he couldn't claim until he had a fixed address?' she asked.

Winnie shook her head. 'Was it the lure of Russell Peters offering him a roof over his head that he craved which resulted in Lincoln ending up in his flat then?' she asked.

Charley smiled. Winnie missed nothing that went on around the Incident Room, but whatever she saw or heard remained within the station. She had earned everyone's trust over the years.

'On the pretext that he would be able to collect his benefits and get himself sorted out, if he had that coveted address? Who knows?' Charley sighed heavily. 'One thing I do know is that there is nothing we can do for Lincoln now, other than bring his murderer to justice. If McDonald's was the place he regularly bedded down, as it's thought, then we might get CCTV footage of them together.' Charley got up from the kitchen table and walked into the larger office, to the map of the town centre. Winnie followed her, duster and polish in hand. 'Look,' she said. 'There is a significant direct "L"-shaped route from McDonald's, Market Street, via the Medway where Cordelia used to sit, past the nearby waste ground where she was found, before joining the main road again to Websters Towers.'

'I hope the CCTV shows you Peters picking him up,' Winnie said.

'I hope so too, Winnie,' Charley said sadly, just as Annie, Ricky-Lee and Mike walked through the door together.

'My office, you three,' Charley told them, as Winnie turned and walked back out of the office, her brief moment of inclusion over.

Russell Peters' bike, his usual form of transport, had not been found at his flat, so there had to be a presumption that he had ridden from the scene. However, where he was planning to go, or when was unknown.

'We still don't know if Peters has any links elsewhere in the country,' Charley said to the team. 'In fact we still know very little about him, even though we have his description, his

DNA, we know where he lived, and where he worked, but we don't have him!'

With everything dependent upon finding Russell Peters, and speaking to him, Charley gave the detectives her instructions. 'Let's go to talk to his boss, Mr Robinson, again. See if there is anything else that he can tell us, anything at all. Just the slightest nugget of information might give us our next lead. Also, get Peters circulated as wanted for elimination purposes, in connection with the murder of Lincoln Heinz, whose body was discovered at Peters' last known address.'

There was no doubt that Russell Peters had been hoping to put the detectives off his scent, by trying to disguise the murder scene, and to make it appear that the victim of the crime was Peters himself. This was done knowing that his attempt to mislead could only be short-lived. Sooner or later, Peters would put his head above the parapet, and when he did, Charley and her team would be ready to grab him.

By the end of the day Charley had the financial investigation team attempting to track him, through the bank account into which his salary was paid.

'We are closing in on him, very soon we will have him in custody,' Charley told the team at the debrief that day, 'but we can't rest on our laurels until we have him locked up. We know he's hell-bent on murder, and we don't want another victim added to his killing spree.' Charley thanked the team for their continued efforts before closing down for the night.

–

PC Helen Weir, along with the CCTV team, had been able to plot Lincoln's movements around the town centre, and updated Charley with their findings the next morning.

'He didn't wander far,' Helen told Charley. 'We see him sitting outside the Medway where Cordelia once sat, it's not far away either from where he usually beds down at night, near McDonald's. He can clearly be seen begging. Just like Cordelia Le Beau…'

'Which is why I think Peters had returned to where he had his previous success with Cordelia,' said Charley.

'Not dissimilar to how wild animals act in their search for food,' replied Helen.

'Exactly. I've also known burglars do the same, and of course Peters has been showing those characteristics, by preying on his victims at the university, the place where he worked.'

'The CCTV shows him actually talking with a lad of Lincoln's description, who is wearing a dark hoodie. He helps him up to his feet, by offering his hand and they walk off together in the direction of Websters Towers.'

'There's a male dressed in a dark hoodie who also features in Cordelia's murder and still remains unidentified from CCTV,' said Charley.

'Yes, and who jumped out in front of my car that time at the university,' said Annie, who had just joined them.

'Do you think it's the same guy?' Charley asked Helen.

'Could be,' she said. 'We can't say for certain it isn't.'

'I want comparisons doing on the person's clothing if there is nothing else,' Charley said. 'If the present CCTV images you've been trawling through show two men leaving the town centre together, where they went after that we do not know, but if it is Lincoln Heinz and Russell Peters, then what we do know is that they ultimately ended up at Russell Peters' flat, where Lincoln's life was cut brutally short.'

'One of the reasons that makes me think that these two guys are those guys, is that Lincoln is noticeably smaller in stature, in comparison with Russell Peters,' said Helen, 'and we know that from what we are told Lincoln was not an aggressive person.'

'You're telling me that you can quite clearly see Lincoln's face on the CCTV footage, but not Russell Peters', as the hoodie covers it?'

Helen nodded. 'Yes,' she said.

'Come on then, find me a snippet that shows our man's face, even if you do have to work backwards through the footage. He's walking about in town, before he befriends Heinz, surely. Let's see if we can find him.'

Charley stood quietly half an hour later, and watched the team working diligently, from her vantage point at her office door.

'We know he's a predator. He plans his crimes. Do you think he might've gone back to the university, where he can mingle with the hundreds of students, without raising much concern as just another worker?' said Annie to her boss, from where she was sitting nearby at her desk.

Before Charley had a chance to answer, a shout came from the far corner of the Incident Room where the financial investigation team was working. 'Boss, you'll be pleased to know that Peters was still around yesterday evening. He withdrew fifty pounds out of the hole in the wall at NatWest, Upper George Street. I'm waiting to hear back from them to find out from his records which is his preferred cash machine.'

Charley hurried over to where Ricky-Lee was sat. 'Does this machine have a camera by any chance?'

'It does, but would you believe, Sod's law, it's faulty?'

Annie walked towards the SIO with a tray of drinks in her hands. Charley's eyes went up to the ceiling. 'Give us a break,' she pleaded with the Almighty up above. 'I was very hopeful then that we were going to get a recent picture of him.'

Annie sighed. 'Be patient, it'll come,' she said. 'That's what you always say. Do you want me to put your drink on your desk?'

Charley nodded. 'Please.'

Ever the optimist these days, Ricky-Lee stood up, took a mug from the tray Annie was holding, and continued talking to Charley. 'The bank say that there's still a chance that they'll have a picture from previous withdrawals. Let's face it, it's hardly likely he's going to give someone else his PIN number and his bank card to withdraw his money, is it?'

'No, but one thing that I have learnt about Peters is that we can't try to second guess what he does.'

Ricky-Lee turned. 'I'll come back to you when we have more info from NatWest. At least we know he's still around and about.'

'That's true,' said Charley over her shoulder, as she in turn headed back to her office. Mike followed her inside, a piece of paper in his hand. He sat down on the edge of the visitors' chair opposite Charley.

'We've got a witness who will say that he travelled up in the lift with Peters and Heinz, on the day that Helen thanks that she's captured them together on CCTV,' he said.

Charley rested back in her chair and took a long sip of tea. 'Can he tell us anything else?'

'Nothing that we don't know, but at least we now know a date and a time when Heinz was still alive.'

Charley's face looked drawn, her expression was one of frustration. 'Peters has got to be lying low somewhere nearby. We know he's a loner, with no links to family or friends elsewhere that we can find, and he isn't going back to his flat, so where is he?'

'Do you think he's secreted himself on campus?' Mike deliberated.

Charley sat up straight, drained her mug and put it down on her desk. 'Annie said that earlier. I think it's a distinct possibility. We know he's a planner. He must have known before he picked Heinz up and took him home, that if he killed him he wouldn't be able to go back to his flat. Maybe he thought that the large police presence would disperse from the university to the new crime scene, and wrongly that we wouldn't be back. Maybe he did go back, but would he risk being seen by his colleagues, or his boss?'

'Let's face it, he was in the perfect job to know where the vacant flats were on campus, and he wouldn't need a key, just an open window,' said Mike. 'He'd probably think that after the attempted murder of Cath Crowther, the scene of a crime would be the last place we would look for him too.'

'That does make sense, because he would feel safe and secure on home turf. Let's make some discreet enquiries at the university and see what rooms are known to be vacant. Then we'll do the necessary. We know he was in the locality yesterday, so the likelihood is that he is nearby, lying low.'

Mike folded the piece of paper in his hand and put it into his jacket pocket when he stood up to leave.

'Like you always tell us, clear the ground beneath our feet before moving further afield.'

'Exactly,' Charley said with optimism in her tone. 'Perhaps we are closer than we know to locking him up.'

Chapter 27

Armed with a list of list of vacant rooms, from their contact at the university, PCs Helen Weir and Lisa Bayliss returned to the Incident Room to update Charley, and get further instruction.

In the meantime, Charley had been reading her morning mail. An update from the Crown Prosecution Service, in the form of a letter via the internal mail, concerning Maddox and Beth Green, suggested that they needed a meeting with her to discuss things further. It appeared that their concerns were regarding how it would impact on any future murder trial in relation to Cordelia Le Beau's death. Charley was fully aware that the details would have to be disclosed to any defence team, so it wouldn't cause her any concern if they decided to prosecute the pair. Irritated, she read on. With regards to Tricia Carmichael and Kirsty Webb, it had been decided that no further action would be taken.

The SIO put the letter in her 'to do' tray. She had more pressing matters to address this morning. Why it had taken CPS so long to come up with the obvious was beyond her.

Conscientious, diligent, and eager to update the SIO, Helen and Lisa were buzzing with the news that although fourteen flats were vacant, one of those was being refurbished, with workmen trudging in and out all day, and could be ruled out.

'Thirteen?' remarked Charley, a brief look of surprise showing on her face. She had expected to have more to search. 'Let's hope thirteen is lucky for us,' she smiled.

Charley briefly looked over the top of Helen's and Lisa's heads at the sound of the door opening, to see Mike Blake enter her office. He closed the door behind him and sat down next to Helen, apologising for his lateness.

'How are we going to approach the vacant flats discreetly?' she asked.

'Perhaps the university have spare keys available to us?' suggested Lisa.

'I'm sure once we get started, the word will quickly spread that the cops are on campus, but how long does it take to check thirteen flats?' said Helen, eagerly.

'I think that's a risk we're going to have to take,' answered Charley. 'If we have enough officers on site, we should be able to check the flats simultaneously for a would-be squatter, in no time at all, don't you think? Get the keys, let's do this tomorrow.'

'Early doors, before admin arrive I guess?'

Charley nodded.

'No worries, I'll get them this afternoon,' Lisa said.

'Just a thought, I wonder if someone could swing past tonight to see if any of the vacant flats are lit up?' Mike suggested.

'Good idea,' said Charley. 'If so we'll have a heads-up on where to start, and if not we've lost nothing.'

Charley's focus turned back to Helen and Lisa. 'Question, are you both working tomorrow?'

Helen and Lisa nodded. 'Yes, ma'am,' they said in unison.

'Helen, I know you're already working with us. Lisa, I'll have a word with your supervisor. I'd like you both involved, in plain clothes.'

Lisa looked a little anxious.

'If supervision has to pay overtime for others to cover your absence, the cost will be covered by us, so don't worry. I'll sort it.'

Lisa's face brightened somewhat. Her shift was short of personnel, with one officer on long-term sick leave, one on a six-week training course, and another at court for a trial.

'One more thing,' said Charley before they left her office. 'We have a map of the campus in the Incident Room. What I would like one of you to do is highlight the thirteen vacant rooms, so that we can see their proximity to each other.'

'I'll do that,' said Lisa, eagerly. 'I finished my shift at two o'clock. I don't mind staying on.'

'Can you get your list of vacant flats copied for us, Helen, and, can you allocate officers to search the flats please, Mike? Briefing prior to the searches... six o'clock tomorrow morning? We will update everyone at tonight's briefing for the operation, so that tomorrow we can get straight off with everyone already aware of their role. Can you arrange that for five-thirty tonight?'

Charley's strength was fading, she needed air. 'I'll be back for the briefing,' she announced, leaving the office, her outside coat billowing behind her.

-

'Hey, Wilson,' Charley greeted the ex-police horse, with a flake of hay, but he knew better and snuffled around her coat pocket, where he knew he would find mints.

Kristine, her best friend and former colleague in the mounted section, was working overtime, so her dad Marty, who was working in the front office, had told Charley on her way out of the building. 'Is it okay if I take Wilson out for a ride?' Charley texted her best friend. Her reply was instant, as Charley knew it would be. 'You don't have to ask. He has missed you nearly as much as I have. We must catch up! I'm off at four.'

In her heightened state of mind, Charley entered Wilson's stall, barely noticing the cold that enveloped her body without wearing all her proper riding attire, as she gathered his reins and thrust her riding boot into the stirrup. Wilson reacted by moving his hindquarters a step sideways as she mounted him. He responded immediately when she tapped her heel against his flank, moving forwards at a quick pace as they trotted out of the stable yard. He knew the procedure when she was vexed, just as well as he knew Charley. Slowly Charley's anxiety began to melt away, as she felt Wilson respond to one after another of her subtle instructions. As her head started to clear, she gave Wilson his head, and he turned onto the moor himself, and his body seemed to stretch like never before when she urged him to a gallop. She knew well that a horse trotted with his legs and galloped with his lungs, and after traversing the soft ground he was breathing hard. She took a leaf out of Wilson's book, and made a conscious effort to release the breath trapped inside her lungs. Dizzy for a moment, her frame trembled in a mix of excitement and fear, as Wilson jumped a stone wall that separated the fields, then another, and another.

On stopping, she knew that Wilson's breath was easing because he snorted. 'Okay, buddy, let's go back to the stables,' Charley whispered to him. As soon as he realised they were heading back he led the way. Patting him on his neck when his stable was in sight, a tear, then another, escaped her eye. Making sure Wilson was cooled off and comfortable, Charley cleaned the tack before the sweat and foam could dry on the leather, and hung up the soaked saddle pad. Despite the soreness in her legs, she ran to the farmhouse, hoping to find Kristine home.

'I heard that you had a breakthrough,' Kristine said when Charley entered the kitchen. She noticed that her best friend's eyes were red and wet, and she knew that she had been crying.

'Yeah, we are going into the vacant flats at the university first thing tomorrow,' she confided. 'Whether Russell Peters has secreted himself there we don't know. It's a hunch, but I have to clear the ground beneath our feet, before moving the enquiries elsewhere like we always do. If I was a gambler it's a strong bet.'

Charley's mobile rang, she took it out of her pocket and looked down at the screen. 'It's Mike,' she said. 'I need to take it.'

Mike had good news, he had received a recent facial image of Peters using the cash machine at the bank.

Within seconds she was showing Kristine the picture of a clean-shaven, fair-haired young man on her phone. 'You'd think butter wouldn't melt in his mouth looking at that face wouldn't you? However, you and I know appearances can be deceptive.'

'You'd better get back to the nick for a shower, and then get that picture distributed amongst the troops!' laughed Kristine, pouring herself a large glass of red wine. She raised the glass towards Charley. 'Oh, I'm so glad I'm not in CID,' she said. 'Give me nine-to-five, Monday to Friday any day!'

Charley threw on her coat. 'Cheers! With any luck I'll be joining you very soon to celebrate,' she said, searching deep inside her pocket for her car keys. 'We just need him in custody for everything to fall into place, and complete the jigsaw.'

'What, if you don't succeed?' asked Kristine.

'If I don't I'll be releasing that picture of him to the media, to flush him out.' With a blink of an eye Charley was gone.

—

Within the hour the SIO was in the office. It was time for the evening briefing.

'All search teams will be in pairs, and you already know who you are to be paired with, the exception being the flats in red block where there are three flats next to each other,' said Charley. 'The searches of the vacant flats should not take a great deal of time, but I want you to check cupboards, beneath beds, anywhere where a person could hide themselves, or secrete anything that would suggest that someone was, is, or has been staying there recently. Each team has been given a photograph of Russell Peters, which is the most recent one we have, taken from CCTV at the bank. If you are successful in finding our man, then I want you to be aware that we have been told that he has a stammer which, given the fact that we will be surprising him, could be made worse at the time of his arrest, so I want you to be patient with him, and listen to anything he may have to say. I want to give him the best opportunity to speak to us if he wants to. Finally, if you didn't already know, Russell Peters is a good climber, described as being of athletic build. We'll have dog handler Mike Sharp and PD Marcel present ready to respond, where required.' A laugh caught in Charley's throat. 'He certainly won't outrun Marcel!' A titter that went around the room told her the team was buzzing. That feeling of being on the verge of feeling the collar of a murderer was like no other.

DS Mike Blake handed out the keys to the flats to each pair of officers assigned to the search, and he reminded them, 'Don't any of you dare forget to hand them back in at the debrief tomorrow.'

Charley looked around the faces of her team, a mixture of anticipation, excitement, and fear in each and every one. 'We will meet in the void, at six o'clock tomorrow morning, and will travel to the university in a convoy. Any questions?'

When all she could see was the shaking of heads, she went on.

'All I need to do now is arrange for the night detective to take a look around tonight, to see if a light is on in any of the vacant flats. If it is, then that will be our main focus tomorrow morning.'

Alone in her office when everyone had left, Charley could feel the adrenaline building. She knew sleep would not come easily. Was she about to come face-to-face with the evil predator she had sought for so long, at last?

Chapter 28

Charley closed the door carefully as she stepped outside into a dark, chilly, still morning. Tiptoeing down the path, she was always mindful not to disturb her neighbours at such an early hour. It was essential to use the element of surprise to apprehend the suspect when he was asleep.

At the station she waited impatiently for the others to arrive. Charley looked up at the clock above her office door when she heard the familiar sound of the CID office door open, followed by the officers' early-morning murmurs as they greeted each other, and the sound of drawers opening and closing. Seeing Charley's office lit up, Annie cheerily called out. 'Shall I put the kettle on, boss? We've time for a quick one, haven't we?'

Charley responded. 'Yes, just a small one for me. I'll be with you in a minute.'

'Me too,' Annie called back. 'Otherwise I'll be needing to wee all morning!'

Smiling to herself at her younger colleague's reply, the SIO collected her thoughts, checked her bag to make sure she had paper and pen, fully charged mobile phone and her radio. A dedicated channel had been organised for the duration of the operation which would be open from the time they left the station, with a running commentary staying live until the conclusion. Checking done, Charley grabbed her coat and walked to her door, put out the light, went out and shut the door behind her.

Within minutes, it seemed that the office had become extremely busy and noisy with the banter amongst highly charged personnel – comrades who were about to work as one unit formed a unit like no other. Charley was pleased to note that all those present stopped what they were doing, and looked attentive when she greeted them.

Proceeding with the short briefing to emphasise her last-minute warnings, and to pass on the information from the night detective, which was that no lights had been seen at any of the vacant flats during the night, she looked at those assembled as she put on her coat.

'Any questions?' was met by silence. 'Ready?' she asked, picking up her bag. A nod of heads was the signal to go.

Charley slid into the driving seat with Annie beside her for the journey. Their breath condensed on the cold windscreen, and obscured their vision. Furiously she rubbed the glass with her sleeve. She cleared it just in time to see the tailgates of the police vans leaving the backyard. On this occasion they were transporting officers not prisoners.

Annie shivered, then yawned loudly. 'Remind me. Why is it best to do dawn raids?'

'You know the reason, to disrupt the suspects when they are less prepared to tool up, escape or dispose of evidence. We hope that it will give us a full working day to deal with the prisoner and any evidence which is produced. Plus, an evening arrest creates all sorts of logistical problems for you, the interviewing officers, mostly because it may encroach on the legal rest periods. Does that make you feel better?' Charley said as they drove onto the site, to join the others at the rendezvous point.

Daylight was beginning to break when she parked beside the police dog-handler's van, its rear windows blacked out, Marcel's cage inside. Dog handler Mike Sharp opened the doors to see Marcel. When Charley opened her car door she could hear Marcel whining with excitement, as he scraped his sharp claws on the bare metal floor of the van. When Marcel jumped out of the van, his tail was wagging furiously, and he was already straining at the leash.

'Let's get this sorted,' Charley said to Annie. She reached for the paperwork to enable her to mark off the flat numbers when the 'all clear' was announced over the airwaves.

The cover of darkness for the search party seemed to have been quickly replaced by grey skies as they moved forwards towards the flats. The SIO's adrenaline started building, her stomach swirled, her chest tightened. Charley watched her colleagues picking their steps with care, using the well-trodden paths on the dewy grass, stooping and clearing the over-hanging trees and bushes that stood in their way. Marcel needed no encouragement to run, he occasionally looked from side to side, his keen eye missing nothing, his nose sniffing until they had reached the destination, then one after another, the officers disappeared from sight.

Eventually the confirmation came over the airwaves that they were all in position, and purely as a precaution, Charley crossed her fingers for luck, and compressed her lips in determination.

'STRIKE!' she called, in a voice she hardly recognised as her own, that came from deep inside her.

Within minutes, messages of 'all clear' started coming in thick and fast. The triumphant shouts that burst from their throats brought a look of anxiety and frustration to Charley's face. 'Come on, come on, where are you?' she beseeched her prey, angrily.

Then suddenly the message that she'd hoped for. 'Suspect found…' However, seconds later the elation had gone out of the officer's voice, and was replaced by exasperation. 'He's out of the window!' A moment passed. 'He's fallen badly. Looks like he's damaged his ankle on landing. He's hobbling, but he's still running…'

Charley was unable to speak, and the sense of frustration flared inside her, like white-hot lava about to erupt from a volcano.

Charley ran towards the scene to see police officers running in the direction of the open fields beyond the campus, their attention on their prey.

The airwaves were busy. Then suddenly, repeatedly, came the shouts from PC Mike Sharp. 'Stop, stand still, or I'll let the dog go.'

As she arrived at the outer edge of the campus grounds, in the distance she could see PD Marcel running at speed in pursuit of a person fleeing, his handler was some distance behind. The surrounding country roads were blocked by police vehicles with flashing blue lights, and other emergency units available should they be required.

Then with a great leap, Marcel pounced and brought the absconder to the ground, but to Charley's dismay she heard the dog give an almighty yelp. Marcel had been injured, and was whimpering in pain, but he still went on; the police dog wouldn't be beaten. The next update over the airwaves told Charley that the officers on site had contained an area surrounding an electricity pylon. Russell Peters was cornered, and he was going nowhere. Peters had quite clearly injured his ankle as previously thought, and Marcel had bitten his arm which was bleeding.

As Charley got nearer she could see for herself that Peters was panicking, still seeking in his pain an escape route. At a stand-off he looked down at the blood that had worked down his sleeve from his injured elbow, the red stain contrasting against the colour of his jumper.

Annie ran up behind Charley, her breathing erratic. The two stood in silence for a minute, then she spoke quietly. 'Have we got him?' she enquired tentatively.

Charley's face was stony. 'Yes,' she said. 'We've got him, but look,' she pointed to see Russell Peters studying the pylon. 'He's looks like he's not done yet.'

A call over the airwaves captured Charley's attention. It was from the officers still searching Flat 22. 'Boss, we've found a backpack, do you want us to take it back to the nick?'

'Get CSI to photograph it in situ first. We'll exhibit the contents when you get back,' she replied.

To Charley's horror, Russell Peters' extra height gained him an easy foothold on the pylon. She watched intently, taking in the warning signs of the upright framework for a few minutes, which clearly warned of the dangers and voltage. Hearing shouting from the officers near the electricity pylon, Annie looked from the back of the dog van, where she had been observing the dog-handler inspecting Marcel's eyes, to the direction in which her boss was staring.

'OMG!' she whispered under her breath. 'Surely he's not that fucking stupid?'

However, Annie's main focus was on the police dog.

The dog-handler's voice shook with emotion. 'His eyes are bloodshot. I don't know what the bastard sprayed him with but there's no doubt he's in pain,' he called out to Charley.

'Blue light him to the vets, and let me know how you get on,' she called back.

Charley took a 360-degree turn, surveying the surrounding area as she updated headquarters control and Bobbie Stokes the Divisional Commander. Northern Power had been informed of what was occurring, and the on-call negotiator Detective Chief Inspector Jack Dylan arrived in a traffic car, at the same time as the ambulance arrived at the scene.

Those living on campus were beginning to walk to their morning lectures, and owing to their interest, it became imperative that the area around the pylon should be cordoned off, and quickly. The last thing Charley needed was a crowd goading Russell Peters on.

Russell Peters was clearly in a lot of pain, and she hoped that he would reconsider his obvious intended actions, but no, as he raised his arm to start his ascent blood started streaming from his wound. When he reached the top his face was alight, flushed with his success even through his pain.

If he jumped from his present position it was highly unlikely he would survive, but Charley was keen to take him alive to suffer the consequences of what he'd done, and explain why.

The noise from the skies was deafening as the Force helicopter hovered above, their observations welcomed by those on the ground.

Over the radio came the request from Dylan for HQ to get a fire engine to the scene, and within four minutes it pulled up alongside the ambulance.

'What does Dylan want a fire engine for?' Annie asked Charley.

'He'll use their turntable to speak directly with Peters,' Charley replied.

Charley's phone rang, and she was relieved to hear the voice of the Divisional Commander. 'I'm en route,' Bobbie Stokes told her. 'I'll deal with the media, to enable you to concentrate on Peters,' he said.

On the ground, Charley couldn't hear the conversation between Dylan and Peters. What was obvious, and encouraging, was that Dylan had engaged Peters in conversation when no one else could, and it appeared that the young man was responding. However, it became apparent that Dylan hadn't quite got his trust, when Peters moved around to the opposite side of the pylon away from the negotiator.

No one knew what Peters next move would be. It was as if the air had been sucked out of Charley, and she momentarily turned away, to see once again to her relief, that Divisional Commander Stokes was at the rendezvous point where he had already gained the gathered media attention, and he was reading a statement.

Stokes made his way to speak to Charley the moment he had finished.

'Is he our man for the murders?' Stokes asked. Charley's eyes never left Peters and Dylan.

'Everything points to it being him,' she said. 'He's bleeding heavily from a bite by the police dog, and I'm concerned about his ability to hold on up there.'

Stokes was pragmatic. 'Doesn't he realise he would have been better being tasered? That pylon carries fifty thousand volts, he'd have been toast if we'd not managed to liaise with the power grid.'

'He's an accomplished climber, according to his boss, he's not fazed by heights and to be honest I don't think right now he gives a shit.'

'Well, the media's sorted for now. I'm heading back to the control room. Let me know if you need anything. One thing's for sure, he won't be up there for long with the amount of blood he's losing.'

For a moment the two stood in silence watching what was happening above. Dylan hadn't given up, and had moved to face Peters.

An hour later, and the necks of those looking up were aching. Dylan had patience in abundance, which was considered to be the most important quality required in a negotiator, and this had paid off. Peters was ready to give himself up. The faces of the officers on the ground showed relief, including Charley, who felt every step that he took on the ladder down, aided by Dylan talking to him along the way, kept him focused. Slowly, he descended and Charley moved forwards with the paramedic. Mike Blake, a few steps behind her, had his handcuffs at the ready to use on Peters, who wouldn't be given another chance to escape.

Peters reached the final ten feet of the ladder; he looked unsteady and he tried in vain to find the next rung on the ladder with a swinging foot. He put his fingertips to the hard metal step, and stopped, looking down at his hand. Blindly, he grabbed the step tightly and instantly let out a shout of pain.

'I think I'm going to…' he said faintly.

Suddenly he slipped.

'Shit!' Charley shouted, seeing legs dangling from the ladder.

Chapter 29

Transfixed, Charley Mann was powerless to stop what happened when Russell Peters let go of the ladder, and slid directly down into the arms of those waiting at the bottom. The officers laid him on the ground. Peters' body was crumpled, his eyelids blinking, opening and shutting seemingly in sync with the movement of the fingers on his one functioning hand. One of the officers produced her handcuffs, and his body suddenly began to jerk and writhe with movement. He splayed his fingers in an attempt to claw at his captors, which jarred the shoulder of his injured arm, dislocated and now useless, forcing a scream of pain from his trembling lips. Flushed from exertion and in a state of panic, he kicked out with threats to kill, in a futile attempt to resist arrest. However, he was no match for the officers in his weakened state. When Peters was handcuffed, Mike and Charley moved to within a few feet of him as he lay on the ground, and watched the paramedic administer first aid. When she had finished she looked up at the SIO. 'He will need hospital treatment for the injuries to his arm and ankle,' she said.

Once he was sitting up, Charley cautioned him. 'Russell Peters you are under arrest for the murder of Cordelia Le Beau, the murder of Lincoln Heinz, burglary with intent to rape, and the abduction and attempted murder of Catherine Crowther.'

He made no attempt to reply, but rather looked away from Charley, coughing and spluttering. He spat blood directly at her feet. Unperturbed, she turned away.

From a few metres away, the SIO watched Peters' pathetic struggles dispassionately as he was taken to the ambulance, then seeing Annie walking towards her, her mind turned to Marcel the injured police dog, and his heroic actions that had no doubt brought Peters into their custody. She was pleased to hear that the vet had told Marcel's handler PC Mike Sharp that the dog would make a full recovery.

Satisfied with the result, Charley turned to see Dylan talking with Mike, and she thanked the negotiator for his prompt attendance, and the patience he had shown.

'He needs watching,' he said. 'I've seldom seen such dark, empty eyes, yet on the occasions that I have, it meant trouble. My advice is to tell your team never to turn their backs on him.'

Charley was thoughtful. 'I'll let the custody team know too.'

After one last look around the scene she walked to her car. With the rest of her team either with the prisoner, or already en route back to the station via other means of transport, she travelled alone, grateful for the time to gather her thoughts. Charley spoke to the Custody Sergeant Percy Shaw to let him know that a prisoner, arrested for murder, would be with him as soon as he was released from hospital, following treatment for an injured ankle and a serious dog bite.

'He has a stammer and made no reply on arrest, although he was given every opportunity.' Before any witticism could escape Percy Shaw's lips, she continued. 'You might have to be patient with him, and Jack Dylan, the negotiator, has warned us not to turn our backs on him.'

'Don't worry, boss, we get all sorts coming through here, he won't be the first, and I doubt he'll be the last that we wouldn't turn our backs on, if you get my drift.'

Percy Shaw had been in the job more years than he cared to remember. He was a little outspoken, and occasionally not politically correct, but no one could deny he was extremely good at his job.

The morning traffic delayed her return to the station, however, she knew the debrief wouldn't start without her.

Silence reigned and Charley was glad of the time to collect her thoughts.

Arriving at the office, Charley liaised with the HOLMES team about the morning's success. It was another forty-five minutes before the briefing could start. Tattie thrust a drink into her hands.

'Non-alcoholic I'm afraid, but I'm sure that will be rectified later,' said the administrator.

The SIO was disappointed to learn that Dylan had been called to another incident, which meant he would not be able to attend. His warning about Russell Peters still rang in her ears, and she would heed it, making it clear to all officers that Peters must be watched at all times. However, what was music to her ears was that Divisional Commander Bobbie Stokes had informed Tattie that he would be attending, to thank all those involved in the operation personally. In her experience, it was rare to see anyone of rank or stature in an incident room. Usually, they preferred to give incident rooms a wide berth, and left the detectives to the job in hand.

Charley's thoughts returned to Peters' backpack that had been recovered from Flat 22, as she walked along the corridor to the briefing room, where already she could hear the noise and euphoria of a successful operation. She was looking forward to finding out what they had found inside from Detective Constable Ania Kierczynska, the officer who had seized it. The moment the SIO walked through the door, her audience fell silent. She stood at the front of the room facing the personnel beside Detective Mike Blake, who was sitting. Divisional Commander Bobbie Stokes chose that moment to enter the room, closing the door quietly behind him, and as he took his seat next to her he whispered in her ear, 'Congratulations.'

Charley began the debrief with a flush of pride upon her face, but caution in her voice. 'Whilst the morning has been a success, we still have a long way to go to prove the offences against Russell Peters, and put him away, hopefully for a whole life tariff.' Her eyes scanned the faces in the room. 'Thank you to each and every one of you for your efforts so far. Now, let us see what else we know after this morning's operation.' Charley found PC Helen Weir's face. 'Helen, you were one of the arresting officers, anything you can tell us?'

Helen chose her words carefully, and was succinct. 'Peters is very much like his recent photo that we have of him, ma'am. He has an injury to his arm where PD Marcel heroically held him, and also another injury to his ankle where he fell when leaping from the window of Flat 22. He was certainly not happy about being arrested. Physically he has broad shoulders, strong upper body strength, and he also has a bad stammer. Presently he is under police guard at the hospital. There are two officers with him.'

Charley took a sip of the drink that Tattie had given her, the hot liquid warmed her stomach. When Helen finished and sat down, the SIO spoke.

'Thank you, Helen. Our police dog, Marcel, is going to make a full recovery by the way,' Charley told them, in answer to the inquisitive faces and unspoken words. 'It appears that Peters sprayed deodorant directly into the dog's face, causing him to be temporarily blinded. Thankfully the vet has assured us that he will be okay.' Charley paused. 'Peters discarded the canister afterwards, which has been recovered and retained as evidence.'

Next the SIO turned to look for Detective Constable Kierczynska. 'You searched Flat 22, Ania, and recovered his backpack. I'm interested to know what you found inside?'

'There was a knife, some rope, a scarf and a roll of gaffer tape. Basically, a kidnapper's murder bag, ma'am. We found no spare clothes for Peters, and there was nothing in the flat to eat or drink except for tap water.'

'Had he got his sights on his next victim?'

'He was prepared, ma'am,' she replied.

'How did he manage to slip the net?' Charley asked.

'He'd been sleeping on the floor under the window. There is no question that he was prepared to make a quick exit if anyone entered the room. Although I don't think he expected that it would be us, ma'am.'

'I'm glad that we were able to stop him from continuing his killing spree.' Charley shuddered as the stark alternative crossed her mind.

After the briefing was concluded, everyone left quickly, each with a focus on their personal task ahead.

A hurried conversation between Charley and Mike resulted in his following her to her office. There was a long day of interviews ahead, and she needed to discuss the pre-disclosure, and interview strategies with the detective sergeant.

Charley informed Mike, 'I know it can be disconcerting interviewing someone with a stammer. You have to be patient, and a good listener, which is why I chose you. However, I want you to choose your co-interviewer. Who do you think will not rush Peters, interrupt him, or try to finish his sentences for him? I want both of you to maintain natural eye contact, no matter how difficult this might be at times. DNA is damning evidence, a great start, but it'll be interesting to hear what he has to say about his victims, or his reason for the attacks.'

Mike looked at Charley quizzically.

'Ever the optimist, ma'am. What makes you think he'll speak to us? As far as we know he has never spoken to any of his victims, has he?'

'True, and talking about his surviving victims, we have the opportunity to test their ability to recognise their attacker. I'll ask the Identification Unit to arrange the necessary. We need as much evidence as possible.' The SIO jotted down a reminder for herself.

When she looked up from her notebook she eyed Mike purposefully.

'Have you decided who you would like as your co-interviewer?'

Mike didn't show any hesitation. 'Annie,' he replied. 'Her timing, and the selective use of silence in interviews is the best I've encountered in a long time.'

Charley turned and caught sight of Annie in the outer office, working with her head down. 'I'll leave it with you to tell her, and I'm relying on you to come up with a strategy. I'll watch onscreen in the office. Let's see how it goes once he gets a brief.'

Mike shuffled to the edge of his seat, and prepared to leave. 'I'll let you know once they're ready to start.'

Charley smiled. 'There's plenty of time. Peters could be at the hospital for some time yet, but at least his custody clock is stopped whilst he's there, which gives you and Annie more time to prepare for the interviews.'

Charley watched Annie's face light up when Mike stopped at her desk to give her the news that they would be interviewing Russell Peters together. She felt a pang of jealousy. The SIO would have liked to interview him herself. However, because of her rank she knew that it would be frowned upon, and deemed inappropriate, and oppressive, according to the Police and Criminal Evidence guidelines.

Detective Sergeant Mike Blake and Detective Constable Annie Glover were both very capable, and like most things, when you do something on a daily basis, it becomes second nature. That didn't stop Charley thinking that she could do a good job, but she had to admit that she was best placed watching the interview. Picking up on things that she wouldn't notice if she were interviewing him herself, because the interviewers would be concentrating on keeping focused, and maintaining eye contact with Russell Peters at close quarters. It always surprised the SIO what she could pick up from outside the room, watching the interview without pressure upon her.

There was no time to sit back and relax. Consultations were required now with Connie Seabourne at the press office. The information given to her regarding the local twenty-six-year-old man, of no fixed abode, who had been arrested in connection with the recent murders and attempted murder, was not however to be released until Charley gave Connie the green light.

Charley added to her to-do-list.

1. Fingerprint samples and DNA to Forensic for comparison, along with the clothes Peters was wearing.

2. Was the zipper on any black hoodie found at his home missing?

The next call that came into Charley's office was from an officer at the hospital. The doctor treating Russell Peters was concerned about possible infection, and giving assurance that there were no windows in the operating theatre from which he could escape, he insisted that the two officers guarding his patient were better placed outside the door.

The SIO's message to the officers was to keep vigilant. Even with one arm, they had seen his strength for themselves, and albeit injured, he was still considered to be a danger to others. 'Take no chances,' she concluded.

'I'll feel a lot better once he's back at the station and in the custody suite,' she told Mike.

It was over an hour before the doctor came out of theatre. He tugged at his mask, and took the hat off.

'The nurse is just finishing dressing the wound, so it won't be long now before he'll be all yours,' he told the officers and PC Lisa Bayliss with a satisfied smile. 'Forty stitches have been inserted into his wound, and a sling will be the man's best friend for a while, until the muscles heal. His ankle is not broken, but it has been badly bruised, so he'll need crutches and care. We've bandaged his foot, and fitted a boot to make it feel more comfortable for…'

He hadn't finished his sentence before an alarm rang out loud and clear. Turning, he saw the red light flashing brightly above the door and his eyes grew wide. Loud clattering from inside caused the officers to respond immediately and burst through the door of the theatre, to find the nurse being held hostage with a ligature around her neck.

Chapter 30

Using a cable wire that he had ripped out of a monitor and wound around Nurse Beth Tyler's neck, Russell Peters dragged her backwards. He held it there with his still functioning arm, increasing the tightness until she could barely breathe.

'T-take o-one step closer and I'll k-kill her,' Peters told the police officers, his voice soft, yet thoroughly menacing.

Constable Helen Weir drew her taser, and forced eye contact. He looked at her with a mixture of defiance and contempt.

'Release her, now!' she ordered through gritted teeth. A few moments later she confirmed her intent. 'Do it, or I'll fire!'

Russell Peters burst into uncontrolled laughter, however within seconds his amusement abated, and he screamed out in pain. As if in slow motion, his hand unclenched and he released the cable just enough to allow Nurse Tyler to stand up straight. She let out a life-saving breath, and with it a strangulated plea for help. Peters lowered his head to Beth's shoulder, and as he did so he tightened the cable around her neck again. He breathed in deeply at her neck, like a man long deprived of a woman's scent. The nurse closed her eyes to the harrowing sensation of his hot, moist breath against her skin. 'No one tells me what to do, d-d-d-do you hear? D-ick tease. Y-y-y-you're gonna die,' he whispered in her ear.

Beth Tyler's colour instantly drained from her face, her lips revealing a tinge of blue. The last of the life-giving oxygen was being forced slowly from her body.

Beth could faintly see the police officer waving her taser through the air, but her shouting was fading, as if she were entering a long tunnel. She saw the doctor's face framed against the bright white lights ahead of her, and she wondered if she was going towards heaven.

'For the last time, release her, now!' PC Weir instructed Peters.

His face reddened.

In a last-ditch attempt to break free, Beth kicked out at his injured ankle.

Peters cried out in pain, and moved as if to yank the wire tighter, but her dead weight was becoming too much for him to bear in his weakened state. When Peters let go of the cable, she fell in a heap on the floor, like a puppet whose strings had been cut. His body now exposed, Helen took the opportunity to fire the taser at Peters' chest.

With the hostage shaking on the floor, and the hostage-taker fazed by the taser, the doctor moved swiftly from behind the police officers and dropped to his knees beside his nurse, to administer first aid.

In frustration, Peters' body struggled to shake off the effects of the taser. He was without doubt exaggerating his contortions, hoping to catch the officers off-guard, but his efforts were futile. Seasoned officers Helen Weir and Lisa Bayliss restrained him in handcuffs quickly, expertly, and without hesitation.

With rising anger at his resistance, Helen reacted instantly, holding him down by the shoulders. She glared at him with a visual challenge to carry on resisting her. 'You're now under arrest for this serious assault,' she said, releasing her anger and frustration in her voice. Russell Peters started to cry, his frustration at being trapped for the foreseeable future clearly in no doubt.

Helen was quickly brought back to reality by the sound of further uniformed assistance arriving on the scene, and Russell Peters was carried unceremoniously by them out of the hospital to the awaiting police van. Satisfied her partner was okay, PC Lisa Bayliss accompanied the prisoner for continuity of the procedure.

He would remain under constant supervision in a cell at the police station.

In the rest room, PC Helen Weir saw Nurse Beth Tyler before Beth saw her. She was sitting holding a glass of water, from which she sipped periodically, but slowly and mechanically, as if she were in a daze. It was apparent to the police officer that she was in shock. Her eyes were still red from crying, and the bruises were coming out on her neck. It took a moment for her to realise that Helen was in the room, but when she did, she looked up and gave her a nervous smile.

Helen approached her slowly, and quietly sat down beside her. Beth looked at Helen but everything was a blur. Her eyes refused to focus. She blinked constantly to clear her vision. The images of what she had witnessed would not go away.

'How're you feeling?' Helen asked.

Beth's lips formed the beginnings of a word, her bottom lip slightly restricting the top to enable her to make a sound. But nothing happened. She tried again, pushing air up from her lungs and across her larynx, but still nothing happened. Traumatised by the horror of what she'd experienced, she had literally been struck dumb. Her eyes took on a look of panic.

Helen reached out and tapped her hand. 'It's okay. You're still in shock,' she said gently.

Closing her eyes briefly, Beth breathed deeply. Random thoughts came and went inside her head.

'Have you been checked over?' Helen asked.

Beth nodded her head. 'Been prescribed painkillers too. Perk of the job,' she managed, with a brief smile. 'I'm going home.'

'Can you remember what happened?' Helen probed.

Beth's eyebrows furrowed. 'I was finishing his dressing, and I told him to keep his arm still. I turned to get the tape, and the next thing I knew…' Beth put her hand to her neck and winced, 'he was strangling me.'

'Did he say anything to you?'

'Yes, he told me he would tell me what to do, not me him.' Beth screwed up her eyes and shivered, although it was warm in the room and there were no draughts. 'His hands were all over me.' She paused and looked at Helen, as though she was considering her next words. 'I know I shouldn't have, but I squeezed his injured arm, and I kicked out at his bad ankle.'

Helen chuckled. 'I know you did. I heard him yelp, and that enabled me to taser him. You did well.'

'I've dealt with violent patients before, but truly he had the strength of an ox. Tell anyone dealing with him how dangerous he is, won't you? I'd hate for anyone else…' Tears welled up in her eyes, and she swallowed hard. 'Doctor Hayes said that I had a very lucky escape.'

Helen nodded sympathetically. 'You did, but you can be assured that Russell Peters will be going away for a long, long time.'

Beth looked satisfied with what Helen had told her.

'Would it be okay if I call and get a statement from you later, when you've had time to recover from your ordeal. We will also need to photograph those injuries on your neck,' Helen asked.

'Of course,' Beth replied.

–

In the office, the phones and printers were busy. Dr Hayes was on the telephone to Charley, when Helen knocked at the SIO's door thirty minutes later, so she stood and waited to be called in.

'I want to thank your officers for how quickly they dealt with the man who attacked one of my nurses, and prevented her sustaining more serious injury. I also want to apologise to you, for asking you to ask them to wait outside the room while he was being treated. I feel somewhat responsible for the whole terrible incident. I'm in no doubt that had they been in theatre, it is very unlikely he would have, or could have, done what he did to Nurse Tyler. I certainly won't make that mistake again,' he said.

Meanwhile down in the custody suite Mr McCloud, the duty solicitor, had rushed to the cells to take instruction from his client, Russell Peters, prior to any interviews taking place.

'I want you to also inform the prison authorities as to how dangerous Russell Peters is, so that they're aware from the start of his incarceration just how violent he can be,' Charley told Percy Shaw the custody sergeant. 'If Peters can be violent towards those that are helping him, then goodness knows what violence he inflicted on those who he chose to kill?' she said.

The thought of his dropping the stone on Cordelia Le Beau's head, and leaving Cath Crowther for dead upside-down in a wheelie bin was abhorrent to her. What did anyone get out of watching people suffer? The murder of Lincoln Heinz was indeed committed by him, solely in an attempt to cause a decoy there was no doubt.

In turn, Custody Sergeant Percy Shaw updated Mr McCloud with regard to recent events, and his client's behaviour. After Russell Peters' private consultation with his solicitor, Mr McCloud confirmed that Peters was fit and ready to be interviewed.

Charley had been sat in her office, anxiously waiting for the first interview with Peters to start, and that time had now arrived.

Her door closed, the blinds shut, and the instruction for her not to be disturbed announced, her eyes were glued to the monitor on her desk.

The first thing she noticed about Russell Peters was his likeness to the descriptions that had been given by his surviving victims, which was indeed a credit to them.

She noticed how calm he appeared, after he had shown that he was also capable of intense violent outbursts.

After Mike began with the necessary introductions for the recording device, Mr Michael McCloud turned to his client briefly before turning to speak to Mike and Annie.

'I have now had the opportunity to have a chat with my client about the serious offences that he has been arrested for, and whilst he is quite able to answer the questions himself, he will decline to respond to anything you ask him, which is, of course, his legal right.'

Mike addressed Michael McCloud. 'Of course, it's your client's prerogative to remain silent, but it does not deter us from putting our questions to Mr Peters, and giving him the opportunity to answer them. After all, he may change his mind when he hears what we have to say. Only time will tell.' Mike shuffled the papers in front of him, and cleared his throat. 'Let's make a start, shall we? Your client has been arrested for a catalogue of offences, of which you are fully aware. I'd like to start with the murder of Cordelia Le Beau, unless you have a preference to start elsewhere?'

Mr McCloud turned to his client. Russell Peters shook his head. 'No, but thank you,' McCloud said. 'The murder of Cordelia Le Beau it is.'

Charley settled herself for the duration of the interview. Interviewing was not about diving straight in, pointing the finger, it was about building a rapport with the interviewee and gaining antecedent history first. There was no confrontation, or any challenges at this stage. A good technique involved patience, it was a slow process, but a necessary one.

Throughout the first interview, Russell Peters' face remained bland and uncaring as the detectives asked their questions. He declined to answer, just as his solicitor had indicated he would.

After forty-five minutes they paused for a short break before resuming fifteen minutes later. In the second interview, the detectives started talking in depth about the murder of Cordelia Le Beau, and it was then that Charley noticed that Peters appeared to become increasingly agitated. He was given every opportunity to speak, with long spells of silence from the interviewing pair to enable him to do so, but he chose not to. Each time the officers revealed further evidence, Peters became animated in his expressions, shuffled around in his seat, or fumbled with the sling on his arm.

The second break was a longer one, then once again the detectives resumed the interview only to be met with the same wall of silence.

When Mike pushed Peters about watching the others walk over Cordelia's body, before he returned to where she lay unconscious, in order to drop the stone on her head, causing the fatal injuries, he could be seen physically squirming in his chair.

'You could have walked away. However, you watched a couple who were worse for drink, walk all over her whilst you hid, watching, and such was your intent to kill her, that you then returned when they left, making absolutely sure she was dead. You'd stripped her in your sexual assault, and left your sadistic work displayed for others to see. There was no need for the extreme violence, or for you to kill her, but it had always been your intention and you did not give up until the deed was done, as you'd planned, to kill this poor defenceless woman.'

Peters shifted his eyes to look down at the floor between his legs, but still he remained silent.

'You didn't know this woman, did you? You simply saw her as an easy target because she was on the streets, didn't you?'

Russell Peters' stare remained one of arrogance, and the serious charges he was facing didn't appear to faze him. There was no sign of remorse, he didn't respond to any of the questions put to him. Yet looking in on the interview, Charley could see that the detective sergeant's questions were getting through to Peters by his body language.

Peters' silence brought the third interview to an end, as the evening drew in. There would be other interviews to follow in respect to the other crimes he had been arrested for. But the burning question remained, would the prisoner keep up his wall of silence?

Peters was returned to his cell, and Charley praised Mike and Annie for their persistence and approach to the interview when she welcomed them back into the office, and Tattie supplied them with a warm drink.

Charley was conscious that twenty-four hours in custody to facilitate the necessary interviews would be insufficient. An extended detention period was available to her via the Divisional Commander, and after consultation with Mike and Annie, she promptly requested the extra twelve hours. This would give them additional time, but still she was aware that even that might not be enough to reach the stage where they were ready to charge Russell Peters with all the offences that he had to be questioned about.

Charley, as the SIO, was looking at a visit to the Magistrates' Court in his final hour of detection to request a further thirty-six hours in police custody to be granted. But Charley would do whatever was necessary to keep him locked up.

It was pitch-black when she left the station that night. The wind had picked up and a splattering of drizzle sprayed her car door window as she unlocked it. Hurriedly getting into the driver's seat she slammed the door shut. A thought sprang into her head and she reached for her mobile phone and dialled the custody suite.

'Although Russell Peters hasn't displayed any suicidal tendencies,' she said to the custody officer, 'I am worried that he might consider his sling a means, should he think about it,' she said. 'I suggest that everyone is extra vigilant with regard to Russell Peters.'

Chapter 31

At seven o'clock the next morning Charley was sitting in her office, with a steaming cup of coffee that Winnie had made for her cupped in the palm of her hand.

Waiting for her computer to boot up, she gave Winnie a grateful smile, and reached out to give the older lady's hand a tight squeeze. 'What would I do without you?' she said.

'And, I you,' she replied.

Whilst Charley read the morning briefing notes, Winnie cleaned the office around her, mumbling under her breath that one day the younger woman might want to stay in bed, to let her get on though.

When Winnie switched off the vacuum cleaner, and gave Charley a little nudge to move so that she could vacuum under the desk, she also retrieved a newspaper from the front pocket of her apron and offered it to Charley. Taking it from Winnie she read out loud the pencilled name in the top right-hand corner. 'Divisional Commander's copy.' Charley looked at Winnie with a raised eyebrow, to see a mischievous glint in her aged eyes in return.

Winnie stood up straight, and continued matter-of-factly. 'Looks like the whole world knows that Detective Inspector Charley Mann, from Peel Street CID, has once again got her man,' she said, proudly, 'and, before you say owt, I'll have it back on Bobbie's desk before he arrives.'

'It's not just me, it's a team effort,' Charley reprimanded Winnie. 'Oh, and it's the Divisional Commander to you and me, not Bobbie!' Charley chortled.

Winnie gave her a cheeky wink. 'I'll have you know that he knows that I know that he could have a criminal record had I reported him.'

Charley's voice rose several octaves. 'What! Bobbie Stokes on the wrong side of the law? No way!'

Winnie nodded. 'The very same,' she said in a conspiratorial way.

Charley was intrigued. 'Pray, do tell,' she said.

Winnie leaned closer. 'His gran lived next door to me, and as a nipper he pilfered apples from the tree in my garden, every time he visited. I never told her, she'd have been horrified, but he knows I know,' she said, tapping her nose.

Chuckling, Charley watched Winnie retreat out of her office with a wiggle of her hips, and a backward glance. Charley turned to her computer and incoming mail.

Instantly she was motivated by the fact that Forensic had acknowledged receipt of Russell Peters' clothing, and the samples that had been sent to them the previous afternoon. With the requested priority status, work had begun immediately. She called Eira, but was disappointed when a recorded message was the only response, which suggested to Charley that she was busy. She left her a voicemail requesting a return call when convenient.

The morning briefing was a short one, and the SIO updated everyone, after which the team dispersed to complete the actions that had been assigned to them.

Dani Miller was the first victim to be given the opportunity to watch a Video Identification Parade Electronic Recording (VIPER), in which she would see Russell Peters' moving image, along with eight other people of a similar appearance. Charley hoped she would pick Peters out as the offender who committed the crime against her, from the series of clips of his face at various angles.

Mike and Annie looked refreshed and motivated, and were happy to continue interviewing Russell Peters. Charley envied them.

Their first interview was scheduled to work around Peters' eight hours' sleep, and breakfast periods.

'Today, I want you to rattle his cage,' Charley told them. 'Just like you did yesterday. I don't wish to teach you to suck eggs, but I would like you to cover the murder of Lincoln Heinz, before moving on to the attempted murder of Cath Crowther.'

'Will you be watching from the office?' asked Annie.

'Too right I will. I want to see his reactions, and if Forensic get their skates on, we will be able to disclose to his solicitor further evidence, prior to any subsequent interviews you may have with him.'

It was mid-morning when Charley received news that Dani Miller had made a positive ID of Russell Peters as the man who had been sitting naked on her bed, inside her flat.

Eira White returned Charley's call minutes later. 'Peters' tracksuit bottoms have revealed a strand of pink hair that is a match for Cordelia Le Beau.'

Charley took a sharp intake of breath.

'That isn't all,' Eira said, with a certain amount of excitement in her voice. 'Lincoln Heinz's DNA has been discovered from blood extracted from a black hoodie found at Peters' home address, and the zipper found near to where Cath Crowther was found dumped and left for dead face-down in a wheelie bin, is a match for the same.'

Charley was speechless for a moment after she had thanked Eira and put down the phone. A mass of conflicting emotions ran through her, euphoria and relief being the uppermost.

'Charging Russell Peters with two counts of murder, one of attempted murder, burglary with intent to rape, and finally the most recent assault on Nurse Beth Tyler is now a possibility,' she told her team. 'Whether Russell Peters speaks to Mike and Annie in the next interview doesn't really matter now. I'll get the Custody Sergeant Percy Shaw to prepare the charges.' She looked at her watch. 'Peters' detention clock is rapidly coming to an end. The extended detention we had planned to take advantage of may not now be necessary.'

Charley felt a tremor run through her body as she focused on the collection and collation of the evidence against Peters.

'I want you to continue to seek evidence,' she told those researching. 'I want as many nails in his coffin as we can get to add to the evidence we already have.'

Wilkie was cynical. 'That said, even with the over-whelming evidence that's been put to him in interview, it still doesn't mean that he'll plead guilty, does it?'

Charley was determined. 'No it doesn't, but when the case goes to court, the last thing we want is for some barrister having room for manoeuvre, from a chink in our armour, which they could drive a wedge through either. So, the more evidence we have the better, and it makes life easier for the jurors.'

Over the next hour the disclosure of evidence to Peters' solicitor was completed, which allowed them to move forwards with what was likely to be the final interview with Russell Peters. However, before Annie and Mike went in to the interview room, Charley spoke to them with passion in her voice.

'We have him bang to rights. You have my permission to let the piece of shit have it with both barrels.' Her face brightened. 'Professionally of course,' she added as an afterthought.

When Peters' solicitor had had time to discuss the disclosure with his client, they entered the interview room together.

Chapter 32

Once in her office, Charley settled back into her seat and turned the volume on her monitor a little higher, to hear what was being said in the interview room. Mike made the introductions, and each person present in turn said their name, for voice recognition purposes.

Eagerly Charley watched Mike and Annie, both experienced interviewers, doing what they did best, and suddenly she felt slightly emotional, but above all extremely proud.

Would he remain silent when the evidence of each incident was laid before him, or would he want his say at this point?

Charley didn't have long to wait for the answer, and in that moment something suddenly occurred to her. Russell Peters, on his own admission, didn't like being controlled, especially by women. It was therefore surprising that, from the beginning, he spoke in Annie's presence, but what became immediately apparent was that his speech impediment was only noticeable when Annie spoke, and he quite clearly avoided eye contact with her.

Charley knew that actions speak louder than words, and after half an hour of the forty-five-minute interview, during which he had spoken little, she watched him lean forwards across the table towards the detectives, and make direct eye contact with Mike. 'The women, they led me on,' he said, in his defence. 'Why else would they walk about half-naked, leaving their curtains and windows open, if they didn't want me to see them?'

He flicked his head in Annie's direction. 'Tell me, what would you do if she walked about naked in front of you?'

All credit to Mike, he refused to be drawn. 'You knew these women then?' Mike asked.

'No,' Peters admitted, 'but, they strutted about half-naked at the gym, teasing me, when I was cleaning the windows.'

'Then you followed them home. That's how you picked your victims is it?' asked Annie.

Instead of making eye contact with Annie, he looked up and glared defiantly at the wall above her with wide staring eyes. 'N... No reply,' he said, eventually.

Peters turned to his solicitor. 'She's trying to control me, I told you, she's just like the rest of them. I'm not fucking stupid you know,' he spat.

Charley, watching the interview strategy from her office unfold, clenched her fist. 'That's my girl Annie!' she exclaimed. 'That's exactly what I'd 'ave said. At last, he's showing his true colours.'

Inviting Peters to sit down, Mike calmly and strategically changed the line of questioning, sensing the growing animosity in the room.

'What about Lincoln Heinz? What's your excuse for killing him? Did he tease you as well?'

Peters slumped back in his chair like a deflated balloon. After a moment or two of considering Mike's words, Peters started to snigger. 'He wasn't just a sex worker, he was also a bloody fool. The pink-haired woman, the town's bike, she pimped him out and rewarded him with protection. Once she was gone he was a car crash waiting to happen. I gave him a place to stay...' After a moment or two he started to shake his head, biting his lip, clearly wanting to say more. 'Then he killed himself.'

Mike continued. 'We know that's not true because he was strangled, no doubt into an unconscious state, which is when you cut his arms in such a way that he would bleed to death, and then you made doubly sure that he wouldn't survive because you put toilet cleaner, containing hydrochloric acid, into his wounds.'

Peters raised his eyebrows and proffered a smile. 'Ingenious of me, don't you think? It's surprising what you can learn from the internet.' Peters shuffled in his seat, and sat upright. 'Oh, come on, he was never going to survive without the pink-haired witch.'

Again, Mike refused to be derailed from the agreed questioning strategy. 'Was your plan always to kill Heinz, in the hope that no one would miss the loner, which would buy you time to move on, using his identity?'

Peter's sighed loudly. 'DNA's a bastard, isn't it?' he said.

Mike pressed on. 'You didn't move on though, did you? You stayed within your old hunting ground to continue your planned killing spree, didn't you? Did you think that we wouldn't come looking for you at the university because we'd think you wouldn't be so stupid as to go back to the scene of some of your crimes?'

Peters screwed up his eyes. 'That, my friend, you will never know, but one thing I will share with you. It's actually the planning that excites me,' he hissed, 'so why wouldn't I carry out my plans to the end?'

'We recovered a rucksack from Flat 22. That rucksack we now know is yours. The items inside were clearly there to incapacitate someone. Had you got someone in mind?' asked Mike.

Russell Peters smiled. 'Your boss, snug-fitting trousers, nice arse,' he said. 'I saw her on the news. Tell me, is she the station bike, or maybe she's a dyke?' This struck Peters as being funny. But it sent shivers down Charley's spine to see him look up to the camera in the corner of the interview room, wink and blow a kiss. 'I know you're watching,' he said. 'You were indeed on my list. I know you... I've seen you...'

He was playing to the audience in an ambiguous way, and surprisingly enough, his speech was not impaired. Was that because he couldn't see Charley?

The detectives in the interview room ignored his outburst, and continued with their questioning.

'Would you have us believe that your victims left their windows open at night just for you, as an invitation for you to climb into their flats?'

Peters remained silent.

'You were hoping to startle them, weren't you, catch them unawares in their sleep, at which time you knew that you would be in control of them?' said Mike.

After a few minutes' silence in which Peters was given time to reply, Mike continued.

'Why are you not answering me? Is it because what I'm saying is the truth?'

'No. I wanted to show them that they were teasing the wrong bloke.'

'You killed them because they teased you?' asked Mike.

'I didn't kill them all, did I? I wanted them to feel what it was like for someone else to be in control.'

'Yet on your own admission you didn't know these young women, never mind knew what they were thinking. Admit it, all this talk of them enticing you, teasing you, it's just another fantasy of yours. It's all in your mind. You targeted the young women purely for sexual gratification, nothing more. Some you killed using extreme violence. Is that what gets you off?' said Mike.

'No,' Peters snapped angrily.

'What then?' asked Mike.

Once again Peters chose to stay silent.

'You thought you'd killed Cath Crowther when you placed her head down in a wheelie bin, didn't you?' said Annie.

Peters was looking down at the floor between his splayed legs. 'And she would be dead if you lot hadn't come along.'

Annie stared in Peters' direction, nodding slowly. 'Yes she would. You bought adhesive, you brought the wheelie bin outside her window the night before collection, you planned her death in advance didn't you?'

Peters raised his eyes to look at her, and hesitated. 'N… N… No reply,' he said.

'She lived on the ground floor didn't she? Was this the reason that you targeted Miss Crowther, because you enjoyed planning the disposal of her body?'

Peters remained silent.

'You videoed her, and stripped her. You asked others in the students' group on Facebook what you should do next, and we know you got sexually excited during this exchange,' said Mike, 'because we found semen-staining on the bed covers which, as you have been informed, has been identified as yours. So all this was about sexual gratification for you, wasn't it? Otherwise why did you ejaculate?'

'I wanted to know what others thought should be done to punish a dick tease. There's a lot of them about.'

'Oh, yes,' Annie said. 'You were warned about being a voyeur, but when that wasn't enough to satisfy your sexual urges, you needed more to satisfy you, and you didn't care about anyone else did you?'

The detectives gave Peters time to respond, but when he didn't they carried on.

'Moving on,' said Mike. 'What about Lincoln Heinz, whom we found dead in your flat? You killed him, and left him there with your university identification card in his back trouser pocket. Hoping that we would think that he was you?'

'I did that when he was dead,' Peters mumbled. Peters raised his injured arm at Mike. 'And if it wasn't for that fucking dog, I wouldn't have had to have stitches. I wouldn't be here, and the nurse wouldn't have got hurt. I should sue you.'

'You resisted arrest, and I don't know if you are aware, but attacking a police dog is classed as an assault on a police officer.'

'It was self defence for fuck's sake. That police officer should have called the fucker off as soon as he caught up with me.'

'It's you who is the control freak. You planned, then killed people for your own self-gratification. You are nothing but an evil sexual predator, and a threat to the public at large.'

Mike could see the look of concern on Peters' solicitor's face as his client's clenched knuckles turned white on his lap. Despite this, the detective sergeant pushed further.

'Go on, give it to him Mike,' Charley said, through clenched teeth.

'The nurse treating you didn't lead you on. She didn't try to entice you, or tease you, but yet you tried to strangle her. Why?'

'Ah, but you don't know that. She was leaning over me, speaking softly to me, flirting with me, letting her body brush against mine. Don't you believe it. I knew perfectly well what she was trying to do. She was trying to get me into more trouble. I had to stop her.'

'If the police officer hadn't used the taser, would you have killed Nurse Tyler?'

'It would have been her own fault if she had died, not mine, I've told you.'

'You mean that you got sexually excited by her close proximity, and that's why you reacted the way you did towards her.' Mike could not disguise the disgust in his voice as he continued.

Once again Peters shuffled forwards to the edge of his chair, but this time the officers and Peters' solicitor were clearly ready for another outburst.

'Sit!' said Mike, with authority, and Peters remained seated.

'If they make themselves easy pickings, then they deserved to be picked. Truth is that they made themselves available. Anyone could have done what I did.'

Annie raised her eyebrows. 'Actually, no, not anyone could've scaled the flats like you did for a start.' She looked puzzled. 'Are you sexually inadequate. Are your inadequacies the real problem?'

'What? Me, sexually inadequate? How dare you?' Peters screeched.

Unconcerned by his latest outburst, Annie carried on regardless. 'Why did you kill them then?'

Peters face became contorted. 'Just because I could. Me. I'm in control. I decide who lives or dies.'

'Do you not feel the least bit sorry for what you did to your victims?'

Charley could clearly see now what people meant about Peters' steely eyes.

'Well done guys,' Charley said on the back of a long breath as the two detectives concluded the interview. When she turned off the monitor and sat back in her chair she closed her eyes, albeit briefly, feeling mentally exhausted. The clock above her door showed her that there was just half an hour left on the prisoner's detention clock before his custody expired.

The two detectives took Peters directly to the charge desk, where PS Percy Shaw read out the charges that were ready and waiting for Peters, in the presence of his solicitor.

Once charged Russell Peters made no comment, but his violent streak was not satisfied until he had lashed out at his solicitor for failing him as he saw it. He struggled with the officers, who were used to dealing with violent individuals and brought him to the floor, then restrained him and carried him in without any problem.

'All I have to do now is let the Divisional Commander know, and Force Control too, for the Chief Constable's Log. Connie Seabourne at the press office will need to be informed that a twenty-six-year-old local man will be appearing before the Magistrates' Court tomorrow morning for a remand in custody. After I've done that then I'll see you at the pub,' she told the buoyant team. 'Russell Peters will no doubt be examined by psychiatrists, who will come up with all sorts of reasons for his behaviour.'

'We all know that his defence team will no doubt shop around until they find a psychiatrist who will say what they want to hear at the taxpayers' cost.'

Back at the CID office, Charley applauded her team.

'Well, that was a hell of an enquiry, every theory we have put together on the case was spot on. Every exhibit we sent to

Forensic produced evidence, which we have in abundance to secure a conviction and put Peters behind bars for a very long time. There is no doubt he is a danger to the public. All we can physically do now is put the evidence before the courts and trust in the judicial system to do the public justice. Will the Divisional Commander be happy to hear the news? I guess I should go up and update him.'

When the rest of the team saw what Annie was doing, they joined in the applause that she was giving Charley. In the next few minutes, everyone with whom she had worked with on the case was standing applauding her actions and abilities. Charley found herself blinking away the tears, and turned a brilliant shade of red. She was embarrassed but she deserved the accolade. The detectives were showing their respect and gratitude to her in the only way they knew how.

'How did you take it?' Winnie asked, early the next morning, handing a strong black coffee to the hungover SIO.

'How do you think I took it?' she said.

'You cried like a baby.'

'I cried like a baby, but not till I got home. We've still a hell of a lot of work to do to pull the file against Peters together speedily. There's no time to rest on our laurels.'

'I don't suppose you went on to stand the first round at the pub last night?'

Charley nodded her head, 'And the second…'

'Not as daft as they're cabbage-looking those detectives,' said Winnie, knowingly.

Charley clutched her throbbing head in her hands when she laughed. 'You're right there.'

When Winnie had left her in silence, Detective Charley Mann looked at the plaque on the wall to the right of her. The supreme test for the detective. She had once again proved herself to be equal to the challenge, whatever that may be. She also knew that it wouldn't be too long before she was put to the test yet again.